To Andrea,

PURGATORY

13 Tales of the Macabre

Best wishes,
'Junior'

A. Lopez, Jr.

A. Lopez, Jr.

ACE-HIL-INK

PURGATORY
Copyright © 2011 by A. Lopez, Jr.
EVIL (poem)
Copyright © 2011 by Julie Falcione

PUBLISHED BY:
Ace-Hil-Ink 2011

ISBN 978-0615-566245

All rights reserved. No parts of this publication may be reproduced, stored in or introduced into a retrieval system, or transmitted in any form, or by any means (electronic, mechanical, photocopying, recording or other forms) without the prior written permission of the copyright owner of this book, except in the case of brief quotations embodied in critical articles and reviews.

This is a work of fiction. Names, characters, places, brands, media and incidents are either the product of the author's imagination or are used fictitiously. The author acknowledges the trademarked status and trademark owners of various products referenced in this work of fiction, which have been used without permission. The publication and or use of these trademarks is not authorized, associated with, or sponsored by the trademark owners.

For any questions about the book or author, please refer to our contact page at: **www.ace-hil-ink.com**

DEDICATION

Thank you to everyone who has supported, been a part of, and listened to me ramble on about my book. Believe me, each and every one of you have contributed in your own way and I couldn't have done it without you.

CONTENTS

Evergreen Road 1
Road Trip 23
Mind Games 46
Tic Toc 72
Weekend Visit 88
Floor Four 117
Purgatory 172
Prized Possession 176
The Crate 198
Ritter House 222
Santa Claws 241
Strangers 254
Don't Bug Me 289

***macabre*:** [muh-kahb] adjective

involving death or violence in a way that is strange, frightening, or unpleasant

EVIL

The screams echo . . . followed by maniacal laughter

His dead eyes peer into their souls

Their last breath he inhales . . . deeply…

Each victim becoming a part of him

He enjoys the terror on their faces…

The pleading . . . The smell of fear

Impending death...

The gleam of the knife...

Ripping flesh...

Watching the blood run warm and sticky...

Igniting his senses...

That powerful feeling . . . dominating the weak...

They are the sheep and he is the wolf...

He likes to tease them . . . Offer hope...

Making them think there is a chance he will let them go . . . making them beg...

He has no intention of setting them free...

He only desires to introduce them to never ending darkness...

For he is EVIL and EVIL is him...

~ Julie Falcione ~

PURGATORY

Evergreen Road

"For those who believe, proof is not needed."

"Do it! Do it! Do it!" Rudy shouted with excitement and anticipation. "Turn 'em off!"

The three high school boys were driving fast down Evergreen Road. The road is infamous in the small southeast Texas town for the myth, or legend of the 'Evergreen Witch', depending on what stories you have heard.

The time had come for Evan, who was driving the Camaro, to turn off the lights for five seconds; that's what you're supposed to do while driving to make the Witch appear. Evan reached for the switch, hesitated, and pushed it in. The road went dark, the car rumbled down the gravel road. They all went silent staring through the windshield into the blackness. The only sound was the motor and the car's tires meshing with the dirt and rocks beneath them. Five seconds seemed like an eternity. Evan's hand hovered next to the switch. Finally it was time, he pulled the switch.

The myth of the Evergreen Witch dates back over forty years. That was when Beverley Peterson was murdered in her small house close to Evergreen road. She had her throat slashed while she slept. She had on a white gown, and since her murder, there have been rumors, or sightings, of her walking the road at night; like she used to do when she was alive. According to legend, if you drive down the road after midnight and turn your headlights off for five seconds while still driving, when you turn them on, she will appear in the road, walking in the blood-stained gown, and holding on to her throat, trying to keep her nearly decapitated head in place.

There has never been any proof of the witch or anything else like that appearing for the drivers that were willing to test the myth. Unless, you blame the legend for some of the accidents that have occurred there at night. Despite it being a myth, the stories of the midnight haunting have been told for forty years.

When the headlights lit up the road, all three boys stared at something standing down the road. As they got closer they saw Beverly, the Evergreen Witch. The car was on her before they knew it and Evan snapped out of his shock in time to swerve the car to miss her. All three boys screamed as their eyes locked on the eyes of the pale-white Witch. The Camaro slid sideways and hit a tree trunk lying on the side of the road. The car rolled several times.

The boys weren't found until the next morning. Rudy was the only one left alive. He had crawled out of the mangled car and got to the side of the road. When the paramedics arrived he was in bad shape. Before he died, he spoke.

"The Witch is real, she looked into my eyes."

Rumors spread fast about the accident, and like gospel, the blame fell on the legend. It fueled the myth into a frenzy that it had not enjoyed in a long time.

Twenty years later . . .

Evergreen Road runs for about two miles along Tabbs Bay. At its darkest spot at night, it is lined on both sides by trees and brush. It's in this quarter-mile section that the Witch is supposed to appear, and it is where most of the accidents have occurred. This stretch of road has been given the nickname, "The Witch's Pass".

Because of the amount of tress in this area it is the darkest location on the road, and even on a clear night there is total darkness. Homemade signs have been put up from time to time over the past forty years, marking the start of the cursed passage. They have been pulled down by residents or curious sight-seers, in the daytime of course, and taken as a souvenir or memento of the legendary piece of road. The signs are usually put up by high school kids, and are usually painted in red letters meant to represent blood.

Some kids believe in the legend and some don't. It has been that way for years. Eighteen-year-old Steven Jacobs is one who doesn't believe in the Beverly's ghost. He has driven down the road, so he says, many times after midnight and has never seen her. Steven has a reputation as being a tough kid on campus, but also loves to pull pranks or practical jokes on his classmates. Despite all of that he is not hated and still holds popularity on campus. He figures it is his last year in high school, and he should have the best time of his life, either by going to all the parties, racing his Mustang, or dating every girl he can during his last year in school. That's how he felt it should be, and that fit his ego well, unafraid and willing to go to the edge to have a little fun.

A couple of months into the school year Steven had a date with Kelly, a senior cheerleader. Besides her looks, he kind of liked her. He took her out to eat and then they decided to see a movie. They both liked horror movies so they chose the new release, "Road Trip"; about a man who drives his brother's dead, decaying body from California to Arizona, and all the strange things that take place during the trip.

They both liked the movie and picked up a milkshake for the road. Kelly had to be in by 1:00 a.m. The Mustang's clock read 12:30 and was a perfect time to test out Evergreen Road, so Steven drove towards the cursed road.

"Ever been down Evergreen Road?" he asked, hoping she hadn't.

"You mean the one that the Witch is supposed to haunt?"

"Yeah that one. Ever been down it at night?"

"Everybody's been down there," she said as she laughed.

"No, I mean, after midnight," Steven said. He was hoping to keep the tone of the conversation a little on the dark side.

"Well I don't really remember the time, but I have been down there at night."

The practical joker in him came out.

"Did you hear about the kids twenty years ago, who crashed after they saw her?"

"Yes, who hasn't?" she asked, realizing that Steven was getting really serious about it.

"They say that the Witch caused the crash. One of the kids told that to the paramedics, just before he died."

"Those rumors have been around for a long time, who knows if he said that or not."

"Let's drive down it. It's after midnight. We could check it out and still have time to get you home by one," he said, offering the dare to his skeptical date.

"Alright, I'm game if you are. Let's go," Kelly said with a smile. She wasn't as scared as he thought.

They pulled down the main road and then turned onto the dark road. They drove over the hill, and gradually the road turned left and then straight again. Now they were approaching the haunted stretch of road. This part was very dark.

"Are you sure you're ready?" he asked.

"Ready as I'll ever be."

Steven sped up and got the car up to around fifty miles-per-hour and looked at Kelly.

"Here goes nothing," he said. He turned the switch off on the headlights . . . darkness. Steven's plan was unfolding perfectly. Very quickly, he reached down on the left side of his seat and pulled out a witch mask and put it on. In the darkness Kelly could not see what he was doing.

"Turn the lights back on, it's been past five seconds," she said. Just as she finished saying that, he had just slipped the mask on his head. He turned the lights on and turned to face her. Steven did his best impersonation of a screaming witch. Kelly was looking at the road as she heard him scream. She turned, saw the mask, and screamed at the top of her lungs as he grabbed her shoulder. It really scared the hell out of her at first before her senses came back to her, and then she turned angry.

"You asshole!' she yelled. She hit him in the head a few times and he tried to deflect her blows as he took the mask off. "You fucking asshole! Take me home!" Kelly was furious. Steven slowed, and then stopped the car in the middle of the road.

"Look, I'm sorry," he pleaded. "I didn't mean to scare you like that."

"Screw you! Take me home now!" Kelly's eyes were on fire. Inside she knew she shouldn't be as angry as she was, her friends warned her about Steven and his immaturity. But he had scared her good. "Please just take me home," she told him as she rubbed her eyes with her head down.

"Okay, I am sorry Kelly," he told her. He actually did feel bad. "Please don't be mad at me. I know the Witch is just a tale. I was just trying to have some fun."

He put the car into drive, and just as he hit the gas to take off, he heard something like a thud sound at the back of the car.

"Did you hear that?"

"I told you to quit it Steven," Kelly said as she looked out the window. Steven continued to drive and looked in his rearview mirror, but saw nothing in the dark behind them.

He got Kelly home just in time and she exited the car without a word, still angry at him, but also angry at herself for going out with him. He drove home feeling bad.

The next morning Steven was called outside by his father.

"Where were you at last night?" his dad asked.

"I was on a date. We went to eat and then to the movies. Why?"

"What's this on the back of your car?" Steven walked around and saw five smeared lines starting at the very back of the trunk and running down to the license plate. He leaned in for a closer look, and to his surprise, the lines looked like blood.

"That looks like blood, son. What the hell were you doing?" his dad asked again, more firmly this time.

"I don't know where it came from dad. I'll clean it off right now," he said as he walked towards the water hose. His dad grabbed his arm.

"Look son, this is blood. If there is something you need to tell me, tell me now. It's the only way I can help you." Steven looked at his dad, but didn't want to tell him that he went down Evergreen road.

"I really don't know where it came from dad. I really don't."

His dad let go of his arm. "Alright son, get it cleaned off."

Steven's dad went inside as he began to unroll the hose. As he pulled it to the back of the car, he had a closer look at the streaks on his car. They looked like bloody finger marks. Was this the sound that I heard last night? He tried to peel some of it off but it was as if it was glued on. He didn't want to think of what or who made the bloody marks. He didn't believe in the story of the Witch, but it did look like bloody fingers that slid down from the trunk to the license plate. He started washing the dried blood. It took some scrubbing but he finally got it all off. This has to be a joke that someone played on me. That's it, a joke. In his mind he had it figured out now.

During the next couple of weeks Steven questioned everyone one he knew about the joke that was played on him. He even asked Kelly if she was in on it. She was shocked to hear him ask her if she was playing a joke. His accusation only made her angrier and she stopped talking to Steven altogether.

To Steven, the blood stains had to be a joke because, if it wasn't a joke, it meant that someone else, or something else, was responsible. He didn't want believe that.

After awhile he put it in the back of his mind and moved on. October came around and it was getting close to Halloween. He made friends with a new girl on campus, Veronica. She had moved to Texas from Louisiana, so she hadn't heard of his reputation of being immature or a practical joker. She had kept to herself and was slowly trying to fit in.

Steven and Veronica had a couple of classes together and became close enough that Steven decided to ask her out to a Halloween party. After some hesitation, she agreed to go. She felt comfortable with it because a couple of other girls she knew were going to be there.

The party was hosted by a few of the parents. It wasn't a wild party like some of the others around town, and this was the reason Steven asked Veronica to this one. He was just getting to know her and didn't want to scare her off. They had plenty to eat. They danced and also sat and talked. Veronica mentioned that she liked the Halloween season and all of the scary movies that came out during that time. Steven immediately thought of the Evergreen Witch. He told her the history of the legend, and asked if she was up for a haunted Halloween drive. She asked him a few questions, but felt good enough about it, so she said okay.

The party died down around eleven-thirty, so they headed out. Steven gave little thought about the last time he went there with Kelly. The blood on his car, and where it came from, was the last thing on his mind. He had no intention on scaring Veronica like he did with Kelly. Steven just wanted to have some fun, and be the first to show Veronica the infamous road.

They made it to the start of the road about fifteen minutes until midnight.

"We are kind of early. You're supposed to drive it after midnight," he said as he pulled the Mustang to a stop.

"How many times have you done this?" she asked him.

"Well, growing up here, and hearing all the stories about the road and the witch, you end up trying it a few times. So, I guess, five or six times since I got my driver's license."

"Have you ever seen anything?" She was getting more curious now.

"Oh yes. I've seen her in her bloody gown walking the road, a couple of times," he said, trying to sound mater-of-fact about it.

"Really? Are you serious?"

"No, I'm just kidding," he said with a laugh, "I've never seen anything down there, but it is kind of scary when you turn the lights off. I don't know if the Witch is real, but the murder of Beverly Peterson that I told you about earlier, is true."

"Sounds creepy, but has me curious."

"Well, it's midnight. Let's go," he said. They started down the road. He drove a little way and then stopped. "Just up ahead is where she is supposed to appear. Ready?"

"Yes I am. Let's see this Witch," she said as she checked her seatbelt.

Steven took off and gradually picked up speed. He got the car up to around forty.

"Here we are." He looked at her just as he turned the lights off.

"One; two; three; four; …" Veronica counted.

Steven waited for her to say five.

"Five."

The sound of her voice made him pause, it sounded evil. He turned the switch and the lights lit up the road, which cast light inside the car. Staring at him was The Witch, her eyes ablaze with anger as she grabbed Steven by the neck.

"Don't fuck with me boy, or I'll come to your house and rip your heart out of your chest while you sleep!"

Steven leaned as far back as he could and screamed louder than he ever had before. He closed his eyes and slammed the brakes. The car skidded to a sliding stop. He opened his eyes and looked over to see Veronica looking at him with a blank expression. Then she turned and dropped her head, not saying a word. Steven cautiously reached over to her and grabbed her shoulder.

"Hey, are you okay?" He was trembling.

"What's wrong? What happened?" she asked. She raised her hands to her face, looking at them as if they didn't belong to her.

"I don't know? You were . . . you were."

She passed out, collapsing, falling towards Steven. He held her keeping her upright. He was afraid to look at her face and was dripping with sweat. Not knowing what to do, he laid her back in the seat and anxiously looked outside the car. What the hell was that? What the hell is going on? The dense blackness outside surrounded them. The only sound was the Mustang's motor, purring in the darkness. Steven put the car into drive and spun out on the gravel, driving as fast as he could to get off of Evergreen Road.

Veronica was waking up when he got back into town and he pulled into a gas station.

"Are you okay?" he asked again.

"What happened? My head hurts, I feel weird. I don't remember anything."

That scared Steven. "I remember us driving down the road and then you turned the lights off. After that, I don't remember," she said as she started to come out of it a little more.

Steven had two things on his mind; Veronica's condition, and what he thought he saw. It had to be real, that's why she is feeling like this and can't remember. It had to be real. No! It can't be real. The last thing he wanted was for her to think that he did something to her. He hoped like hell that she wouldn't think that.

He got her a bottle of water and waited until she was feeling better before he took her home. The next thirty minutes were focused on her, and she eventually came around to the point where she wasn't questioning him anymore. He didn't know if that was good or bad.

After she went into her house he drove off, and all the visions of the Witch came back to him. He cleared his eyes, but his eyes weren't the problem, it was his mind. Steven wanted so badly to believe what he saw was just his imagination, or a joke of some sort, but it scared him too much to be anything but real.

Steven slept very little that night and sent Veronica a text message the next morning to see how she was doing. She didn't respond until later that evening, saying she said a headache and would talk to him at school the next day.

Veronica didn't make it to school until Tuesday. She was not herself, and when Steven tried to talk to her, but she was very distant and asked him not to text or call her for a few days. She said she had a lot of school work to do for the week. He knew better, and his patience grew smaller by the day. All he wanted to know was if she was mad at him, or thought he had done something to her. All of this was driving him crazy knowing that the reason Veronica wasn't feeling well was because he took her to see the stupid Witch. The Witch that he didn't believe in!

That night he went to bed early; the lack of sleep over the last few nights finally caught up to him.

The weather was bad that night and it stormed hard, but it didn't awake Steven. He was so tired, that the lightning and thunder that the storm produced went unnoticed. That was until the door to his room slammed shut with a bang. Steven jumped up in bed, startled. He looked around his room and saw his closet door half open. The lightning flashed outside as he slowly got out of bed. It felt like someone was watching him from the closet. He grabbed his baseball bat and made his way over to the closet door.

Standing in front of the door, he wiped sweat from his face, and gripped the bat's handle. Using the head of the bat he started to push the door open. The creaking sound of the door inching open was deafening, sweat poured from his face. The door was completely open and the darkness of the closet showed itself.

"Still don't believe in me Steven?"

The voice came from behind him. Steven froze as his heart raged inside him. He knew the voice, it was the Witch. It can't be. He turned around quickly, bat pulled back, ready to swing. To his horror the Witch was sitting up in the middle of his bed, staring straight at him. Blood covered her neck and gown, one hand holding her throat, the other stroking her stringy, bloody hair. Even in the dark, he could see her eyes as they looked right through him

"I told you I would come for you," she said calmly.

Steven, still stricken with fear and disbelief, attempted to strike down at the witch, but his arms wouldn't move. His unbelieving eyes were locked on hers.

Suddenly she rose from the bed like magic, and was standing at the side. The Witch took her hand away from her neck, and as soon as she did, the gash in her throat opened completely and her head fell over to one side, still attached by a piece of skin. Blood spilled out, but her eyes remained glued to Steven's. Steven finally found his courage and took a swing at her. It was too late, she had disappeared. The bat connected with his dresser, wrecking the lamp shade and shattering the bulb. In his frightened state he turned around and took another swing. No one was there.

"Steven! Are you okay?!" his dad yelled, as he swung the door open and entered. Steven stood still, bat still in his hands, looking at the spot where the Witch had just been. "What's going on? What happened Steven?!" His dad was upset and still clearing his head from being awakened in his sleep. Steven dropped the bat.

"I don't know dad. I had a nightmare, that's all. It's okay, it's over now. Leave me alone," he said as he sat down on the edge of his bed. His mother entered the room.

"Oh my God, what happened?" she said, looking down at her son. Steven's dad knew his son was going through something, but now wasn't the time to ask him.

"Let's go Barbara. We'll talk about it tomorrow."

Steven's mom kept looking at her son with a concerned look as she left the room with her husband.

"He'll be alright." He knew something was wrong, but he also knew how to handle his son. Their talk would come in the morning. "Have to give him some space."

He closed the door. Steven was numb. In his mind he had only been imagining it all. In his heart, he knew what he saw. He had to admit to himself that the Witch was real. IT CAME TO MY HOUSE! Scared and not knowing what to do, he paced his room for the rest of the night. He thought of a plan.

I'll talk to Veronica tomorrow. If she is doing better and doesn't remember anything bad from the other night, I'll know that I am just seeing things, all in my imagination. If she is still sick, then I know it's all real and I'll confront that demon bitch, one more time!

He knew this was all too crazy to talk to anyone about, but he also knew that he had to do something about it.

After Steven got up the next morning he knew that he would have to answer his dad's questions. He wanted to get it over with. His dad was waiting for him in the kitchen and Steven apologized before the questions came.

"I'm sorry for last night dad. I had a real bad dream and I thought someone was in my room."

"It must have been really bad for you to take a bat to your dresser," his dad told him in a calm and understanding way.

"Yes I know, that's how real it was to me."

"Your mother went to the store, but she worried me the rest of the night, wanting to make sure you were okay. You will have to tell her and reassure her that everything is okay. Understand me?"

"Yes sir, I do."

That was simple enough Steven thought. Now he needed to call Veronica, with her he would know what he had to do next.

Veronica answered. "Hello, Steven?"

"Hey Veronica, it's been awhile. How are you doing?"

"I'm okay, I'm feeling okay." Steven immediately felt the pressure lifted off of him. "It's just; I have had some strange things happen to me, weird things." The pressure that had just left him was now back and much heavier than before.

"What do you mean weird things?" He needed an explanation; he needed to know what to do.

"I've had weird dreams and have been just sitting, like in a trance. My mom says it looks like I am meditating. I don't feel sick like I did at first, but this other stuff is strange. I'm sorry Steven, I wish I was better."

"It's okay Veronica, I understand. I mean, I don't understand but I know how you feel."

"Has it happened to you too?" she asked, hoping for a common bond with him.

"It doesn't matter, it's okay."

"Please tell me," she said desperately. "Tell me what you have experienced Steven." Her voice changed. It was the voice of the Witch. "Yes, please tell me Steven." The Witch's laugh was sinister and evil. In shock, Steven ended the call and dropped his phone.

There was no doubt now that he had to end this. He didn't want to give the demon another chance to haunt him at home or scare his parents. He knew that if he could stop this, Veronica would be okay. He was going to take care of it that night.

His plan was simple; tell his parents he was spending the night at a friend's, and then be at Evergreen Road by midnight. The problem was that he didn't know how to fight the demon, or how to end it. What he had heard from the rumors was that, almost all of the kids who had crashed had always swerved their cars at the last second to miss her. Steven didn't plan to do that; he planned to run her over. His mind was tired and weary with all of this. He decided to take a nap, content with his plan.

Steven left home around ten that night and went to his friend's house. He hung out there until just after midnight, no one knew of his plan.

He wanted to clear his head so he drove down to the bay, parked the car and sat on the hood, just overlooking the water. The night was cold, cloudy and dark, no moonlight to help with his quest.

The time was now 1:00 a.m. Steven got in his car and drove to the start of Evergreen road. He coasted his car slowly down the dark road until he was close to the spot where everything had happened. He put the car in park and was more determined than ever, he wouldn't let anything distract him from his plan. He had to see that the curse, or whatever this was, ended. He felt totally responsible for Veronica, and felt that because he hadn't believed in the myth, and had mocked it, that it had cursed her and him.

Steven grew more determined each second. Tears wailed in his eyes; he put the car into drive and punched the gas. Gravel spit from under the rear tires, the motor roared to life, and he was off. As the speed of his car increased, the tension mounted and his determination and anger grew stronger. Forty miles per hour, fifty miles per hour, the Mustang hummed perfectly down the cursed road.

The time was now, he turned the switch, the lights died and he went into complete and total darkness. For the first time he was beginning to feel nervous. He knew he was tempting fate in challenging the demon, but he had to, and now it was too late. He had to face his fear.

He made sure five seconds had passed. He turned the lights on; his car was speeding at sixty miles per hour. At first he saw nothing, but then, down the road, he saw white. Her gown! He had her now. It got closer and closer, closing in on him fast. He sped up.

"Get ready bitch. Here I come!"

He gripped the wheel tighter, leaned forward, and sped up. The tears in his eyes turned into rage. The witch's gown grew brighter, closer. Holding the wheel with one hand, and clearing the tears of anger and fear with the other, Steven headed straight for her.

"Looking for me Steven?" Steven screamed and his body stiffened. The witch was sitting behind him, leaning forward, and spoke in his ear. "Here I am."

His arms locked straight, holding the wheel, he dared not look behind him. The light that he saw on the road was headed straight for him, he swerved. The two cars just missed each other.

"Asshole!" was screamed from the other car as it passed, full of kids.

Steven's car spun in a circle until it came to a stop, his foot mashing down on the brake pedal. Scared, sweating, and going out of his mind, he got the courage to turn and look in the backseat. The seat was empty.

Relief.

He could see the taillights of the other car fading in the distance, and he could hear the kids yelling and laughing as they disappeared down the road. He tried to slow his heavy breathing to catch his breath. The dust cloud caused by the other car and his sudden stop, was settling around the car. Once his senses came back to him he felt stupid, it was all in his head.

That's what it is; it's all in my mind!

"Damn Steven! Get your head together," he spoke aloud. "I just have to be stronger than you, I can beat you. You're only in my mind bitch!"

He sat there for a minute and almost laughed at himself for letting his imagination get away from him like that. He deserved it, he thought to himself, especially for all the practical jokes he had played on others.

Karma, he thought.

He put the still running car in drive, and turned in the direction he was headed originally. His thinking was becoming clearer and his rationale, that he'd had his scare, based on karma, was now over. He was glad to be getting off the road and back to the city, to his home. He vowed to himself to keep the demon out of his head.

He drove down the road with growing confidence, he was gonna beat this thing. Suddenly, a small animal shot across the road in front of him. He quickly swerved the car to miss it and then straightened the wheel safely. He looked back and laughed at the sudden scare. It made him think of his seatbelt. Looking down, as his car sped down the road; he grabbed and locked the belt into place. He turned his eyes back to the road, and standing no more than ten feet in front of his speeding car, was the Evergreen Witch.

"Oh shit!"

This time when he swerved, he lost control.

His overturned car was found the next day in the middle of the road. The driver's side door was open and a trail of blood led from the door and into the woods. There, tied to a tree trunk was Steven's dead body. He was held upright by long strands of vines, which wrapped around his waist, neck, and tree, in a twisted mess. His eyes were open, locked with fear and stared blankly towards the road. His shirt was ripped open, and carved down his chest and stomach, the letters clearly visible in his dried blood, was the word, BELIEVE.

Road Trip

"And I looked, and behold a pale horse: and his name that sat on him was Death."

The dead body of Joe Cantu, forty-one years of age, was found in a pig pen in one of the feeding sloppers on a farm just outside of Bakersfield, California. Luckily, if you can call it that, he was found before the pigs were able to feast on more than the parts of his legs and sides of his torso that they had already worked on. The coroner called it a homicide discovering he had been shot twice in the head and more than likely dumped there hoping the pigs would enjoy their new found meal and cover most or all of the evidence of a murder in a feeding frenzy. Joe was found face down in the mud and slop and had been there for at least three days.

Originally from Arizona, Joe moved to California four years prior hoping to get a fresh start and try to stay away from the troubles that had found him in the Phoenix area. The rest of his family of one brother and two sisters along with his mother and father all resided in Mesa, Arizona. The Bakersfield authorities and county coroner's office were at a loss in locating his next of kin having found him naked and with no identification. It wasn't until a missing person report that was filed by his brother seven days later that a connection was made through a description provided by his brother, Manuel.

Manuel explained to them on the phone that Joe had no wife or kids. They asked him to come out and identify the body. Not knowing for sure if it was his brother or not he told only his wife and sisters of his plans to see if it was Joe. He did not want his parents to know what was going on and they had no idea he was missing. No need to worry them until he knew for sure. With that a very nervous and unsettled Manuel Cantu gave his wife and kids a kiss and got in his 1988 Ford station wagon hoping it would make it the long one-thousand-plus round trip miles.

Manuel set out west on Interstate 10 with a million thoughts running through his mind. His sisters had offered to help him with a plane ticket but he thought of it as too expensive and a waste of money, when he could drive there instead. Manuel and his siblings were second generation Americans having all been born in the United States. His parents were born in Mexico, and carried the old traditional ways of their heritage, culture, and religion. Manuel, his older brother Joe, and his sisters, Ana and Marcela all had went to school here and learned the American culture to go along with their upbringing in a traditional Mexican household. All four spoke Spanish fluently but knew English just as well or better. Manuel had four daughters to support and found it hard to make ends meet having been the least 'Americanized' of the four, but he always managed to find work, paid his bills, and put food on the table. Now with all these thoughts running through his head, and driving to a place he had never been, combined with the uncertainty of the body not being his brother, it all had him a bit unnerved.

The road trip was going well all the way to the Arizona-California border and periodically Manuel would call his brother's cell phone hoping for a miracle. Instead his calls went straight to voice mail time after time, lowering his confidence and expectation of Joe being alive. After almost four and a half hours of driving he was growing hungry and although he didn't want to stop he was starving and pulled into the town of Indio, California. He pulled into a typical roadside diner that you see in many movies and decided to go in and rest his tense body and mind. He ordered coffee and a ham and cheese omelet. He glanced around feeling out of place but did feel better putting some food into his stomach before the next leg of his journey. He looked around hoping by chance to spot his brother. Manuel knew that was a long shot. After finishing his coffee he headed back out on the road towards Bakersfield.

Three hours later he arrived at the coroner's office. Feeling the tension and apprehension Manuel sat in the station wagon for twenty minutes ringing the steering wheel like it was a wet rag. He finally made up his mind to go in. Wiping his face with a towel as he walked to the front doors he felt nauseous. Making his way in he spoke with the receptionist and she directed him to the coroner's office down the hall.

"Mr. Cantu? I'm Dr. Stevens, county medical examiner," he said as he offered his hand to Manuel. Manuel shook his hand nodding yes.

"I know this is a very difficult thing for you and I understand you have driven a long way to find out if this is your brother so I can understand if you need more time before we go inside."

Manuel had his head down at this point, and after looking up said "I am okay. I'm ready."

"Very well let's go inside and we'll try to make this as brief as possible Mr. Cantu." The coroner led Manuel into a cold, well lit room and walked him over to a table in the corner. Manuel stared at the corpse, covered in a white sheet, his legs frozen in place.

"Please if you will Mr. Cantu, step forward. We will need to make a positive identification. Only when you are ready."

The coroner had his hands on the edge of the sheet and prepared to lift it when Manuel gave him the okay. Manuel felt his nausea build again, but nodded okay and the coroner lifted the sheet, with only the face visible.

It was his brother Joe. He looked severely beaten and his face was dry and withered, but there was no mistake, it was Joe. Manuel nodded, and waved for him to drop the sheet. The doctor obliged and covered Joe. Manuel couldn't hold it anymore and bent over to throw up on the floor. The doctor came around and gave him a towel and told him that he was sorry.

"I know this is the hardest thing to do, and you are a brave soul to do this on behalf of your family, I applaud you for it. We can continue when you are ready. Let me know."

Manuel raised his head up, "I am very sorry for making this mess."

"No worries," the doctor said. "Are you okay?"

"I am okay sir," he said as he wiped his mouth one more time still starring at the body under the sheet, the body of his brother. "It is him. It is my brother sir."

"Are you absolutely sure Mr. Cantu? We can have another look if you need."

"No need, I am certain doctor."

"Okay Mr. Cantu, we can step outside and go over the paperwork, and I have to notify all the agencies involved." They walked back out into the lobby and had a seat at a desk. Manuel's head was spinning in shock and horror, and the realization of his brother actually being dead had not set in on him yet. The coroner made several phone calls.

After a few minutes, and enough time for Manuel to clear his head, the coroner was right back to business with him. "How will your brother be transported back to Arizona?"

That was a question Manuel had not thought about at all. How was he going to take his brother back? There had to be a way that wasn't too expensive. His head spun again.

"What are the best ways to do that?" he asked.

"Well, you can get a funeral home to make arrangements, but traveling from here to Arizona will be expensive. I can make some calls if you like?"

"What if I take him back myself? Can I do that?" he asked the coroner.

"Yes you can if you get a transport permit, but I would not recommend it." The coroner looked at the puzzled and concerned face of Manuel and tried to give him the best options. "Let me make a few more calls and see what I can do. Okay?"

"Okay thank you." He was lost now not really knowing what to do and knowing he still had to make phone calls to his wife and sisters. It was overwhelming. He made the phone calls he hoped he would not have to. He called his wife, and then his sisters to give them the terrible news.

Because of all the legal issues, and the ongoing investigation involving his brother's murder, Manuel had to stay overnight while they were worked out, and the medical examiner had to make sure all evidence was taken from the body in hopes that a murderer would be caught. Around eleven the next morning he got a call from the coroner telling him it was okay to make arrangements for the transport back. After giving Manuel all his options, Dr. Stevens told him the best price he could get for transport. The price was way too expensive for that, so he asked about the permit to take his brother himself. The doctor made a call using his contacts, and had the office fax over a permit to help speed the process.

By this time Manuel was a very anxious man and wanted nothing more than to be back home with his family. The doctor wanted to load some ice in a tray into the back end of the station wagon to keep Joe's body cool for the trip. Manuel, being scared and in a hurry, said thanks, but would rather pick some up if he needed. He said he would be okay with his cold body wrapped tightly. It would be only a few hours. Reluctantly the coroner loaded Joe Cantu into the back of the station wagon and handed Manuel the permit.

"I wish you and your family the best of luck; please make sure you call me if you need anything, or if anything goes wrong on the trip."

"Thank you, doctor. I will get him home soon and give him a proper burial." Manuel closed the back of the wagon and gave Dr. Stevens one last look before he got into the car.

Manuel had fueled up earlier in the morning so there would not be a delay in driving back. He had not told anyone of how he was going to bring Joe back. He had only said he would be back today. He looked at his watch and it was 12:30 in the afternoon and already getting hot. It would be hotter in Arizona by the time he got there. Mesa was expected to hit 110 degrees. Even with a full tank of gas he knew he would have to stop at some point on the road to fill up, so his plan was to get to Blythe.

As he was getting past Los Angeles and heading back towards Indio his thoughts were on his parents. He had asked his sister Ana to tell them, and now he felt bad that he hadn't done it himself. He noticed his temperature gauge getting a little hotter and thought it was probably because he was running the air conditioning, which he normally wouldn't use since the car was so old. But, he wanted to keep the car as cool as he could so Joe's body wouldn't begin to smell. His cell phone rang it was Ana.

"Hello, how did it go with mom?"

"It's very bad; they are crying and asking so many questions. They are in shock. We are all in shock. I can't believe this. I just don't understand." Manuel had to be strong and cut her off.

"Once I get back I will talk to them and try to explain what all has happened. Then we can make arrangements. I want us to do everything so they won't have to deal with it," he said trying to ease her mind, and wanting to be the glue for all of them. But even he knew it was a very tragic and horrible situation.

"Are you driving back? When will Joe be here?" Ana asked, trying to hold back tears.

"Yes I'm driving back now and I hope to be there by dark. Joe will be there around the same time." He couldn't tell her. His plan was to drive straight to the funeral home and have it all taken care of before anyone knew the difference. He looked at his temperature gauge again and it was getting hotter. Too far above the normal temperature so he had no choice but to turn the air off and hope it cooled the engine enough to continue. He was fifty miles out from Blythe so he figured he could make it there and then check the car out.

It was almost five o'clock when he pulled into Blythe. The temperature read 104° on the gauge at the gas station. He was sweating from the last leg with no air conditioning and was glad to stretch his legs. He quickly fueled up and parked the car away from the walking paths of customers. For the first time he began to smell the rotting corpse of his brother. The stench hit him after he came out of the store. When he opened the door the smell was the horrific. Quickly, he opened the windows, but could not lower the back door window because it was broke. He couldn't believe how bad the smell had gotten, and the doctor had warned him once the body got to a certain temperature it would begin to decompose at a fast rate. Now he had to check out the water and antifreeze to make sure he could make it back to Mesa. Manuel was getting more nervous by the second. So many things could go wrong with what he was doing. After checking the water level and oil, he couldn't take it anymore. He had to check Joe to make sure he wasn't rotting away.

When he opened the back door of the wagon the smell was worse. He was parked far enough away that he could partially unwrap his brother without anyone noticing. He gently pulled away some of the top covering then got down to the sheeting. With the smell being almost unbearable, he held his breath. Joe's face was almost as it was back in the coroner's office except it looked to be softer, almost like it was going to rot or melt away. Manuel fought back tears and uncovered more of Joe, his curiosity getting the best of him. The places where the pigs had eaten were wet and beginning to liquefy. They had chewed on his brother and torn away almost half of the right side of his stomach. He had seen enough, but knew he had to do something. He went back into the store and bought ten bags of ice and tried his best to lay them around and on his brother. Manuel was frantic, but did the best he could.

By the time he set out on Interstate 10 East it was almost dark and the temperature was now at 109°. It was a typical July summer. He had maybe three more hours to drive and hoped the ice would hold up long enough to keep his brother from getting worse. Even with the windows down and driving at 70 mph the smell was still bad. He called his sister letting her know he was running late and not to expect him until later that night. Manuel had talked to three funeral homes about pricing and arrangements while he was in California, and of course he had to settle for the best price. It was a place in Mesa so it was close. They were waiting for him there. He continued driving, and combined with the weight of all of this and his pure exhaustion, he was tired and getting sleepy.

While his thoughts were running in and out of his head his cell phone rang. It was Joe's number! His hand shook as it continued to ring. Manuel pressed the button to answer and put the phone to his ear.

"Hello?" was all he said. There was silence. "Who is this? Who has my brother's phone?!," he demanded. Still no answer. "Whoever this is…"

"Manny?" It was Joe's voice. "Where are we going hermano?" Joe's voice again. Manuel began to shake listening in silence, unbelieving what he was hearing. He didn't know what to do or say. The speed of the station wagon slowed. No one was on the road but Manuel and Joe. He glanced at his rearview mirror with the phone still to his ear, and to his horror he saw Joe's body begin to rise as if sitting up. The phone dropped from his hand as he screamed, and pulled the car to the side of the highway.

His scream woke him. He looked around the inside of the car, hysterical and startled, and opened the door. He got out as quick as he could and looked into the back window to see if his brother was sitting up like he thought he had just saw. His body lay still and unmoved. Now he realized that he had a dream. He was indeed pulled over on the side of the road and checking his watch to see that it was now eight o'clock. He vaguely remembered pulling over earlier when he was getting tired. He figured he must have been asleep for at least two hours. Afraid, and feeling like he was losing his mind, he got his cell phone and checked for miss calls. None. His first instinct was to call his sister, but he decided to get back in the car and just drive straight to the funeral parlor.

The Grimes Funeral Parlor, formerly known as Grimes Mortuary, off of Main Street in Mesa had been there for over fifty years, and is one of the oldest funeral parlors around with its roots going back to the 1920's in various locations. This location was the oldest. The building was white with a covered drive-thru at the front door. Tall white pillars stood tall on each side. The building looked different in design than any other one in that part of town. The prices there were cheap, but their reputation had always been in an ominous light, and there have been rumors of strange and abnormal practices in their dealing with the dead. There is a very popular rumor that they preserved a two-year-old baby at the request of the parents, after their infant's untimely death. The baby is rumored to still be preserved inside the mortuary, in a 'special room', so the parents can visit her. That rumor helped spur the already rampant speculation that the place was haunted. By the time Manuel pulled up, there was no doubt that the station wagon was ruined with the smell. He had no idea how his brother's body was doing and the back of the wagon was soaked and dripping liquid, either from the melted ice or from Joe's decomposing body. He didn't want to look so he went to the door to get someone from the mortuary. He pushed on the door after he didn't get an answer, and it opened slowly. The first thing that hit him was the odor coming from inside. It wasn't the same smell coming from the back of his car. This was different, more of an old, musky smell.

"May I help you?"

The voice startled him and came from the direction of his car. Manuel turned to look and standing next to his car was a very tall, very pale skinned older man in a black suit. Manuel turned toward the man and the door slowly closed behind him. As he walked over he noticed that the man's eyes never left his. They had a strange and distant look about them.

"Hello I'm Manuel Cantu. I spoke with someone here about my brother."

The man smiled in a way that gave Manuel the creeps.

"How are you? I'm Jeric Grimes. I own the mortuary. Nice to meet you," the man said, extending his hand to Manuel. "I believe you spoke with one of my assistants. We've been expecting you."

Manuel shook his hand and noticed right away how cold it was.

"Pleasure to meet you sir. I think I have a problem. I am not sure what condition my brother is in. I drove him here from California."

"Please ease your mind Mr. Cantu. We will take great care of your brother Joe. He will be in good hands, but I would suggest that you leave the car here with us overnight, so we can have it cleaned and take care of your brother properly. Your car will be ready for you in the morning," said the old man as he looked directly into Manuel's eyes with a smile. Manuel noticed that the man's eyes were almost completely black. Maybe he was tired, but he was sure that his pupils were completely black, and that sent another chill through his body. "I have arranged a ride for you." He pointed as a taxi pulled up. "Please do not worry. We will take care of everything."

With that Manuel shook his hand and got into the taxi, not wanting to leave his brother, but he had a feeling of confidence in the way the pale, tall man handled his business. He felt everything would be okay.

He called ahead and told Ana that he would meet her and Marcella at her house to explain what he was doing. It was in an effort to make things easier on their parents. He had a tough time convincing his sisters that this was the best way to do it. Their parents had little money and had no burial arrangements for any of them. So they agreed that what he was doing was best, although they were very upset at him for driving Joe back in his car. They all three cried in the emotion of it all. They decided to all go to their parents the next day and tell them of the arrangements with the funeral parlor.

The next morning they told their mother and father, Jose and Alicia, about the funeral parlor they were using and that they didn't have to worry about anything. The three of them would take care of all the arrangements and cost. Their mother made the sign of the cross and said a quick prayer in Spanish when she heard the name of the mortuary. She too had heard the rumors. She protested and wept hoping her husband would feel the same way. She was a devout Catholic and felt the place was evil. A weeping Jose Cantu stood up and walked his kids to the door. He said he would talk to their mother.

Manuel got a call from the funeral home saying that he could stop by to make the arrangements, and also that his car was ready. His sisters did not want to go, they weren't ready to see their dead brother yet. He got them to drop him off.

He went in through the front door and noticed it was almost completely dark inside except for a casket in the corner with a lamp next to it. Manuel slowly walked towards it. There was a paper attached to it that read, 'Mr. Cantu'. He debated opening the shiny jet-black casket. Reluctantly, he reached for the lid. Just as he grabbed hold of it, a hand tapped his shoulder and squeezed.

"Your brother is not in there Mr. Cantu. He is in back, follow me." The old man let go of his shoulder and turned and walked towards the double doors in the back. Manuel never turned around while he was speaking. Jeric had scared him so bad that he didn't want to see those eyes again. He followed him through the doors and into a short hall that led to a room with four caskets. Jeric walked to the center of them and turned with a smile.

"Which color do you feel will suit your needs Mr. Cantu?"

The caskets were gray, white, blue, and brown. As nervous as he was at this point it really didn't matter to him, but he summoned up his courage as the man waited for his answer.

"What about the black one outside?"

"Ah yes, the black one. For the moment, that one has been mislabeled. These four are what we can offer you."

Manuel looked once more at the gray one. I'll take that one there."

"Excellent choice Mr. Cantu. It is our most popular. You may view your brother's body now if you like." Jeric took one step towards the gray casket reaching out his long arm and lifted the lid. He stepped away to allow Manuel room. His mind was spinning again. How could I have chosen the exact coffin that my brother was in?

He stepped forward a few steps and looked down at his brother Joe. It was Joe, but he didn't recognize him this way. He looked different.

"They never look the same do they? But I can assure you, in the condition he was in when you brought him here, we did a very nice job," he said, looking proud.

The smell was not nearly as bad as it was in the car, but you could smell him. He had the smell of Death. His face and hands looked decayed and dry. He couldn't take it anymore and closed the lid.

"This will be fine," he said, never raising his head.

"Very well, let's step over to my desk."

Jeric's desk was in the corner of the room. The dark brown desk was very big and looked out of place. They sat and went over the details of the burial. The old man was very business-like, but very much to the point. Manuel couldn't wait to get out of there.

Because of the condition of the body, the viewing and Rosary would have to take place soon, with the burial the next day. He left the same way he came in and couldn't help but glance at the black coffin in the other room. His station wagon was parked out front, very clean and shiny, just as Jeric had said. To his surprise it did not smell at all. He looked in back, and it was as if nothing ever happened. Manuel was amazed, but didn't question it.

The next two days of the Rosary and funeral passed very slowly. Manuel had to deal with his sisters, and had to console his mother and father, trying to help them understand what happened to Joe, and why he brought him back the way he did. His mother said she would not go to the funeral home, that it was evil. They tried to convince her to go, but she refused. Manuel's father was not happy about the arrangements either, but he had to see his son.

Thursday came and it was finally time for the viewing. The Cantu family went together early for the family's private viewing. As they walked up together, just outside the mortuary, the first thing they saw was the hearse parked out front. It was white in color and had purple curtains. As they walked by it, Manuel noticed that the paint and curtains were faded and old. The hearse was an older model, and seemed like it was from another time. As soon as they walked in they were met by Jeric. He offered his condolences and stepped aside to let them pass.

Joe's body was in the gray casket that Manuel had picked out. One by one they stepped forward to see their son, brother, cousin, and uncle. Joe's father didn't look at his son for long. He cried as he walked away and held his hand over his nose. Joe's sisters cried along with the rest of the family. Manuel was last to step forward not knowing if their cries were from seeing Joe dead, or from the way his body looked. His brother looked worse than he did on Wednesday. He smelled worse and his face looked more decayed than he did the day before. His skin was dry and cracked, but Manuel had wanted an open casket so that his family could see Joe before he was buried. He walked straight up the isle to talk to Jeric.

"What the hell is going on?" he demanded. "Look at my brother. He looks terrible."

"I am sorry Mr. Cantu, but is this not what you wanted? An open casket?"

"Yes but I thought there was something you could do to keep him looking better for my family. You told me that everything would be alright."

"I have done everything in my power. His body was not in a good state when you brought him in. If you like we can have it closed for the service."

"No just leave him," he said as he turned to go back inside.

"Mr. Cantu." Manuel turned around angry and looked right into the old man's eyes. "I know this is a difficult time. But as life is not fair, there is one thing that always seems to come to light in my business."

"What would that be Mr. Grimes?" Manuel said. His filled with anger.

"Death is something no one get used to, and unfortunately, death will find us all when its time." His delivery was cold and chilling, almost sounding prophetic. Manuel felt it. He turned and walked away.

When the priest arrived to bless Joe's body he was shocked at what he saw. He had only come to the funeral parlor on behalf of the Cantu family and their loyal following at his church, but felt the same evil that Joe's mother felt. He spoke with the family choosing not to speak to Jeric directly. He didn't ask, but ordered it to be a closed-casket service. Manuel felt worse and knew the blame of everything would come down on him. The priest blessed Joe, and closed the casket.

Nothing else seemed out of ordinary for the rest of the night and through the funeral service the next day. His mother went to the church and then to the cemetery for the services. Manuel felt better about that, but as with any funeral there was sorrow, grief, and crying.

He went back the next day to the funeral parlor to take the rest of the money for the services. It dawned on him that Jeric always said 'we' in referring to the mortuary staff, but Manuel didn't remember ever seeing anyone else working there. The strange thought played in his mind as he waited in the office. He looked up over the counter at the bulletin board pinned with papers and other business items. Partially covered behind a billing slip, he saw a picture of Jeric. He looked around, stood and reached over the counter to look at the newspaper article about the history of the place. Sure enough it was Jeric, or he thought so. The picture of the man was dated 1929.

But it can't be, he thought. Those eyes and that cold stare belonged to Jeric. He felt uneasy and pinned it back on the board and sat down.

Jeric made it in a couple of minutes later. Manuel was hoping for a fast transaction and got it. He gave Jeric thanks, and as he got up to leave, Jeric extended his hand. He looked Manuel in the eye and said, "See you soon, Mr. Cantu." He squeezed his hand and Manuel felt that familiar chill that he was used to around him, and without saying a word, walked out the door, planning to never come back again.

After his wife went to sleep Manuel stayed up and tried to recycle all the events that had begun less than a week ago. Even though his brother was now resting, his stress level was still high. He played everything back through his mind, from the road trip, to the nightmare he had on the side of the road. Then, finally the mortuary, especially Jeric Grimes. That had to be him in the picture, or the date was a mistake. Everything about it all was strange and bizarre. He was exhausted and decided to go to bed.

Still bothered by the news clipping he saw earlier at the funeral home Manuel did some research on the internet and found out that the history of the mortuary went back over eighty years, moving from place to place. And then there he was, Jeric! Only in this article, his last name was spelled Grim not Grimes. It was the same photo that he saw at the mortuary and showed him to be the original owner, circa 1930's. The man in the photo had to be in his sixties or seventies, but the resemblance was too real, too perfect. He knew then that Jeric wasn't a person, but was some kind of ghost or demon. He wasn't going crazy, he knew!

Manuel rushed into the funeral parlor's front office and grabbed the picture from the board. A sense of fear hit him knowing now for sure that Jeric was the same person. He opened the doors to the viewing parlor and to his shock he saw his family sitting on both sides of the isle. They had their heads down in mourning. At the end of the isle he saw it, the open, shiny, jet-black casket from before. It was on display for his entire family to see. He slowly walked towards it; his family never looked up at him. As he got closer he saw that there was a body inside. Then he stopped cold in his tracks. Inscribed on the side of the casket was 'Mr. Cantu'. He took one more step, and to his horror, he saw himself inside. He felt as if he was going to pass out. Things became blurry and then he heard his family weeping behind him. He turned to try to get some type of explanation from it all. No one could see him. He spoke, no one could hear him. They were there to attend his funeral.

The lid on the casket slammed shut behind him. Frightened, Manuel turned around quickly, and standing over his casket was Jeric, one arm over the lid.

"I told you I'd see you soon Mr. Cantu!" said Jeric. Fire burned in his eyes.

Manuel woke up in bed startled, covered in sweat, and his heart pounding. His chest was heaving up and down as he tried to catch his breath. He realized now that he was having a nightmare, and although his mind was racing with thoughts, and trying to comprehend this latest twist, he was relieved that it was only a dream. He wiped his sweaty face with the sheets, his body still trembling, and walked to the window to look outside.

Parked at the neighbors house across the street was an ambulance and a police car. A body, completely covered in a white sheet, was being carted towards the curb. To his shock, pulling up and parking alongside the ambulance in the street was the very familiar faded, old-white hearse with purple curtains from the funeral home. Manuel's heart began to race again. Getting out of the hearse and standing in the open doorway was Jeric, brushing off the sleeves of his black suit. Then, Jeric looked directly into the window at Manuel. Even at this distance Manuel could see the blackness of Jeric's eyes staring at him. Bearing his rotten, yellow teeth and pale lips, Jeric Grim spoke, and although he couldn't hear him, Manuel unmistakably read Jeric's lips, as if they were in slow motion.

"See you soon, Mr. Cantu."

Mind Games

"We the jury find you innocent, by reason of insanity."

There's a saying that goes: "What you don't know won't hurt you." But in this case not knowing, specifically, who the person is sitting next to you, may put you in a very dangerous position without even knowing.

What we fail to think about, is that those people who we don't know, the ones who are complete strangers, could be judging us the same way that we all know we have judged others. Imagine if they were making assumptions about you. What if their assumptions were much more violent and diabolical? What if the person sitting next to you was crazy, insane or a murderer? What if everything that you saw in them and everything you judged them by was real? What if that one person you avoided talking to because you were so judgmental about them had a doctor's appointment just like you one day? What if that person was sitting right next to you?

Our odyssey begins with George Milton. An average man, of average height and build in his upper forties, slightly balding, and wearing eyeglasses. A truly innocent and kind man to everyone he knows. He is single and lives alone in a small one-bedroom house. George works for an accounting firm, one of the many accountants on staff. He works in an eight by eight cubicle not unlike many of you do. We find George going to a doctor's appointment. He is always very prompt and leaves nothing to chance in the planning of his day. He doesn't like delays, and always has a schedule to keep.

We don't always know what's going on in another person's mind. Some thoughts could be pleasant, some could be very bad. We never really know do we? Let's take a look into the mind of George Milton.

Dr. Office

I can't believe they scheduled this many people on the same day! This is fucking ridiculous. It's so crowded here, and they put these chairs so close to one another. I have a right mind to change doctors if this is how it will be here. The air conditioning must be going out too. So damn hot in here. Look at that lady, probably breathing up half the air in here as it is. BITCH! Listen to this guy next to me, loud, obnoxious, and just won't stop talking. He better not even try to strike one up with me. I'm just here for a doctor's appointment, but these people act like it's a social event for gossiping. Damn if this guy doesn't shut up! Okay great, now we have the crying baby. Why am I mad at the baby? I don't hate babies or children, but they can be a royal pain when their parents won't take responsibility and keep them quiet. The parents, yes it's the adults who are to blame! Now I'm starting to itch. I wonder if this asshole has some type of contagious disease. Probably does, just look at his arms, and how he is scratching them along with his coughing. I'll just keep my mouth shut and act civil unlike these animals. Either they're yacking on their phones or yacking to one another, or a baby is crying, but you can be sure that they won't be QUIET! I just had an amusing thought. What if I could loop a long rope around this guy's neck? I could somehow tie it to a machine at the end that would yank it hard causing the rope to choke and strangle him. I can see it now, his neck being choked down as he struggles to find air. He reaches for the rope that is causing him to finally be quiet. His eyes begin to bulge and water, and start to turn a nice shade of red. Oh yes, I can see it now!

"Mr. Milton? George Milton? The doctor will see you know."

Damn her! I was just about to see this man's eyes pop out from his fat head! Maybe next time.

"Mr. Milton. How are you today? You look happy," the doctor said.

If only you knew what I just did to your idiotic patient in my mind. Hhmm, for you, my most favorite, sarcastic, and fake person in the world. The man that keeps bringing me back here month after month, taking my money for useless checkups. Yes for you, I would simply grab your scalpel and slice open your carotid artery until you bleed out over your pretty tiled floor. The light in your eyes would dim as you fall to the floor. Nurses would scream, they would run out to the lobby, only to see the massacre I just created. Ah yes! That's what I would do to you my doctor!

The next visit for George was the store. He needed a few things, and had to fill the prescription that his beloved doctor had given him.

Grocery Store

If I didn't have to get this stupid prescription I wouldn't even come to this store on such a rainy night. It amazes me how many people are still out with it pouring down like it is. I don't like the looks of this place, I should have drove to the one I usually go to, closer to home. Looks like there could be a wino hanging around the parking lot, probably begging for money to feed his addiction to staying drunk and lazy. Look at those two making out in their car. People like that really disgust me. Just can't stay loyal to their partners. Lying, cheating, whores and bastards! I ought to go over there and... Calm down George, you've got more important business to take care of. I'm gonna get soaked just from running into the store. Damn! Now these damn automatic doors won't open right! Piece-of-shit rundown store! Shit! I forgot a basket. I'll just use this one. Let me turn in this prescription from that money-hungry doctor. I'll get him one day. One day soon. Look at the low-life people in here. Sooner I get out of here the better. Now what?? They can't even keep their carts in decent shape. Fucking squeaking wheel is gonna drive me over the edge! I swear!

Might as well pick up some meat while I wait, if this cart will even make it over to the meat counter. Look at this meat department. No upkeep here.

"May I help you sir?"

"Yes you may. I'd like 3 pounds of 90/10 hamburger meat in three separate packages please. Then I'll need two ten ounce rib-eye steaks. The best cut you can make if you don't mind. Thank you."

"No problem sir. Be right out."

He looks okay to be working here. But you never know about people behind closed doors. I'll freeze this meat and just eat some soup tonight, since it's cold and raining. Can't wait to get home and unwind, get out of the stressful atmosphere of this world.

"Here you go sir. Best cut of steak in the house."

"Thanks," George said smiling.

He seems like a very happy person. Only if there were more people like him. My scrip should be ready by now. That's if that young girl doesn't fuck it up. She's probably texting or talking on her phone while my scrip sits unfilled in back.

"Hello, I'm George Milton, here for my prescription."

"Oh yes, Mr. Milton the pharmacist would like to speak to you."

What the hell now?? I knew I shouldn't have stopped here.

"Mr. Milton? Hi, I'm the on-duty pharmacist. I will need to confirm something with your doctor before I can fill this prescription. It's not your fault or anything, just a technical issue on his choice of medicine. I am so sorry for this mix-up, but I won't be able to do anything until tomorrow, after I speak with him. I can give you a supplement for tonight if you like."

You fucking bitch! Just looking at your eyes I can tell you don't really give a damn about me or any medical condition I may have.

"That will be fine. I'll pick it up tomorrow," George said, hiding his inner rage and looking as pleasant and kind as ever.

Bullshit I will! I don't need those stupid meds anyway.

"Okay sir, I'll have it done by ten in the morning."

Look at her fake expression of concern. I ought to take my fist and drive it right into her nose, and crush her face until blood explodes everywhere.

"Thank you, you have been very kind." he said as he turned and walked away.

Actually, no thank you, bitch! I need to get out of this place. Luckily there is no one in line at this dump of a grocery store.

Oh now look at this winner doing the check out. I should have tried to pay at the meat counter. With those fat fingers he'll probably ring my bill up wrong.

"Price check on four please," the cashier announced through the p.a. system.

I knew it!! "Is there a problem?" asked George.

"No sir. It's just that this meat was on sale only until yesterday. I'm just gonna make sure we can give you the lower price."

Well just ring it up as the lower price dipshit! If it's not one thing it's another. This is the last time I come to this damn store!

"You know what sir? I'll just ring it up at that sale price. Sometimes they take too long."

That's all you had to do in the first place asshole!

"Thank you for your help. I appreciate it," George said in a very pleasant tone while paying, then walked out of the store.

Oh great now here comes the homeless guy.

"Look, I don't have any money to give you, so don't ask!" George said.

"Well thanks mister," the wino said as George walked by in a hurried pace.

I ought to string him up on that light pole by the neck and watch him scream and convulse until he strangles to death, fucking low-life!

Home

Finally home. What a day. It's an older home but who cares? It's paid for! Ah the sanctity and peacefulness of home. No one to stare at me, no one to disturb me and my dinner. This is the only place where I feel at peace and safe from that unruly outside world.

Oh, what do we have here? A roach? Even this roach isn't going to ruin my time, in my sanctuary.

Without wasting a second longer George stepped over and squashed the bug ending its life with a couple of twists back and forth, making sure it ground down into the wooden floor. George seemed to take satisfaction in the popping sound the roach made as it died. Just then, the microwave's timer pinged, letting him know his frozen dinner was ready.

Ah yes, my dinner! Small, but efficient and neat. I must take my hat off to the inventor of the microwave! Let me wash up before dinner.

As George turned the faucet to wash his hands a flow of rust-colored water began to flow out.

This same shit again! How many times do I have to call the city to get this fixed?? I knew that bitch I talked to last time wasn't paying attention. Typical city employee.

Just then the water turned to the normal clear, chlorinated flow.

I'll call those bastards again tomorrow.

George began to wash his hands with a smile on his face. A smile saying he knew something the rest of the world didn't know.

No sense letting others, and their lazy stupidity, ruin my time in my house, in my sanctuary.

With a sense of satisfaction he dried his hands and took his microwave dinner to the living room to his favorite chair. He placed the dinner on the TV tray in front of it. George always found peace here at home, and for the most part, let his mind be at ease and tried not to let the outside world into his four walls. He didn't have many things here, but they were enough to satisfy his needs and get him through his nights and weekends. He hit the remote to turn the TV on and flipped through a few channels, until he settled on a western.

Who needs those high priced, fancy TVs? Black and white is the way to go. Old classics, the old way.

Another smile of satisfaction came over his face as he stared into his small, 13" black and white screen.

<u>Work</u>

Some people hate their jobs. For one reason or another it has changed from what it once was, and has become almost unbearable to be there. For George, it wasn't the job; it was the people he worked with. The man he despised most is Carl Hubbard. Carl is an accountant, like George. He has been with company for ten years. He is a happy-go-lucky fellow, but his social skills are lacking, and despite his knowledge as a CPA, he communicates very slowly when talking. Let's check in on George as he arrives at his office.

I hope she doesn't say hi, or good morning, or hello George! I can't stand a fake person like her. I know she is the receptionist, and that's all part of her job but...

"Well good morning George," Doris the receptionist said, in a cheerful voice.

"How are you today?"

"I'm fine thank you," is all George cared to say, be it in a polite and cheerful way. He hurried by her desk and into the minefield of cubicles, chairs and computers.

I just don't understand how a person can be so damn happy all the time! Luckily I made it here early, and should be able to make it to my desk without anyone else holding me up.

George made it to his desk undisturbed. His cubicle had a small amount of clutter, but nothing like most of the desks in the department. George always kept his things in order, and things were exactly where he knew they would be. His main working tool was his computer.

This computer better not crash again like last week. I.T. better get their act together, and do their damn job!

As the computer booted up, George took a visual scan of his work area to see if there was anything missing or out of place from the night before.

Everything looks to be where I left it. Never know about that damn cleaning crew. Let's see here. Email from my asshole boss. Wants to meet with me today as soon as I get settled in. Ha! I think I'll delay that for a bit and go to take a piss. Yes! Take a leak and not wash my hands, then walk up and shake his hand!

George walked to the restroom; his little ploy for delaying his boss was in full motion. Just as he entered he ran into Carl.

"Hey George! Good morning."

There stood Carl. George's plan ruined. Carl always carried his ridiculously large 60 oz. refill mug wherever he went, even in the bathroom. The mug was old, dirty, and stained.

Now this mother fucker!

"Hey Carl. How are you?" George asked while trying to hurry past Carl to the privacy of the toilet stall.

"I wouldn't go in there if I were you," Carl said with his infamous Santa Claus laugh.

This guy is really gonna try to hold a conversation with me here in the bathroom??

Carl is known around the office as obnoxious, with nothing really in common other than being a CPA like most others.

"How was your drive in George?"

This big, tall, fat bastard is really gonna stay in here and talk through the stall door!? Damn, it stinks in here.

"My drive in was fine, but if you don't mind I'd rather do this in private." George said as professionally as he could.

"Oh, okay right. I'm sorry. I'll see you out on the floor," Carl said as he walked out the door.

Yeah I'll see you on the floor alright. Lying on the floor with your face buried in your own stinky shit, suffocating to death while I hold you down in it.

George smiled at the thought. He finished up, waiting longer than usual to make sure Carl was not lingering outside, and then headed to his boss's office. Next to Carl, his boss was the second most hated person in his life. He always handled himself professionally and polite so they never knew, no one ever knew his hatred and violent thoughts towards them. George entered his boss's office with his normal smile and greeting.

"You wanted to see me?"

"Hello George, yes I did. I have Bill working on another project so I need to cover his work on the Brown account. You're familiar with it so I'll need you to keep up with it as you can," his boss, Mark Willis said, never looking up from his desk.

Man, the nerve of him! If I had a sledgehammer in my hands right now... I would slam it down and squash his head flat like a watermelon, all over his precious paperwork and desk!!

"It shouldn't be a problem Mr. Willis."

"Good, keep me informed," Willis said, still not giving George the courtesy of eye-to-eye contact.

Asshole! I don't think a sledgehammer would be good enough now. George thought as he walked out of the office.

Movies

Being a Thursday, it is movie night for George. He doesn't go to the trendy overcrowded places. No, he prefers the quiet and less crowded dollar theater. He doesn't go every Thursday, but when there is a movie he likes, you'll find him there. George stands outside the ticket window contemplating his choice when his cell phone begins to buzz in his pocket. He doesn't recognize the number but answers anyway.

"Hello?"

"Dad? This is Marsha."

George stood in silence, not knowing how to respond. He has not spoken to his daughter in five years. There falling out was his fault, he knew, but he still found a way to blame her for their discontent.

"Dad?"

"Yes? Yes I'm here."

"Dad I know we haven't talked in a long time, but I felt I should call you. It's been too long."

George was still in shock and didn't know what to say.

"Yes it has been too long." That was all he could think to say as his mind raced with thoughts that something could be wrong with Marsha.

"Dad I called to tell that you are going to be a Grandpa. I just found out that I'm pregnant."

Silence, silence only on the phone, but George's mind was running wild with shock, surprise, and anger.

What the hell?? I haven't heard from her in five years and now I do, and I'm thinking the worst, and all it is, is that she is knocked up?! How dare her scare me like that!!

George kept his inner emotions inside his head.

"Wow, congratulations. I guess I'll be a grandfather soon." His words sounded so dry and fake, but it was better than saying what he really wanted to say. "Very well. When are you due?"

"I'm only two months right now, so around November. The father is my boyfriend. I've been with him for three years now."

More silence.

"That's very good Marsha, I'm happy for you."

Marsha could sense that he was very surprised by the call and the news. Both were so out of the blue that she decided to try and end the call on a good note.

"Well I just wanted to let you know. I'm so glad you have kept your old number so that I could reach you."

"Yes, well I'm glad you called," said George, trying to sound convincing.

"Okay dad, well I better go. Maybe Robert and I can drive up someday and visit you, if you think that will be okay?"

"Sure anytime."

Not convinced, Marsha continued on anyway.

"Of course we would call ahead. Nice to talk to you Dad, I hope everything is okay with you."

"Everything is fine. You take care now," he said as he hung up.

"Bye dad."

George stood outside the theater in amazement. Part of him was so angry at his daughter, who he had not heard from in years and part of him very proud at the thought of being a grandfather. Mixed emotions for a man who never has a nice thought for people around him. This was different. This was...

I can't believe she called out of the blue like that. But damn! Why hasn't she tried to call me before this? All this time has gone by and then there she is calling. She must think I'm some soft, easy-to-fool old man. She's got another coming!

With that, George entered the theater. He got in line to get popcorn and a drink. The young cashier spilled some of his popcorn on the counter.

Stupid kid! They don't care. They're not taught any respect or common sense.

"I'm sorry sir, let me top that off again," the cashier said.

George took the popcorn and walked to his movie. It's was a lot more crowded than usual, and that had him a little on edge as he took his seat.

Don't these people have anything else to do then to be at a movie on a Thursday night?? And if this fucking idiot doesn't stop kicking my chair I'm gonna strangle his pathetic ass!

A man sitting two seats over coughed, and tried hard to hack up his mucus.

Asshole! Why would you come to a public place and do that?

George looked over at the man with a cold, almost wicked stare. The stare sent a chill through the man's body. The man looked away.

Damn right. You know what's best for you. Look away like the little punk that you are.

The lights dimmed as the previews started. As usual, lights from cell phones popped up all over the theater.

The same thing every week! No respect for others. This bastard next to me better not even think about pulling out his phone or I'll slam his head into the seat in front of him and split his head open!

A theater attendant came up the isle shining a flashlight at the various cell phone users. There must have been one behind George because the beam of the flashlight hit him right in the face. As angry as it made him, he offered a small smile until the attendant redirected his light to the real culprit.

I appreciate him doing his job, but he is an idiot too. If he kept that light on me one more second I would have...

Just then the movie started. As if on cue, a baby two rolls back began to cry.

Immediately George turned.

"Hey. Do you mind??"

The lady looked embarrassed and rocked the baby trying to stop it from crying. George took a quick glance at the newborn and turned around. A strange feeling hit him as he watched the movie. He didn't feel the anger anymore. He felt connected in some way to the baby, my grandbaby, he thought as he turned again for a quick look. His heart filled with a different kind of emotion, compassion, and maybe even happiness. He quickly turned back to the movie.

But that's not Marsha, or my grandbaby. Just some lady with a crying kid interrupting my movie!!

George was back to his old inner self. He made it through the movie without incident aside, from the mucus-hacking man munching his popcorn at the most quiet moments in the movie. He let it pass without action and only played it out in his dark mind.

After the movie George went home to contemplate his daughter's call. His anger would build then subside. His emotions rode him like a roller coaster. They say a daughter's heart can tame the most rugged of fathers, and in George's case, potentially the most violent. Yes, women have a way with men, but it wasn't only his daughter. The thought of having his next generation starting, his granddaughter, gave him a feeling of great pride inside. He spoke out loud so the rest of his vacant kitchen could hear.

"I'm gonna be a grandfather! Finally something goes right for me."

He finished his cup of coffee and called it a night. He lay in bed feeling better about himself knowing that he was able to fight his violent, inner demons, and turn into the nice and innocent George that everyone else knew on the outside.

He slept well that night and woke up ready to try out his new found inner-spirit on the world. Until...

"Where in the hell is all this water coming from? I'll be damned! It's leaking from the same spot the plumber fixed last week. That no good prick! I'll have his ass when I call his boss."

George turned off the main valve on the water line and got ready for his day. He planned to call the plumber on the way to the DMV. He asked for an hour off to renew his driver's license.

As he pulled out of his driveway he was already dialing the plumber. He got the message service answering machine and angrily flipped the phone shut and threw it on the passenger seat.

What's the use of having a business number of you aren't going to answer the damn phone!

He finished his drive to the DMV and called the plumber one more time.

"Hello, Ace-Hil Plumbing. How may I help you?" the friendly voice on the other end said.

"Well you can start by patching me through to the owner if you don't mind?"

"May I ask who's calling?"

"This is George Milton. His guy did a repair on my pipes, and now it has leaked all over my kitchen floor."

"Oh yes I remember your call last week. I'm very sorry for the problem. Please hold."

Now I'm on hold?? Unbelievable!

George could feel his bad, inner side beginning, for the first time, to creep out into the real world.

"Mr. Milton? Can I get your number and have Mr. Johnson call you right back? He is on a call at the moment."

Son of a bitch! You can't even get good customer service in this world anymore.

"I'll tell you what, why don't you give me his direct line and I'll talk to him man to man. Enough with all this horse shit!"

"I'm sorry sir?" the shocked secretary asked.

For the first time the demon inside George showed itself to the outside world.

"Look, just tell him I won't be home for another two hours and I would appreciate it if he could have someone there at that time. Think you can do that!? Think you can handle that?!"

George was starting to lose control as he hung up the phone, while she sat in stunned silence.

Fucking idiots! Now the line will probably be a mile long to get my license!

<u>DMV</u>

George walked into the DMV and was about tenth in line. The place was already crowded with people waiting to be seen for one reason or another.

This is fucking worse than the doctor's office. Probably the same type of people who were there, always looking for a handout. Assholes!

George was letting his anger get the best of him. He got to the front of the line and got his ticket, # 29A. He found a seat and sat down. The plumber was still on his mind and making him angrier by the second.

Damn this place is loud. People have no respect for others, and no social awareness.

"Now serving number 12B at window 31," the robotic voice on the speaker said.

I'll be here all fucking morning! I'll probably miss the plumber and my house will be ruined.

So many things were going through his mind, and all of them made him angry. It made him feel out of control.

Look at these kids. No belt, pants hanging down, and they think they're cool. My dad would have put a belt to my ass so fast if I had dressed like that.

Just as George was turning his head around he was accidentally bumped by a Hispanic woman with her kids. He looked up at her expecting an apology, but got none as she sat down.

I didn't really expect an apology did I? People are animals!

A cell phone played a loud musical ringtone behind him. After it was finally answered, the young man spoke loudly into the phone.

I guess he has to let everyone in on his conversation. People think they can just be just as loud or obnoxious as they want in public.

Just then, his chair was accidentally kicked by the young man on the phone. George then turned to him with a smile, but the most sinister of smiles.

"Do you mind not kicking my chair, and keep your voice down a little?"

George's stare never broke from the young man's eyes. He had a way of conveying his anger and violence through his eyes. The young man shook his head yes and turned his eyes away from George, and spoke much softer. Satisfied, George turned around. His heart was beating fast, emotions on edge, struggling to keep it all together. Even though the man complied, his temper was raging inside. He was reaching the breaking point. The point where people snap, and do violent acts. Now, he felt like hurting someone. His hand trembled with anger.

"Now accepting #29A at window 14," the speaker blasted in his ears. It pulled George out of his violent thoughts and he looked up at the flashing display, then down at his ticket. Finally, his turn. He had to clear his head before he got to the window.

Still emotional and angry he made it to window 14. He put on his nice-guy outward appearance but his face was still red and his hand still shook.

"I'm here to get my license renewed."

"Oh my. They gave you the wrong number at the help desk. They should have given you B. I can't renew licenses here sir."

The rage inside came back full-force. His hands were now on her desk and he was trying to not shake. His face reddened as he looked down at her, not having taken his seat.

"What do you mean you can't help me? I've been waiting for over an hour."

"I am really sorry sir. My computer can't access, or give out renewals. If you go back to the h..." George interrupted.

"Help desk. Yes I figured! This is typical of people not paying attention to their jobs."

He turned and walked toward the help desk, but had no intention of stopping there. He went outside to his car and opened the trunk. He reached down and pulled out the machete that he carried in the trunk, slid it inside his jacket, and zipped it shut. Rage filled his mind now.

I can't take it anymore! I can't stop it! That little bastard on the phone sitting behind me will be first!

He began to walk towards the doors, oblivious to anyone around him. He was not the same anymore. He finally gave in to his inner demons. He opened the glass doors and walked back to where he was sitting. He saw not only the young man that was on the phone behind him, but the two other thugs, the ones he saw earlier with the ridiculous pants. As he got halfway the three young men stared at him. One waved him over in an arrogant way, and ended the wave by giving George the middle finger. George slowed for just a second, as the rage grew more intense. He was now about thirty feet from them and picked up his pace.

A much more determined pace. His mind had him now. A truly innocent and nice man on the outside, now about to turn into a mass murderer, starting with those three thugs. As he got halfway there they sat up realizing he was not scared and he was coming for them. George was not bluffing. He began to unzip his jacket and reached in to grab the handle. They had no idea what was about to happen to them. As he reached to get the machete, a Hispanic girl about five years old, ran to him with a cell phone. She reached up to him, proud and smiling, with her mother watching close by. George was taken back. He stopped and let go of the machete handle that was still out of sight in his jacket. He reached down to the little girl and took his phone. She smiled real big, and then ran a few steps back to her mom.

"Well thank you. I didn't realize I had dropped it. Thank you very much," he said as he smiled back at the girl.

So young, so innocent, no fear. That is something special that kids have.

His thoughts turned to his future granddaughter. He now realized what could stop his inner demon at any moment. Even in his most unstable of mindsets, just like now.

He smiled big realizing he had beat his demon, and looked at the three young men, all three looking ready to take him on if needed, but still a little confused by the interruption. George walked over to them. They stood eye-to-eye with George. He smiled and said: "Have a nice day gentlemen."

He turned and walked away. He could hear them making vulgar, demeaning remarks. He saw it as a test and thought of his unborn granddaughter. He now saw the light and realized there was much more life left to live and be a part of his next generation. He continued smiling with the machete tucked safely in his jacket, as he made his way to the door. George pulled out his cell phone to dial his daughter's number as he walked by the help desk and smiled at the lady who had given him the wrong info earlier.

As he looked down at his phone to dial Marsha's number, a man not unlike the dark, violent inner George, was entering the building, his face full of rage and anger. From his long black trench coat, the man pulled out a sawed-off shotgun and aimed at the first person he saw...George.

George looked up just in time to see a blast of fire explode from the barrels of the gun. The shot hit George in his chest and sent him backwards. The sound of the blast sent people running and screaming in every direction. Laying on his back, in a pool of his blood, and in shock, George looked up at the fluorescent bulbs burning above, and wondered if he was ascending into heaven. His vision was beginning to cloud as he heard another blast from the shotgun. Out of George's sight, an on-duty constable, fired at the gunman, hitting him in the neck and chest, sending him flying back and on to the floor, the shotgun dropping at his side. George looked up one last time, and standing over him was the little girl that found his phone.

Without knowing, he had shielded her from the initial blast and saved her life. His last vision, as his eyes closed, was her looking down at him with a shocked, blank stare. The last thing he heard, was not little girl's mother screaming for her, or the people running around afraid for their lives.

The last thing he heard was his daughter's voice, coming from his cell phone.

"Dad? ...Dad?"

Tic Toc

"Anything lost can be found again, except for time wasted."

Since September 11, 2001, people are much more aware of their surroundings in the places they travel, be it by plane, train, car or boat. Even a leisurely walk down the street can be dangerous these days. Make no mistake, the enemy is always out there. We are more aware of that fact, but sometimes we get caught up in our everyday lives and forget that no matter what, the enemy never sleeps. Sometimes . . . we are our own worst enemy. The clock is always ticking.

The ringing in his ears was more than bad, it was deafening. Car alarms sounded from every direction. The white haze of a dim light surrounded his truck and burned his eyes, as if the sun was shining directly into them. Small pieces of glass and dust were falling all around Brian as he woke up behind the wheel and airbag of his truck. His vision was slowly coming back to him. He looked down at his watch; it read 12:00 p.m. He thought he heard the sounds of screams, but wasn't sure. The ringing in his ears was now centered in the middle of his brain. The high-pitched alarm sound pounded his head like a sledgehammer. As his vision became less blurry, he noticed, through his shattered windshield, that a figure was walking towards him. Brian was pinned in and his body ached as he tried to move free in his badly wrecked truck. He again tried to focus on the figure walking closer and closer. If his eyes were right, the tall dark figure was hooded, wearing black, and carrying a long-handled blade. Even in all the confusion, and not remembering what happened to him, the hooded figure walking towards him looked like the Grim Reaper.

What the hell, Brian thought. The figure moved slow and methodically and was now only twenty feet from him. Brian tried to get free of the seatbelt. His senses were quickly coming back to him.

BOOOM!!

All the sounds and all the sights around him disappeared. The Reaper was gone, and the only thing left was a light, a brighter light than before. Brian felt no more pain, no more discomfort. The light flashed brighter, blinding Brian. Then, everything went dark.

The darkness brought voices, or more like whispers. "You must return, you must return." Is what it sounded like. "Not much time. One more chance, one more . . ." Then the voices faded.

He woke up again, this time at the intersection of Murrell and Greenway. Brian was again behind the wheel of his truck, but this time he was at a red light. He looked down at his hands, then at his face in the mirror. Was it some kind of dream? He thought to himself. He looked at his watch, this time it read 10:00 a.m. Confused, he looked around him. The people in the cars next to him were doing the same as him, waiting for the light to change. Brian shook his head quickly in an effort to loosen the cobwebs.

The view from his seat looked very familiar, a location on the outskirts of town. Then he remembered, he was just at this intersection a short time ago. This was the route he traveled when he was headed downtown.

The sound of a car's horn behind him broke him from his thoughts. The light was green; he hit the gas and put on his turn signal to pull over to the right. He needed more time to evaluate what was happening. He quickly pulled into a gas station and parked. After rubbing his eyes, he looked again at his watch. It now read 10:08 a.m.

"What is going on? It can't be a dream, it's all too real," he said out load. The dust, the Reaper, the light, and the accident had to be a dream, I'm not hurt or anything. Had to be a dream, he thought. Brian looked at his clothes, same shirt, same pants, and same shoes. "I come this way to work every day. I remember I had a doctor appointment this morning, that's why I'm at this intersection later than normal," he said, trying to rationalize his situation. He pulled out his cell phone and dialed his doctor's number.

"Dr. William's office, how can I help you?" the young female voice on the other end of the phone said.

"Yes, my name is Brian Jacobs. Did I have a doctor's appointment this morning?" he asked.

"Is this Mr. Jacobs?"

"Yes I am," he said, feeling very stupid for calling about his appointment that he was just at earlier.

"I remember you sir. My name is Adriana. We spoke on your way out. Is everything okay?" she asked.

"Oh yes of course I remember, I believe I dialed your office instead of my dentist. Everything is okay. I'm very sorry for the confusion," Brian said.

"No problem Mr. Jacobs. Have a good day."

Brian hung up. Still stunned and very confused, he checked his phone for calls that may have already happened. He was grasping, but he needed to find out if this was real or maybe, he had fallen asleep at the light and had a quick dream. That could be possible I guess, he thought. The only call listed was the one he just made. Still thinking, he checked his text messages. He had received one this morning from his wife and he had sent one. Both messages said: I Love You.

Brian looked at the clock in his truck. 10:25 a.m. He talked to himself. "If this is, or was a dream, what day did my accident happen? Or was there an explosion?" Again, he looked down at his clothes. He knew the answer before he looked. They were the same. "What the hell is going on? I can't remember a thing!" Brian ran his hands through his hair. He put his truck in drive, deciding to continue on his route, hoping to remember something or figure out what was happening.

Brian's cell phone rang, he looked down at it, his wife was calling, and the time was 10:34.

"Hey babe," he said.

"Hey there. How did it go?" his wife, Terri asked.

Brian was still confused, but didn't want to let Terri know anything was wrong. "It went well babe."

"Well what did they say?"

"They said I'm okay, nothing wrong." He didn't know if he was telling the truth or not, but he had to say something. "I'll tell you about it later, I'm driving right now."

"Okay, okay, I won't bother you. I'm glad it went well," she said. "Are you still going to pick me up for lunch?"

Her question sounded familiar to him. He felt that whatever was happened might start coming back to him. "Yeah I'll be there. What time again?" he said trying to not sound stupid.

"At noon, like always. Are you sure you're okay?" Terri sounded concerned.

"I know babe. I'm just messing with you. See you at noon."

"Okay bye. Love you," she said and hung up. Meet her for lunch? If I could only remember what we talked about leading up to that, Brian thought.

He kept driving towards downtown. Terri's office was there, but he was still at least forty-five minutes away at best. She worked for a customer service center. It was only 10:50, hopefully enough time to figure it all out.

"She said noon. Noon? Wait a minute; it was just at noon when I was at the accident. Where the hell was I?" His thoughts were coming clearer. "I need to get to downtown to see if it helps me remember."

Brian, a man who knew he had to do something by noon, but he was also a man who didn't understand how or why. He headed for the freeway; it would be the fastest way to downtown. The traffic was flowing well for about three miles, but before he could exit he found himself in the middle of a traffic jam caused by an accident a quarter mile up.

"Shit!" He slammed his hands on the wheel and checked the time, 11:00. The sounds of horns honking brought on the memory and vision from earlier. They sounded much like the car alarms from his dream, or whatever it was. The familiar sounds jolted his brain. He could now see where he was after the crash, with debris falling around him, trapped in his truck. It was all happening so fast in his mind, but yes! He could recall what happened.

"Okay, just before the crash," he said. He was thinking hard, eyes closed. "Just before the crash I was driving." Brian was playing it back in his mind like a movie. "I was going to pick up Terri. I was on Congress St. heading west when a big cargo truck in front of me suddenly stopped." He was remembering it all. "I couldn't stop in time. I swerved to the right and up on the curve, just at the corner of Terri's building. I hit a newspaper stand at the corner and then ran into the front glass of Terri's building. Yes I remember now.

"Now I remember crashing into the lobby windows. There must have been an explosion in Terri's building! Oh my God, I have to call Terri and warn her," Brian said, frantically looking for her number on his phone. He called her but only got her voicemail. "I have to get out of this traffic." He looked around, searching for the nearest off-ramp. "I only have forty-five minutes!"

Brian twisted and turned his truck in and around cars to make his way to the outside lane. People cursed and honked at him as he squeezed by. Sweat was pouring down his face as he attempted another call, this time to her office phone. He got the same result . . . voicemail.

The off-ramp was full with cars and trucks, but there was enough room for him to try and get by on the left side. He had to do it. He had to get to Terri.

Brian thought briefly about calling 911 to report what he thought was going to happen, but he knew how it would sound to the operator to make that kind of statement. He would wait until he got closer to the location to be sure.

11:25 a.m.

He finally got his truck to the bottom of the ramp. At least here on the surface streets he would be moving. Brian headed straight down Jackson St. This was the fastest route considering the long sections of road between lights. He was driving well over the speed limit and making good time. He tried Terri's phone again.

"Hello, Brian? Coming to get me?" she said.

"Terri. I've been trying to get hold of you," he said as he saw the traffic piled up at the next light.

"What's wrong? Are you okay?"

"Listen, this is going to sound bizarre. I want you to get out of your building now. I'm not sure yet, but I think something bad is going to happen there," he said.

"What? What do you mean? How do you know?" Her voice sounded much more concerned.

"I don't know what it is or was. I had some kind of dream or nightmare, but I just know something bad," he paused contemplating whether to say it or not, "maybe even a bomb may be in your building." He couldn't believe he actually said it.

There was a short silence.

"What did you just say? A bomb? In my building?" Terri's was shocked, and her tone was lower, not wanting anyone around her to hear what she was saying.

"Listen Terri, just get the hell out of there now. Please! Something is going to happen around noon."

"I don't understand. How do you know all this?"

"I really can't explain Terri, just get the hell out! I'll be there soon."

11:40

Driving down Jackson St. was faster than the freeway, but was slow in places, so Brian tried to make up time when he could by ducking in and out of traffic and speeding through intersections. He hoped like hell that Terri did as he asked.

Brian's memory was coming back to him more and more. As he drove, his mind was bringing back his drive from earlier. He had turned down Congress St. and was looking forward to meeting Terri for lunch. If their timing was right, he was going to park out front and catch her as she left the building. He remembered that he was on time, he wasn't in a rush. He was driving slowly, as not to get there too early. Recalling his vision, Brian could see Terri's building in the distance on the right.

Brian had to slam his brakes as the car in front of him came to a sudden stop. Brian's truck screeched to a halt, and reality came back to him. Is this really happening? Or was this really a dream?, he thought. He looked around the intersection, scanning the crowd at the corners, impatiently waiting for the light to change, when he is eye caught a dark figure. He refocused on the tall figure that stood just off the sidewalk and close to the door of a business. Brian shook his head. This was the Reaper, the one he saw in his vision or dream. The tall, dark figure in black never looked up at him, just stood there facing Brian. Chills ran up and down his spine.

The light turned green and the car in front of him was well through the intersection by the time Brian noticed. He hit the gas, still focusing on the Reaper. The eerie site continued as the Reaper turned, facing Brian as he passed.

"Damn!" He had to swerve to get back into his lane as he turned his eyes back to the road. A quick glance back revealed no Reaper in sight. If there was any doubt before, this new vision erased all of it. He had to get to Terri fast.

11:48

Terri had to really think about what Brian had told her. She heard the conviction in his voice. She knew him well, and although he liked to joke around, this was different, she could feel it. She knew it.

In the time since he told her, she ran to her boss' office and tried her best to explain to her that the building had to be evacuated. It had to be cleared out by noon. There was no time to waste. All these things were said to her boss, and with the same conviction or more, as Brian had said.

Fortunately for Terri, her building was small, and only two floors were being used. Her boss, Jennifer, hesitated, not knowing if it was a joke or some kind of prank. Jennifer also knew that Terri wouldn't joke about something like this, and when the word terrorists was mentioned, Jennifer didn't care where Terri got her information from, or what the motive was, nor did she waste time getting her staff and workers off the floor and down to ground level. Jennifer relied on her instinct in believing the conviction and sincerity of Terri's words. It was the same instinct that helped her move into the high-level position that she held with the company. Jennifer called 911.

Terri and Jennifer worked together to get the one hundred or so employees rounded up and down the stairs to the bottom floor. Terri was very thankful that there wasn't a lot of questioning or panicking. She also had the frame of mind to trip the fire alarm to get a quicker response. Fire alarm drills were very common in their building and everyone knew what to do when they heard it. With their insistence, the people quickly filed out the door and on to the sidewalk and street. Traffic stopped and people were realizing that it might be more than just a fire-alarm drill. She was also very nervous about what she had started. She trusted in what Brian was telling her, but she knew if this was a mistake, she probably would be fired.

11:55

Brian sped up as he got close to the building. Everything that was happening and everything that he was seeing felt just like before. He might as well have put it all on cruise-control. Everything was very clear now, and for the last ten minutes he knew that he was living his fate. All he hoped for was that Terri had gotten herself out of the building. As he approached in the heavy traffic, he saw some commotion outside the front of her building. People! Terri had listened! He felt relieved and turned the wheel to move into the left lane, but was almost hit by a passing car. He had to turn the wheel quickly back to the right to avoid the car and when he focused his eyes straight ahead, he saw break lights. The van in front of him was at a complete stop.

Brian had no time to stop and had no choice but to steer his truck to the right and out over the curb to the sidewalk. A couple of people screamed as they jumped out of the way as Brian tried to bring the speeding truck to a stop. He had no idea he was already at the intersection when he jumped the curb. By the time he hit the brake in his panic, he was crashing through the first floor windows of Terri's building.

His foot was pushing down as hard as he could on the brake. Broken plates of glass, as well as shattered pieces, rained down all around him as he came to a stop, just before the airbag exploded into his face and knocked him out temporarily. Brian's truck had went about twenty feet inside the first floor. His truck was smashed on the driver's side door, the motor was pushed in towards him and pinning his legs.

11:59

Police sirens were approaching from all directions. Terri, with tears in her eyes, held her phone to her ear as she called Brian. She heard the crashing sound of glass and steel, but could not see who or what the cause of it was. People scattered further across the street, and by now along with curious bystanders, the crowd had swelled to twice the size.

The ringing in his ears was more than bad, it was deafening. Car alarms sounded from every direction. The white haze of a dim light surrounded his truck and burned his eyes, as if the sun was shining directly into them. Small pieces of glass and dust were falling all around Brian as he woke up behind the wheel and airbag of his truck. His vision was slowly coming back to him. He looked down at his watch; it read 12:00 p.m. He thought he heard the sounds of screams, but wasn't sure. The ringing in his ears was now centered in the middle of his brain. The high-pitched alarm sound pounded his head like a sledgehammer. As his vision became less blurry, he noticed, through his shattered windshield, that a figure was walking towards him. Brian was pinned in and his body ached as he tried to move free in his badly wrecked truck. He again tried to focus on the figure walking closer and closer. If his eyes were right, the tall dark figure was hooded, wearing black, and carrying a long-handled blade. Even in all the confusion, and not remembering what happened to him, the hooded figure walking towards him looked like the Grim Reaper.

He refocused, now remembering what happened before. He had it just like he wanted. He spoke to Mr. Death.

"Come on bitch. You wanted me, come get me. But you can't take everyone, they're outside now. Come get me!!"

Brian knew that if he couldn't cheat his death; he could at least try to save his wife and anyone else who would listen.

The Reaper was closer, now at the front of Brian's truck. He lifted his head and Brian could finally see the stare of death in its black holes it had for eyes. The skull and face of the Reaper were more powerful and horrifying than Brian had imagined.

Brian stared in amazement as the Reaper turned just at the front of the truck, and it began walking towards the crowd outside, towards Terri. The messenger of death looked like he had a smile on his face as he walked past Brian. Brian was now in shock, realizing that the one thing he could never figure out, where the bomb had exploded, was now very clear to him. It was never planted inside; the bomb was actually outside, in the street.

What have I done?? Have I sent everyone to their deaths?

He tried to free himself again, but he was pinned and unable to move. All he could do was watch the Reaper move towards the crowd. Brian screamed . . .

"NOOOOOOOOOOOOOO!!!!"

BOOOM!

Brian awoke from the terrible nightmare. He had soaked his gown and the sheets of his hospital bed with his sweat. His eyes came to focus at everything surrounding him. He wasn't in his truck anymore. He wasn't in that hellish nightmare. He saw no Grim Reaper. Thank God. He was in a hospital bed.

Standing, looking out the window was a woman. Her back was to him and the light from the window made her more of a silhouette than anything else, but he recognized her. It was his wife, Terri.

"Terri? Honey?" he called out to her.

"I'm glad you're awake," Terri said as she turned to face Brian. "I need to talk to you." Her features were still shadowed because of the light from the window. She walked to Brian. He smiled, happy that she was okay.

Her lower body came into view first as she walked into the light shining from above the bed. He noticed that she was wearing the same dress as she was the day of the explosion. Terri's upper body and face came into view next.

"Why did you do that Brian?" she asked. She walked closer to the edge of the bed.

Terri's left arm was missing, completely gone. The entire left side of her body was charred black and burned. Brian's eyes went wide and in complete horror as he brought his shaking hand to his mouth. The left side of Terri's face was also gone, totally blown off. Only her right eye remained and it focused on him as she stood three feet away. She spoke again through what was left of her jaw and mouth.

"Why did you send me to my death hun? I thought you loved me." She reached with her blackened and blistered right hand and touched his cheek.

Brian screamed . . .

Weekend Visit

"We do not have to visit a madhouse to find madness."

I am a private investigator hired by the family of Richard Johnson. I have obtained information that I am making public in an effort to help with this case. This is what was turned over to me, as written by Mr. Johnson:

"My name is Richard Johnson. I am of sound mind and body. I am not crazy."

I never thought much about clowns before this all happened. I always saw them as something that might be at a kid's party, or something you would see at a circus. Well, maybe one other time, when I read Stephen King's "It" and that wasn't a pleasant clown, nothing like I had seen before anyway. Since that time clowns had all but vanished from my mind . . . until that day.

This is how I remember it.

<u>Friday</u>

My girlfriend Lori has an aunt who lives in the backwoods of Big Lake in the White Mountains of Arizona. She is closer to her than her own mother, based on the few years we have been together. Aunt Carol invited us up from the valley where it was already warming up in April. The drive up was nice, not too much traffic. Lori and I have made this trip; it seems like a million times. I know it now by heart.

Carol's place is very nice and very cozy. It's a small two-bedroom house that sits back from the road, nicely nestled into the pine trees. Driving into the cooler temperatures felt good even though summer hadn't hit the Phoenix valley yet. Lori and Carol had been talking a lot during the week. Carol had told her about letting a friend of her brother's stay on her property in a small travel trailer. Brady had been there for about a month.

When we pulled into town it was just getting dark. Carol was so glad to see us. We talked for awhile and decided to get something to eat. As we were leaving we saw Brady in front of his trailer and Carol waved. Brady looked down, giving the slightest of waves back.

"He kind of keeps to himself," Carol said.

"Seems strange, doesn't he Aunt Carol?" Lori asked.

I didn't think much of it and we headed on our way to have dinner. Lori was more concerned about her aunt being around a stranger, so she asked a few questions at dinner. I kept nudging Lori under the table to stop being nosey, but once I got that, let-me-handle-this look from her, I left it alone. According to Carol, she had met him a couple of times, through her brother, before all of this came up, and he had always been respectful and kind. Her brother had actually been by to visit a week ago, to see how things were going.

"Like I said, he pretty much keeps to himself and doesn't bother me at all. He seems very nice." Carol told us.

"Well how long does he plan to stay Aunt Carol?" asked Lori.

"He said at the latest until the end of this month. It does feel having a man here for the first time since Jim passed."

Jim was Carol's husband before he died in a car accident two years earlier. Lori felt bad at that point and stopped asking her questions.

We left the restaurant and went back to Carol's. I was tired and was falling asleep as Lori and her aunt talked the night away. As I dozed off on the sofa, for the third or fourth time, I was awakened by a blood-curdling howl. It sounded sort of like a dog, but more like a wolf, or something else. It lasted a few seconds, but was long enough for me to tell that it was nothing like any animal I had ever heard. I looked up at Lori and Carol, they heard the same thing. Carol had a strange look on her face.

"It's just a mountain animal or something. I've heard it before plenty." She said

I wasn't convinced by the way she reacted, but she lived on the mountain and I didn't so as soon as the howling stopped everything was back to normal. After awhile longer we went to bed. Lori was still worried about her aunt and asked me to go meet Brady the next day while they went shopping.

"Are you sure babe? I think we should wait until your aunt introduces us to him before I go talk to him."

"I understand but I would feel better if you kind of surprised him, just to see what he is like." She said

I knew there was no need to argue the point and said okay.

Saturday

I woke up before Carol and Lori and put some coffee on. I walked over to the kitchen window and looked out towards the small travel trailer that belonged to Brady. You could tell it was a small one room set up on a double axle. He had made a makeshift back patio by running a tarp out from the back along with a couple of chairs and a small table. I saw a clown mask propped up on the handle end of a rake. Then I saw a lot of, the best way I can describe, small clown heads hanging by string from the makeshift porch under the tarp. There had to be at least fifty or more. Different sizes, different faces. With that I was getting a little curious as to what this guy was all about. Maybe he was a clown as a part time job.

Carol was up soon after, then Lori. She doesn't drink coffee, but we chatted for a little while as Carol made breakfast.

"I'm going to see if Brady would like some breakfast. I'll be right back." Carol said as she went out the back door.

I turned to Lori and asked if she had seen all the clown stuff out back. She walked over to the window and it made her feel as I did, strange. Maybe it was something he did for a living. Carol was knocking at the trailer door but got no answer. She came back in and said he must have already left for the day.

"I don't mean to be nosey Aunt Carol, but what are all those clown heads about?" I couldn't help but to ask, and it surprised Lori that I beat her to the punch.

"He collects different things besides those clowns. He just recently put those up. They don't bother me any, so it's no big deal. He's had a lady friend over a couple of times and from what I can tell, she really likes them. Maybe that's why he has them up." Carol shrugged.

"It looks weird Aunt. Are you sure you are okay here."

"I said I'm okay dear." Carol's voice sounded annoyed now. "Well Lori we better get going so I can get back and make some dinner."

Aunt Carol was always worried about making sure we were taken care of and we always told her not to worry, but that was to no avail. Carol went out to get the car and Lori turned to me to remind me to go talk to Brady when he gets back. I nodded yes.

Carol's home is very cozy, and a perfect place to relax and get away from the fast paced life in the valley. I always enjoy my time there, and when they go off on their shopping sprees I really find it nice to just sit down and read, or do absolutely nothing. That day I planned on doing absolutely nothing. A few minutes later I heard a truck pull up and looked out the front window and saw a man and a woman pull down the side of the driveway towards the back where the trailer was. I walked to the kitchen and on to the back window and found myself being nosier than is my nature. Brady was a short man, average size, maybe 5' 6", and had a very colorful shirt. It looked like a clown costume shirt. I figured that must be his profession considering everything else that was out there. The woman with him was tall, very close to six foot and she was barefoot. She had a thin dress, dirty blonde hair, and what appeared to be blue eyes. All this I saw in a few seconds then moved away from the window as they went inside.

Now I had a decision to make. Go over and introduce myself to Brady or leave it, since he had company over. I decided to wait until they came outside and casually walk out to meet them. I walked to the refrigerator and looked inside for something to snack on, when I heard knocking at the door. I walked into the front room and looked through the blinds. It was Brady! How did he get to the front so fast? I thought. I just saw him walk inside his trailer. I opened the door and was met with a surprised face.

"Hello I'm Richard." as I offered a handshake. He shook my hand very soft and quick.

"Hello I'm Brady. Is Carol in?"

"No, I'm sorry Brady, Carol and my girlfriend Lori went into town to get some things. Carol is our aunt." I explained. "Can I do something for you?"

"I just got back in from town myself and forgot to get a couple of candles. I was gonna see if Carol might have one I could use. I have a friend over and thought it would be nice to have dinner by candlelight. I also left some steaks to thaw with Carol yesterday and didn't want them to spoil in my trailer. If you could see if she has them in her refrigerator, I would appreciate it," he said.

I asked him to come in while I looked, but he said he would stay outside. As I looked for some candles and the steaks, my mind was in overdrive thinking that he did seem very nice and normal, but there was just something about him I couldn't figure out. I found a couple of candles and some matches and gave him his steaks that were in a Safeway bag.

"These were the only steaks in the fridge."

"Yes these are the ones thank you very much; nice to meet you and tell Carol I said hello and thanks," he told me.

"I will," I said, "Nice to meet you too."

I closed the door and rushed to the back window to see him enter the trailer and had a weird feeling about it all. Something just didn't sit right with me. At least I had met him like Lori wanted. As much as I was curious about Brady, I knew it was a good time to relax and watch some TV or read. The place just felt so homely to me that it made it very easy to unwind. Plenty of times before, Lori and Carol had returned to find me snoring on the couch. I grabbed a couple of snacks, put the TV on, and sat down to read. I had started a very good Richard Laymon book a few days earlier and it was getting better with each page. I got through two or three chapters fairly quick before I started dozing off. I was awakened by the sound of a man yelling, well maybe not yelling, but talking very loud and it sounded kind of hysterical. It was coming from the back. I walked over to the kitchen window and just as I looked I saw Brady going into the door of the trailer talking, maybe even persuading, his lady friend back inside, and what was really weird was that he had a clown mask on. Right away I started thinking they were into some really weird stuff, but they had just been arguing. It was strange. Just as I was looking away I noticed the mask that was on the rake was gone. It gave me the chills. Again I found myself being nosier than I am, and I hung around the kitchen waiting to hear or see something.

Nothing happened and I finally heard Carol and Lori pulling back in.

I was torn between telling Lori what I saw and minding my own business like I know I should but I knew she was going to question me.

"We're back!" Lori hollered from the porch. She sounded happy and was smiling, part of the reason why I am so attracted to her.

"How did it go?"

"It was good. We did a lot of looking and talking. We bought some things for dinner if you don't mind helping my aunt with it?"

I headed out the door and grabbed a few bags and brought them inside.

"How was your day Richard?" Carol asked.

"It was good just read and relaxed." I felt like I was keeping a secret by not telling her and Lori about what I saw. I just felt it wasn't my business, and I really didn't feel Carol was in any kind of danger from it.

"Brady stopped by to pick up his steaks and asked if he could borrow a candle or two. I found a couple you had and gave them to him. I hope that was okay?"

"Oh yes, I forgot about his steaks and of course the candles were fine. I have plenty of them. What did you think of Brady?" Carol asked.

I could feel Lori move and shift her body so she could hear my answer.

"He seemed like a very nice man. Kind of shy and reserved but very kind." What else was I supposed to say? Lori was watching me like a hawk to gauge my response.

"Well I'm glad you got to meet him. Is his friend still over?"

"Yes she is there as far as I can tell," I said as I felt Lori could tell I was not telling everything.

"Even though they have those steaks I'll see if they want to join us for some dinner," she said as she started getting things out that she needed for cooking.

Carol made up dinner fast. She knew how to cook and it was like an art form as she threw the food together out of nowhere. Lori and I talked awhile and I was debating on telling her about the weird feeling I had. She knew something was up. Lori knew me too well, but I was surprised she didn't challenge me more on it. Once I walked into the kitchen and casually looked out the window to see if I could see anything going on out there. All seemed quiet.

There was a knock at the door and Carol asked if I could get it. I answered and saw it was Carol's neighbor Earl. He lives next to her lot, but the lots are spread much more then you normally see in the bigger cities. His lot was at the end of the road marked, DEAD END.

"Hello Earl, how are you today?" I shook his hand "Come in."

"Thank you. Is Carol in? I have these pecans she asked me about earlier in the week."

"Yes she is in the kitchen making dinner."

Earl went into the kitchen and spoke with Carol and Lori. I overheard Carol say something about making a pecan pie, which didn't hurt my feelings none. I walked outside to the front yard to enjoy the cooler temps while they talked. I started thinking, everything else seemed so normal here so why was I worried about some guy and his girlfriend out back in a trailer. Truth be told, we were leaving tomorrow, and I just wanted to enjoy the rest of the weekend, so I was determined to put what was bothering me out of my mind. It was nothing.

The smell of the food being cooked inside started hitting my nose and helped me to further forget everything else. I walked towards the road and noticed bear tracks in the front yard. Bear tracks weren't uncommon at certain times of year in the mountains, but it was always nice to see something that was natural and something that couldn't be totally controlled by man at every turn. We were in the mountains after all. The area where Carol's house is has about six roads that intertwine and follow two main roads out to the highway. I enjoy taking evening walks up and down the roads to think and kill some time. Most of the places in the area were trailers which made Carol's place special because it is a log cabin and is placed in a perfect spot. I saw some snow piled, and still frozen next to a trailer. In the mountains snow can stay that way if it stayed in the shade for most of the day. I made it around the block and heard Lori calling for me.

"I'm on the way!" I shouted so she could hear me as I was still coming up the road towards the house. Lori waved and went back inside. I couldn't help but glance towards Brady's trailer but didn't see anything or anyone.

I went inside and Lori greeted me with a kiss.

"How was your walk?"

"Always good, feels nice up here. What's for dinner?"

"You know. My aunt's favorite casserole," she said laughing.

"Okay I'm gonna wash up and be right there," I said and went to the bathroom to wash my hands and face.

When I came into the kitchen I saw Lori looking out the window.

"What's up?" I asked.

"Nothing, I'm just watching Aunt Carol talking to Brady. She took him some dinner."

"Your aunt is the nicest woman I know, always thinking about others."

I looked out the window over Lori's shoulder and saw Carol and Brady talking just outside his door. The conversation seemed friendly enough with lots of smiles. I shifted my stare over to the rake handle and noticed the clown mask was still missing. That knowledge I kept to myself and I backed away from Lori to get a quick bite from the casserole dish. Lori turned around and slapped my hand but it was too late I had already scooped up some of Aunt Carol's famous chicken casserole with a chip and I walked away laughing.

Carol came in and asked if we were ready to eat. I told her I was starving.

Carol as always, served me up a big plate of food. Her servings were usually more then I could eat, but it was always very good so I didn't have a problem putting it away. We sat and ate making small talk until Lori couldn't take it anymore.

"How's Brady doing?" she asked Carol.

"Oh he's fine. I took him and his friend a plate of food and he told me because it was already getting late, that she may stay the night. He seemed happy and likes her, but I did ask about the clowns."

When she said that I felt my face suddenly get warm and knew she was looking at me. I looked up from my plate and Carol was throwing a, "I can be nosey too look" at us. It felt awkward.

"Brady said his friend really likes clowns and he wanted to make her happy. I didn't get her name, but I did ask about the clowns, so maybe you two can rest your busy minds a little and see that there is nothing wrong out there." She kept her look on us for just a second longer holding her fork full of casserole in her hand, then took a bite as she smiled at us.

Lori and I both knew something was weird about Brady, but we didn't dare bring it up after that. I continued eating, but my mind went back to wondering why he had that mask on and walking her back into the trailer. Unless they had some weird sexual thing going on, there had to be a lot more to it. I debated on telling Lori what I saw.

After dinner we washed dishes and watched a movie, then called it a night. Carol was already making plans for breakfast in the morning so Lori and I went to the guest bedroom and changed. We lay down and talked in the dark.

"Lori, I'm gonna tell you something. Earlier today I heard some yelling coming from the trailer so I looked out and I saw Brady, with a clown mask on, he was kind of pushing her back in the door. I know it sounds like nothing, but seeing him with the mask on didn't seem funny. It felt creepy. It was like he was putting her back inside so she wouldn't come out."

"Are you sure they weren't just playing around?"

"No, I don't think so. I couldn't see his expression because of the mask, but his body language was as if he was scared." I said as I sat up in the bed.

"I know I was more skeptical when we got here, but I think my aunt has it under control. She would know if something bad was going on," Lori said. I almost couldn't believe that the tables had turned and I was the one who was more curious and skeptical now. My instincts are usually right on and they were telling me bad things now.

"I'm just going on the record now saying something isn't right. I can't believe how you have changed your opinion now." I was frustrated, now having told her what I saw and how I felt, and her not taking it seriously.

"They're probably just some freaks and the mask it part of it," she said laughing as she rolled onto her side and said goodnight.

I stayed up awhile staring up into the darkness of the room. My mind was racing and for whatever reason I couldn't let it go. I was glad that we would be leaving the next day, so I tried to relax so I could get some sleep.

The howling I heard was unmistakably something evil. Sometimes you just know. I rose up in bed and looked around, my eyes trying to adjust to the faint moonlight coming in from the windows. The howl was loud and seemed to cut right through the air, and straight into my soul. The howling was more like a beast than an animal. That's the best way I can describe it. I looked over at Lori who had not awoken, wondering why she didn't hear it. I got out of bed just as it stopped. It sounded like it was coming from out back by the trailer. I hesitated then decided to walk to the kitchen and look outside. The light on the side of the house shined down on the trailer, but it was not bright at all. I saw nothing, no one. I took a quick glimpse towards the small window on the trailer. I was just focusing my sleepy eyes on the makeshift curtain that seemed to be moving when… a tap on the back of my shoulder made me jump halfway to the ceiling. I let out a yell.

"Hey what are you doing?" It was Lori. She saw the scared and angry look on my face and then her expression changed to concern.

"What's wrong? Did you see something?" she asked.

"Jesus Lori! You scared the hell out of me!" I was mad because she scared me when I thought I was about to see who or what was making the curtain move, and with one tap on the shoulder I missed it all. "Don't do that again." I said angrily.

"Didn't mean to scare you..geees."

"Look, I'm sorry. I woke up hearing that howling again and it sounded like it was coming from out there, so I came over to see if there was anything going on and you scared me." I told her in a calmer tone.

"I'm sorry I didn't know." Lori said as she began to walk back to the room.

I took a quick glance outside, then followed her to the room.

"You didn't hear the howling?" I asked her.

"No, I woke up and saw you weren't in bed, so I was going to the bathroom when I saw you in the kitchen. I didn't mean to scare you."

"I know. I was just a little on edge before you touched me, it's okay. Let's try to get some rest before your aunt starts waking us up at six a.m.," I said. I was trying to put a funny spin on it and break the cold air around her. She gave me a half-assed smile and we went back to sleep.

<u>Sunday</u>

Sooner than I could believe, for lack of a full night's sleep, it was morning. I woke up before Lori and found the sofa in front of the fireplace a great spot to read my book. I didn't even hear Carol stirring around, but I did smell coffee being brewed in the kitchen. All was quiet so I took advantage of the time to catch up on the book I was reading and enjoying the peacefulness of the fireplace burning. I looked outside at the temperature gauge; it read 36 degrees, not freezing but cold enough to appreciate the heated living room. I poured me a cup of coffee and lay down on the couch. I got through a couple of chapters when I heard Carol come in the back door with some groceries. I got up to help her.

"Good morning Carol."

"Good morning Richard. Could I get you to help me with the other bags? I went to the store to get some things for breakfast," she said dropping four bags on the kitchen table.

"Sure, I'll take care of them," I said as I went out the back door and around to the side of the house where her driveway runs into a makeshift garage. This side of her house is on the opposite of Brady's trailer. I grabbed what was left in the back of her SUV and looked up and I saw Earl sitting on his back porch in his wooden rocking chair. He kind of startled me at first. He had his old fishing hat pulled down over his face, obviously enjoying a morning nap. He was facing towards the woods and had a beer can and ashtray sitting next to him on an old crate with the name Graham stenciled on the side. I was going to call out and say hello but I know how I feel when someone wakes me up from a good nap, so I decided to let him rest.

Better get these inside to Carol, I said to myself as I shut the rear hatch to the SUV. As I walked back inside, I couldn't help but glance over at the trailer.

Carol was already making breakfast when I got back inside.

"I saw Earl sleeping on his back porch. He's not one for talking is he?" I asked Carol. She laughed.

"Earl has been living up here for a long time like me and is a very quiet man and loves sitting on his porch. I guess he thinks about his late Alice, usually until he falls asleep. They loved it up here and that's why they moved here after they retired," Carol said. She had given me a quick rundown, in her own way, of how nothing was really unusual with the way people acted and lived around there.

Lori came into the kitchen and gave me a morning hug and kiss.

"Aunt Carol you didn't have to make anything. We could have treated you to breakfast in town," Lori told her as Carol stirred the pan full of frying potatoes. "You're making enough to feed an army."

"It's okay I'll have plenty just in case Brady or Earl care to eat. Can you hand me that lid?" Carol asked Lori and used it to cover the potatoes. I made my exit back to the sofa with coffee in hand as they finished getting breakfast ready.

Breakfast as usual was very good, and again I over did it. If I lived up there and was around Carol too often I would go from slim and fit to fat and lazy. We sat around and talked; I finished my second cup of coffee, rinsed my cup, and went to the bathroom for a quick shower. When I got out there were two plates of food covered with saran wrap on the table. I saw the look on Lori's face and knew I was about to be asked for a favor.

"Will you please take this plate of food out to Brady? Aunt Carol is going take the other to Earl," she said as she gave me a kiss on the cheek and a pat on the back. The kind that says, you really don't have a choice.

Carol came back to the kitchen with a couple of bottles of water and took a plate to Earl. I grabbed the other and headed out the back door. My mind was racing again, back to the weird feeling I had got from Brady and his friend, the thoughts that I had been able to block out earlier. As I walked towards the trailer I saw Brady sitting in a chair facing sideways. He was leaning forward, rocking forward and back and had the clown mask on his head. A sight that most of the time would seem comical or crazy, but this was scarier then I can describe. He was talking, no, chanting something towards the other side of the makeshift wall he had made using a piece of blue tarp. I slowed my walk and looked down and I saw what looked like blood on the ground. There was a good amount and mixed in with it was pieces of something scattered along the way towards Brady and the other side of that tarp. He never looked my direction and I stopped midway, my eyes were fixed on what I could not see behind the blue tarp. Brady began waving his hand back and forth as if to say no to whatever was behind the tarp. He leaned back and as he did I saw fingers on a hand. Fingers, hideously long, with nails that looked like sharp blades. They were dripping blood. Slowly the hand emerged from behind its cover inching towards Brady. I was brought out of my disbelief by the most painful scream I have ever heard.

"Noooooooooooooo! No no no no!"

Carol was screaming from the next yard over at Earl's. The combination of her screaming and me seeing the bloody claw, caused me to drop the plate of food, and instinctively I turned and ran to Earl's house to where Carol was. Lori opened the back door as I turned to run.

With a panicked, scared look on her face Lori yelled "What's happening??"

I pointed to the house as I ran by. "Get back in the house, lock the door and call the police! Now!" I yelled I ran by Lori not knowing if she did what I said. I jumped over the small fence and into Earl's yard and ran up to the back porch where I had seen him earlier. Carol was on her knees in a praying position, clearly hysterical.

"Oh dear Lord, oh dear Lord…"

Then I looked over at Earl. He was in the same position as before, only now the fishing hat he was wearing was on the ground and stained with blood. His face was, the best way I can tell you now, was ripped off. He had no eyes, no mouth, no nose, just a big hole where it all used to be. As you can imagine, I was in shock and trying to figure out what I was looking at. Blood had run down where his chin used to be, and I could see right into the back half of his brain.

The sound of Carol's sobs brought me back to reality and I turned only to see her running towards her house with her hand raised to her mouth, running for her life and in total disbelief. My senses came back to me and I ran after her, yelling at her to stop. Whatever had done this to Earl was lurking behind that tarp.

Carol never made it to her back door. Just as she reached for the knob she was ripped apart by the demon that was Brady's friend. The monster was now in full view as it sliced Carol with its long fingernails with such speed and precision, it worked like a machine. The last cut was to Carol's shoulder, and as her arm dropped to the ground so did her body. What remained of her slumped in a heap at the doorway. Her arm was on the ground twitching and moving as if still attached to her body. Lori was screaming from inside the house and I looked up and saw her at the window, looking out at the monster and having witnessed the same thing I did. Her screams were muffled by the devilish sound of the creature howling that same sound that I had heard the last two nights. The demon was looking up towards the sky howling, with its long skinny arms raised above. The beast was nearly seven feet tall and was a sight that defied all belief. I was terrified.

Lori's screaming from inside brought the beast's attention to her in the window. She was looking at me with panic-stricken, horrified eyes. I motioned for her to run out the front door…the demon was too fast. It crashed those insanely hideous hands or claws through the glass and grabbed her by the neck, pulling her through the window. I was still in shock and scared out of my mind and out of the corner of my eye I saw Brady running at the beast. He was charging at it wearing the clown mask and chanting again, but this time he was carrying a huge machete. The beast let go of Lori, her body falling limp over the window seal. Brady hit the beast full speed bringing the machete down towards it, but was flung away with ease as the monster lifted its long arm, throwing Brady back several feet in the air and onto the ground. It walked towards Brady.

Still in shock, I looked up and saw Lori was no longer in the window, so I ran around to the front of the house and through the front door. Lori was lying on the kitchen floor in a pool of blood. The blood was such an intensely red color; I had never seen anything like it. It poured from her neck. She was clutching her cell phone in her hand. I could hear the voice of the 911 operator, but paid it no mind as I kneeled beside her. The demon howled again. Lori was mumbling something as she looked up at me. Her eyes were in another place, she was dying right in front of me. I was holding her, I was shaking, her eyes closed as she tried one last time to say something. I got close to her, now crying, trying desperately to hear her last words. All I could hear was "...you" and with that, her eyes closed and she took her last breath in my arms. I was in despair, filled with sorrow, covered and kneeling in a pool of my love's blood.

I could not believe everything that had happened in the last ten minutes. My mind was spinning when my sorrow and sadness suddenly turned to rage and anger. The reality of everything came back to me and as blood dripped down from my arms, I raised them in the air with clinched fists and screamed at the top of my lungs, letting all my emotion out in one angry moment. I knew then that the demon would be coming for me. I got myself to my feet, tears still filling my eyes and looked out the window. Brady had his back to the fence yelling something at the beast. It had its back to me, arms hanging down to its side, staring at Brady. I ran out the back door and stopped halfway between the house and where they were standing. Brady was looking up at the monster, still wearing the mask. He slowly began sliding along the fence moving out and away from it as it stood there, still unmoving.

"I stopped it, I stopped it!" Brady was saying in a low, but excited voice. He walked very slowly towards me and stood about ten feet away, machete still in hand. I stared into the clown eyes still trying to wrap my head around all of it.

"You see, it's afraid of clowns, I don't know why, but that with the chant…." Just as he said that, the beast turned around so fast I didn't have time to warn him. It took one short step and sliced Brady's head off with its long razor sharp nails. The machete fell as his body stayed upright for a brief second and his head rolled right to my feet. Shock and the most fear I have ever felt set in on me as the beast now stared directly at me. Time seemed to stand still as we looked at each other. It was still a hideous monster but I could see in its face that it was changing or transforming back into the woman. I woke up from the trance it had put on me and instinctively picked up the machete and ran towards the half-human, half-beast and before it could react to me I slammed the blade down on its shoulder, just missing the neck. A dark demonic sound rose through its body from deep within as it grabbed me. I knew I had one last chance to end it so I drew the blade back and took my best shot at its neck. I didn't miss, striking it midway on the neck and the blade sliced right through cutting its head off. Its claws still dug into my ribs so I kept chopping at it over and over. Blood spewed everywhere.

I guess in my state, I hadn't heard the police pull up to the house. Just as me and the beast were falling I heard someone yell.

"STOP or I'll shoot!!" I couldn't stop. I kept chopping.

I was shot four times, two in the back and two in the legs. Just before I passed out I saw the beast's head. It was no longer the monster that I had cut up, but the face of a very pretty woman, as I can best remember. She had a smile on her face and her eyes were looking right into mine.

It has been six months since it all happened, so they tell me. It has actually been five months and three weeks. The first four weeks of that I was in ICU. I am paralyzed from the waist down and in a wheelchair. Two gun shots in the back tend to do that to a person. They say I was lucky that no major organs or arteries were hit. You see they think I've lost my mind here with all that has happened, that I'm crazy. They also think that I am a murderer, that I somehow went insane and killed five people including the love of my life. The doctors and the police all think my account of what happened is a delusion, and that I am out of my mind. They laugh at my mention of clowns and how that was involved in this tragic event. Only, if they could have been there. I think they are the ones who are crazy. So they have me locked away in here in this mental institute under heavy observation and under house arrest, until they can sort out all the events of that terrible Sunday. They call it an institute; I call it an insane asylum. My attorney wants to fight the case in a way that makes me look insane as well, but I'm the only one who truly knows. I remember everything that happened that day. I remember it as if it happened yesterday. They just refuse to believe me.

They told me I could have anything I wanted in here, within reason. I asked for only one thing . . . a clown mask like Brady had when he tamed the beast that I killed. They said okay, thinking that it would help me with my therapy and with recalling exactly what happened. I need it for the beasts or demons that are still out there. I hear them howling at night from my bed in here. They tell me it's just some of the patients on the fifth floor, but I know better. I know what lurks out there waiting to finish me off for killing one of their own. I must confess, I did ask for two other things, a pen and paper, so I could write to you as I am now. I was denied for fear of me using the pen to harm myself. So they gave me a box of chalk and a small chalkboard. Funny how they fear me, when what they should fear is outside that window somewhere. I guess I will end my story here as I have filled the fourth and last wall of my room with my story. Also, I am about to run out of chalk, space, and now …time. The beast is on its way, I can feel it. Just as well, I have told you all I know. Plus it is getting dark out, and I must assume my position in front of the window to wait for the beast. But before I take my place in my chair, with my clown mask as I have done every night since I've been here, and before I begin my chant the demons, strangely I can now recall every word of it. I must ask you; now that you know the truth . . . Do **you** think I'm crazy?

"Those are the words of Richard Johnson, the man accused of the multiple murders of two and a half years ago in Big Lake, Arizona. He wrote his account of what happened that gruesome weekend on the walls of his room at the Arizona Mental Institute of Health just before he disappeared. It has been two years since his disappearance and this information has been kept private until now. This is the first time this it has been made public.

According to the files on this case, at around 11 p.m. on April 29 the night of the disappearance, patients and staff heard a scream or howling coming from outside the building, just before they heard a crash, in what turned out to be the window in Mr. Johnson's room. Some reported hearing a brief scream soon after the crashing sound. By the time staffers made it inside the room, Mr. Johnson was gone. The window and part of the wall below it were smashed into broken pieces of brick and glass. The only things that were found were Mr. Johnson's blood-stained wheelchair and a clown mask that belonged to him. Blood was also found on the grounds outside the room. The baffled staff and police searched the building and grounds all night and into the next day. Mr. Johnson was not found. I have asked if there were surveillance cameras that may have recorded the events. I was told that information was not available as the incident is still under investigation. You are the first to read publically of Richard Johnson's account of the grisly multiple murders almost two and a half years ago in the White Mountains. It makes little sense to me that the institute is releasing only this information, but not the video from the surveillance cameras, or anything else to the public that may help in finding Mr. Johnson.

Mr. Johnson is accused of the murders that day, but was under evaluation to determine his mental health status before appearing in court. After reading his account, along with the pictures of his room just after his disappearance, and along with the pictures from the crime scene in Big Lake, I plan to investigate this matter further. I feel there is more to the events of that horrible day than are being portrayed by the doctors and police.

Currently there is still an official missing persons report on Mr. Johnson, and at the same time he has made the 'Most Wanted' list in Arizona. As I record this on my digital voice recorder, I am pulling into the Winter Pines subdivision in Big Lake, and very soon will be pulling into the driveway of the still boarded-up home of Carol Benson. I have been told that half of the properties and all of the ones directly surrounding the home, where the murders took place, have been vacated. It is a very eerie sight driving here to see the vacant trailers with overgrown grass and weeds. People in town say the place is haunted, and that screams can be heard from the Benson home at night. I will be using a video recorder to record my night's stay in the house, so I will sign off now before the last day's light fades. I want to have a look around before it gets too dark.

Some say you can hear the howling of wolves, and that bears have been seen roaming here after dark. Others say it's the Demon. Maybe, I will find out first hand, tonight."

Floor Four

"Is it true that ghosts are only seen by one pair of eyes?"

The rain continued to pound the top of Mary Tompkin's car while she sat in the parking lot of her client's restaurant. She was talking to her husband on the phone. She needed to finish this business dinner and after that she would be done for the week and get to spend time at home, while enjoying a long three-day weekend. It wasn't too late for a Thursday night, but she wanted to get this meeting over with as quickly as possible. Lightning flashed outside as she finished her call. Mary took a quick look up at the dark sky as the thunder from the lightning finally made its way to her. The thunder was loud and she could feel it vibrate in her chest. She grabbed her umbrella, opened the door, and the strong, gusty wind hit her face. As she closed the door and pushed down on the alarm remote, she heard the sounded of a chain hitting the ground behind her. Before Mary could turn to see what it was, she felt a sharp, hot pain in her back. The pain was intense; her head shot back as she felt the middle of her back split open. The umbrella dropped from her hand and was blown away in a gust of wind and rain. She didn't even have time to scream, her eyes closed as she died while still standing.

The killer held Mary's body upright, with his tool of choice, a razor-sharp farming sickle, still lodged in her back. He wrapped the heavy chain around her head and neck and pulled the sickle from her back. Her body slumped and the slack in the heavy chain tightened around her neck as she fell. He dragged her with the chain to a dark corner of the parking lot that opened into a vacant lot, and then down a ditch that disappeared into a small creek. Dark red blood from Mary's body stained the path the killer had taken, but it was quickly washed away in the heavy rain.

It was a perfect night to commit a murder, dark, rainy, and very few people out. Mary Tompkins was the eighth victim of serial killer, David Henry Coleman, also known as The Mangler. His murders were always very well planned and executed, and took place in different cities and states. Authorities were having a hard time tracking him. Coleman was a violent serial killer, much more violent than most. His murders were described as angry outbursts by the F.B.I., but he wasn't sloppy, he never left clues behind that would get him caught. He always left a calling-card though. It's what made him the most feared serial killer in years. When Coleman killed his victims, he took the bodies to a place where they would be found the next day. His calling-card was the sickle. In each murder, the victim's face was sliced and cut, beaten, and mangled beyond recognition. The sickle would be lodged in the chest, his trademark. It was determined that some of the victims were alive when he cut up their faces, some were already dead. Authorities had their murder weapon, but could never get anything from it. The Mangler was toying with them and knew exactly what he was doing.

The Mangler's murderous run had gone on for four years. He averaged about two killings a year, with his path had taking him from the east coast, to the Midwest, and down south. Mary Tomkins lived in Florida. There was no way to tell when and where he would strike next, and this made it hard to pen him down.

Police got their first break in August of 2002. They received a call from a resident in Liberty County, Texas. The resident told police that a suspicious man had been up and down their road at night a couple of times. This was a farming area and was generally not walked on by anyone but the few people who lived there. They sent out a patrol car with the officer treated it as a routine call, but everyone had the serial killer in the back of their minds at all times, especially the police. The patrolman didn't find the man, or find anything out of the ordinary. A call went out to surrounding counties to be on alert in general, but most kept in mind that the serial killer was still out there somewhere.

Coleman chose his victims at random, but planned their murders in a very precise way. There was no connection between the victims, no similarities. Half were men and half were women. They ranged from married people with kids to single without kids. Those things, combined with him traveling from place to place to find his prey, left everyone on edge from the authorities to the public. They were all waiting for him to make an unlikely mistake. The break the police got began with the resident spotting the stranger walking the country road. Without making the communities anxious, law enforcement moved to a higher alert level.

"David Henry Coleman planned his ninth murder in September of 2002, close to the Old River-Lost Lake area in Texas." The old man began telling the story to the boys. "A very small, quiet community, Old River found itself in the middle of a major manhunt. Coleman chose the time just after dusk to make his way to the home of a Mark and Jean Ellis. They had just finished working outside around the house and were cleaning up for dinner when Coleman peered into their kitchen window. They didn't see him, they were lucky; The Mangler had not planned out this murder like the rest. He was rushing it and it didn't fall along the same time frame as the others. He felt the need to kill and murder again, maybe to get more notoriety than he had before. He wanted to be taken more seriously." The boys listened intensely.

"He watched the older, married couple get things ready for dinner. His plan was to wait until Mark came back outside, as he usually did, and then use his sickle and chain to end his life. Coleman waited patiently, watching from the window. A sly smile came over his face as their dinner ended and Mark got up from the table and walked to the back door. Coleman moved into position in the shadows. Mark grabbed a water bucket from the back porch and headed towards the stalls. Coleman waited until Mark entered the stalls and then walked in his direction. Just as he was about to enter the stalls a truck came driving up the dirt road to the house. The sound of the truck brought Mark back outside just as Coleman was entering. Coleman had no choice but to strike down at Mark with the sickle as he entered the stall. Mark screamed out, shocked and surprised by the stranger. The blow from the sickle hit Mark on his left shoulder after he partially blocked it. The momentum of Coleman walking in and striking down on Mark pushed them into the doorway and inside the stalls just as the headlights from the truck shined on them. They fell to the ground; Mark struggled in pain as Coleman lifted the sickle out of Mark's shoulder and prepared to strike down on him again. Mark shifted his body enough to cause Coleman to barely miss as the pointed end of the sickle slammed into the dirt floor. Dust rose around them in the struggle, the long chain clanged between them. Coleman was going to make one last attempt at killing his prey when he heard Jean's screams behind him. He took one last swing down at Mark and hit him in the forearm. The sickle sliced halfway through. Coleman got up, grabbed his chain and ran towards the back of the small barn. The driver of the truck was a neighbor from down the road. He grabbed his shotgun from his truck and ran to where Jean was screaming. He made it just in time to see Coleman running to the back of the barn. He fired a shot and hit Coleman in the right leg. The shot knocked him forward, but he didn't lose his footing and was able to run out the back of the barn and into the surrounding woods. The bloody sickle standing on its own was stabbed into the dirt floor with blood. Mark was the only victim to survive an attack by the serial killer. He was taken to a hospital as the manhunt began."

The three boys, still curious and listening, looked at each other.

"Two things worked in favor for the police you see; the suspect was shot and bleeding, and for the first time, he had left his murder weapon behind. At this point they didn't know if it was The Mangler or a copycat, but this man had to be found and arrested. The manhunt continued through the night with police using helicopters and dogs. With dogs locked in on the scent, the trail seemed to head in a southwest direction. Around four a.m. police were called to a neighborhood here in Baytown. A suspicious man was spotted walking through an alley on the east end of town. By the time police arrived, the man was gone. They decided to seal the area for four or five miles and work their way in."

"Just as dawn broke, and the sun began to rise, another call came in to police just a short distance away from the original call. A resident was taking out his garbage when he saw a man sitting in a brushy, wooded area across the street from him. He couldn't give a good description, but he thought of it as unusual. Again, when police arrived, he was gone, but this time, the dogs picked up a scent. The helicopters were called in and the hounds barked and howled louder than you ever heard before. They felt that they were closing in on him. The wooded area led to another neighborhood just on the other side." The old man was very dramatic in telling his stories.

"This area had less people, and with daylight on their side the police felt that they would find him as they approached from both directions. The hounds closed in on a garage that was detached from a vacant house. After getting in place, they burst into the garage and found some bloody clothes and a mask that matched the description that Mark Ellis had given them earlier. The suspect was not in the garage, so they focused on the vacant house. Surrounding the house, they broke through the front and back doors at the same time," he said with excitement building in his voice.

"Gunfire erupted in a backroom as police were shot at. They had no choice but to fire back hitting the suspect several times until he was unconscious. They called an ambulance to try and save the man, who they suspected to be The Mangler. The ambulance crew stabilized him on the way to Saint Vincent Hospital," the old man said as he pointed across the main road, "right over there." The boys looked over their shoulders at the vacant hospital.

"After arriving, Coleman's condition worsened, but not before he told a F.B.I. agent that he was indeed David Henry Coleman, The Mangler. He confessed to all the murders as two other agents looked on. Coleman's expression was heartless and one of an unremorseful murderer."

"An day later and still in ICU, Coleman's hand began to shake violently." The old man paused here, looking at the ground in front of him. "The nurse walked over to him and he grabbed her arm quickly, just in reach of his handcuffed wrist, looked her in the eye and said, 'I will be back, and I will return, and kill again and again. I will haunt this place forever!' They say his eyes stayed open, staring at the nurse, until he died. She screamed and shook her arm away from his grip. The FBI rushed in, but The Mangler was already dead. They say he walks the halls of the old hospital with his sickle and drags his chain. The anniversary of his death is coming up this week."

The old man paused and lit his cigar. "That's the story of The Mangler." Old Man Jake knew how to tell a story.

The three, wide-eyed, thirteen-year-old kids, on their bikes, stared at Jake. Two of them, Kyle and Doug, heard stories from him before, but it never got old. The other boy, Brandon, was new in town. They brought him to Jake's so he could hear the tale of The Mangler.

Jake, an older black man in his sixties, has lived in the neighborhood across the street from Saint Vincent Hospital for thirty years. He knew the hospital in its hey-day, when it was the only hospital in town. He saw the demise, as the new times rolled in and newer buildings were built, all in the name of business and opportunity.

After hearing Jake tell them the story, the boys headed out on their bikes towards the hospital, but not without one last word from Jake. "Ya'll be careful now," he said, as he took one last puff from his cigar before smothering it under his shoe. The boys waved back as they sped off. The boys were way up the sidewalk by then. "Best be careful," Jake said quietly to himself.

Saint Vincent Hospital was built in the late 1940s, and still stands tall at five stories, overlooking the town. At the time it was built, it was a massive hospital, for the small town, covering over 280,000 square feet. It stayed in business until 2004, when its ownership had completed the transition to a newer, more modern version of the hospital built on the other side of town. Since the closure of the original hospital there have been many reports of it being haunted. The building was used, for a short period after its closer as a private business. Most of the reports of hauntings in the building came from staff and late-night security guards. The old building was finally shut down in 2006 and sits on top of a small hill making it seem taller and bigger than it is. Set against the western sky, it is a dark and menacing site for those who believe the place is haunted. Most of the windows have been boarded up, and the grounds around the property were fenced to keep trespassers out.

As recent as a year ago, a contract company was hired by the property owners to do some minor structural repair work on the lower level. Just as the three-week project was about to end, contract worker Ed Payton was found one morning, hung to death from an overhead rafter. A chain was wrapped around his neck. There was no suicide note, or any reason in his personal life as to why he would hang himself, but the death was ruled a suicide anyway. His death sparked the rumors of The Mangler still haunting the building, especially since a chain was involved, one of his trademark tools. The thing that made his death peculiar was that there was no stool, no box, or no ladder for Ed to climb up on to do it himself. He just hung freely, in his work clothes, his feet more than five feet from the ground. Rumors circulated that his face had a look of fear and terror, not the look of someone who wanted to kill himself. After the investigation was complete, more fencing was put up to secure the old building. But during the summers, it was hard to keep junior high kids like, Kyle, Doug, and now Brandon, from finding ways in and exploring. High school kids were the bravest, and were always being run out of the area by police.

David Henry Coleman died on the fourth floor in ICU. That floor is said to be most haunted. The reports have been of people hearing chains rattling, to the sound of a sharp scraping sound, supposedly that of a sickle being dragged against the concrete wall. Rumors can get exaggerated over time, but when there is said to be a haunting, like that at the hospital, the sounds of a chain, or of a piece of metal scrapping the wall, are much more believable. An assessment for structural integrity was required for the building once a year. Over that time only once have any of the people in that group reported something strange. A woman who was inspecting the fourth floor said she heard noises coming from near the old ICU hall. She walked further down the dark hall with her flashlight. About halfway down she said she heard the sound of a chain dragging on the floor coming from the next room up. That scared her enough for her to turn around and head back down to the first floor. She wouldn't go back on the fourth floor even after her coworkers went up there and found nothing. Not many dared to go up to the fourth floor.

Kyle and Doug took Brandon over to the back of the hospital so he could get a good look at the scary side of it. Even in the day, the hospital took on an ominous look. The backside of the hospital is where all the kids snuck in through a spot in the fence near the sidewall. Brandon stood, straddling his bike, with one foot on the ground. His eyes looked over the building from top to bottom. Kyle and Doug were riding their bikes around the fence line to the far corner of the fence. He quickly jumped up on his seat and peddled towards them. The lower portion of the back of the hospital was like a huge patio. The covered area was extended out to provide shade from the evening sun, making it a makeshift break and lunch area. A couple of the concrete tables and chairs were still there. Even in the day time, this area seemed dark. They hid their bikes behind some overgrown shrubs and snuck in through their secret spot in the fence and walked towards the covered area.

"You're pretty brave Brandon. I never made it this far my first time," Doug said.

"Quit trying to scare him," Kyle said. "It's okay, nothing to be scared of," Kyle said to Brandon, as they walked further in. The covered area was at least sixty feet wide and another forty feet from the edge of the cover to the back entrance. The further that they walked, the darker it got, despite the afternoon sun. They stopped a few feet from the entrance. The doors were boarded with plywood and locked with small chains.

"Most people think you can't get in, but we know a way. Want to go in?" Doug said as he looked at Brandon.

Brandon was usually game for things like this, but he was a little nervous and Doug seemed to be pushing him to go further. "Yeah, let's go," Brandon said. Kyle looked on.

They had done this a few times before, and it was always fun to show someone the haunted hospital for the first time.

Doug led them to a corner where the walls intersected and disappeared behind a piece of plywood. Brandon and Kyle waited for a moment before Doug reappeared smiling. "We can still get in." Then he promptly disappeared again. They followed him behind the plywood and through an old rusty door that opened enough to allow them to pass through.

It was dark and damp inside and the hall they were in had a wet, musty smell. Doug and Kyle turned on their flashlights. Graffiti lined the walls in various colors and styles. Some represented gangs, some professed their love, and others were just there in the form of street-art. They could hear water dripping at the end of the hallway. Most likely caused from the rainstorm the day before.

"Still looks the same as before. The fourth floor is where The Mangler died," Doug said, looking at Brandon. "The only way to get up there is through the stairs down the hall."

He pointed the flashlight in the direction of the stairwell. Brandon's heart was beating fast with excitement, but he was a little scared now that they were inside. Shinning their lights in all directions, they started walking towards the end of the hall. Old pieces of metal and pipes, detached wiring, and broken sheetrock filled the floor and forced them to steer in a weaving pattern as they closed in on the door to the stairwell. Despite Doug's brave appearance, he stayed pretty close to the other two.

Finally, they were at the door. "Here it is," Doug said. He pushed the door and surprisingly; it swung easily on its hinges. The rusted, metal door came to a creaking stop almost all of the way open. The stairwell was completely black. They stepped forward and shined their lights upwards. The light cast shadows on every wall and corner that they could see. It was an eerie-looking sight.

"You ready to go up?" Doug asked Kyle and Brandon, but secretly he was just as scared as them. They nodded okay without taking their eyes off the stairs above. Kyle held tight to his flashlight as Doug led the way. Brandon trailed Kyle as close as he could. Once they got to the second floor Doug paused. "Shhh, checking to see if we can hear his chain dragging on the floor."

"Come on Doug, quit trying to scare him." Kyle said on Brandon's behalf, but also reassuring himself.

"There's nothing to be scared of, until we get to the fourth floor anyway," Doug said with a laugh.

"Have you ever been to the fourth floor?" Brandon asked them.

"No, not . . ." Kyle began to say, before being cut off by Doug.

"Sure, many times. We've never seen The Mangler, but we know he's there." Doug said, trying to keep the tension up.

A loud bang was heard from above, it scared them and they quickly shined their lights up the stairwell. The clinking sound of something falling down the stairs followed until it stopped and everything went dead silent. They continued looking up and noticed dust being stirred up by something above and floated across the beams of their lights. Someone or something was up there. Doug tried to hide his fear and stepped up a couple of more steps. Kyle and Brandon looked at him, their feet locked into place, they had no intention of going any further.

"Probably just a cat or something," Doug said. He took another step up and craned his head at an awkward angle trying to see what was stirring up the dust.

"Maybe we should go Doug, it's too dark," Kyle said.

"No, I want to see The Mangler," Doug said in a deep haunting voice, trying to scare them.

Just as he finished his sentence and began to laugh, the unmistakable sound of a chain being dragged down the stairs hit their ears and wiped the grin off of Doug's face. Frozen into place, and listening intently, the boys heard the clanging sound of the chain drop slowly, one step after another. They looked at each other with the same look and at the same time, as if to say, Let's get the hell out of here!

Their flashlights no longer shined above, they didn't want to see what was coming, but the dusty light that shined on their faces showed the fear that neither of them could hide any longer. The sound of the chain was getting louder, he was getting closer. Then, the high-pitched, screeching sound of metal grinding against metal, accompanied the sound of the chain. Simultaneously, all three boys turned and ran out the stairwell door and straight to the door that they snuck in from. The sound of the metal grinding on the handrails of the stairway, in the boys minds, was that of The Mangler's sharpened sickle. There were no words as they squeezed out the door; they were thinking the exact, same thing . . . get out!

Brandon was the last one out. He couldn't help but look down the hall to the stairway door. Just as he made his last push to slide out, he saw the stair door being pushed open. He screamed, turned away, and ran to his bike.

Seniors in high school, Russell, Jesse, Craig, and Christy, had been friends since fifth grade. They've never gotten into much trouble at all. They did the normal high school parties and get-togethers, but for the most part stayed away from trouble. They hung out with other friends a lot of times, but they had their own little circle. One thing they did like to do for kicks was to sneak into the old hospital. They had done it three or four times, but never went deep into the upper floors. They loved testing the rumors of the haunting by wandering around the first floor and most recently, going to the spot where the worker was hung. Russell and Jesse were teammates on the varsity football team and kept their options open on the dating scene. Craig and Christy were dating and looked forward to going to college together.

With the anniversary of the The Mangler's death coming up over the weekend, they had plans to throw a private party on the fourth floor with some more friends. None of them had ever been to the fourth floor, but figured, as a group, that it would be fun and adventurous, and a lot safer than going alone. Russell and Jesse were letting only a handful of close friends know of the party. They didn't want to have too many people there, or for any one to find out, especially the police. Their plan was to have a keg of beer, some precooked food, and music to make it all fun. They also planned on having a few flashlights and candles to make sure there was plenty of light. With Russell, Jesse, Craig, and a couple of other guys, along with the girls, they wouldn't have any trouble getting all of their party décor up there on one trip. It was Friday afternoon and their plans were going well. Keeping it a secret was a must.

Jake loved telling the story of the serial killer to the kids that stopped by. He did it to try to scare the kids enough for them to stay away from the old hospital, but he knew that the killer's ghost only haunted the building on the anniversary of his death. He knew kids snuck in and out of there at different times, he couldn't stop that, but he would make sure they couldn't get in on the anniversary day, that one time a year. Since Jake lived across the main road from the old hospital, he always took a walk to the park that was set along the creek behind it. The walks helped him free his mind of his wife passing away three short years ago. His favorite spot at the park was the gazebo. The octagonal-shaped structure was set out over the water, about thirty feet from land. A nice, cool breeze usually accompanied anyone who stood or sat there. Jake always enjoyed watching the kids play basketball on the concrete courts, or the sounds of the younger kids playing on the playground. This was his place to get away from it all, at least for a short time. He hadn't taken his normal walks in the last few days because of the thunderstorms that recently hit the area. Jake never told the kids, or anyone he has told the stories to, that he was the one who called police when he spotted Coleman in the alley that day. He had a personal attachment to the murderer, but saw no reason why to tell anyone about it. Jake had never been visited by the ghost of Coleman at home, so his thought was, it only existed inside the walls of the hospital. After all, he was the one who called police and got him caught. Jake figured if there were anyone he was going to haunt and seek out for revenge, it would be him. The anniversary of that day was coming Saturday, and he planned to do his usual walk for that, which was walking all along the fence of the old building and checking to make sure that the door the kids used to get in was locked down. This was Jake's ritual.

Saturday morning brought a sunny sky and upbeat attitude to Russell. He was looking forward to the party that night, and also looking forward to having a little scary fun with some of the party-goers. He and Jesse needed to sneak into the hospital before the party to set some things up that would help scare everyone. What harm could it do?, he thought. It would be all in good-natured fun.

Doug woke up Saturday morning and rode his bike the short distance to Kyle's house. Kyle was still getting out of bed.

"What are you up so early for?" Kyle asked him as Doug sat down at the computer desk in Kyle's room.

"Guess what I heard? Russell and some of the other guys are planning a party for tonight," Doug said with excitement in his eyes.

"So? They always have parties on the weekends. What's the difference?"

"The difference is that the party they having will be at the old hospital, on the fourth floor."

Doug waited and watched Kyle to see his reaction.

"Are you serious? They plan on having it there?" Kyle looked surprised, but with a little gleam in his eye.

"Yes, I heard my sister talking on the phone about it. It starts at ten tonight. I think we should go around ten-thirty and sneak in," Doug said proudly.

"I don't know Doug. How will we be able to stay out that late with our parents expecting us in by then."

"Simple." Doug already had a plan. "We say we are spending the night at Brandon's and he says he is staying at one of our houses." Doug smiled again. Proud of his plan.

"I don't know if that will work. Did you ask Brandon?"

"No, but I will this morning."

"What about all those noises we heard when we were there? You were just as scared as us," Kyle said.

"Come on. Do you want to do it or not? Russell and the rest will be there anyway. Nothing to be scared of, right?" said Doug, doing his best to convince Kyle.

"Okay, if you can get Brandon to go along, I'll go."

Kyle hid his excitement, but if Doug could make it work, then he knew it would be a fun night. The only question was; what was making those noises in the stairs the last time?

The party was going to start at ten, so Russell and Jesse planned to meet at the hospital just after dark to take some things inside, set up for the party, and maybe plan a few pranks. The day darkened earlier than usual because of a thunderstorm in the afternoon that left the skies cloudy and overcast the rest of the day.

Russell and Jesse arrived at the back entrance to the hospital in Jesse's truck. The truck bed was filled with a few chairs, a table, and a small sound system for the music. "We'll have to take this stuff in two loads. The truck should be okay parked here," Russell said.

The faded, dark blue paint on the truck blended in well against these dark bushes.

"Yeah, we just need to be quick," said Jesse. He was excited about the party and the possibility of having some fun with the rest of the group that night.

They grabbed the chairs and the table first. As they made their way to the hidden spot where they always snuck in, they noticed it was open. They always closed the door completely shut when they left. This meant that someone was inside, or that someone had been their recently. They pushed through with more caution than usual, just in case they ran into to someone. Russell carried the four chairs, two in each hand. Jesse held the plastic table at his side as they moved along the first room towards the stair case. Both boys carried flashlights, but Jesse, holding his light out with his freehand, led the way with the beam of his light. After a bit of a struggle they were standing at the stairwell door. The old door was also open, when it was usually closed, they looked at each other, but then laughed it off. They were scaring themselves before they could even pull the pranks on their friends.

Jesse went in first and shined his light along the stairs as they walked one step at a time, to the next floor. Their shoes slid against the dust and grit that has built up on the steps over the years. Their steps made a loud crunching sound in the dead-quiet stairwell. The boys tried to break up the awkward silence by joking about the upcoming night.

As they got to the third floor Jesse stopped suddenly. Russell bumped into him. "What happened? What's wrong?" he asked.

"I don't know. I thought I heard something."

"Come on. Now you're sounding like someone in a scary movie. Keep going." Russell said. Unaware that something was stirring above them on the steps leading up to the fourth floor, he nudged at Jesse's back to move him forward.

"Listen! Can't you hear it?" Jesse said. His heart was beating fast in his chest. His eyes focused on where his light was shinning above. Russell looked above with him, but neither could see anything. There was dead silence for a moment. Then, the sound could be heard again, the unmistakable sound of a chain dragging the floor. Russell didn't want to show his fear, but his heart was beating as fast as Jesse's. Russell set the chairs down and grabbed his flashlight. He shined it alongside Jesse's light. They could only see dust particles floating around and the rails that led to the fourth floor. The sound of chains grew louder and coming closer. The boys were frozen, but Russell was able to find some bravado, despite his fear.

"Who's there!?" he demanded. "You better show yourself or we'll kick your ass!" The sound of the chains dragging the floor stopped one flight of stairs above them.

More silence.

The clinking of the chains began again. The source behind the sound was about to show itself. The boys wanted to run, their minds told them they had to run, but they just couldn't. Their hands shook, causing the beams of light to dance around the walls like strobe lights at a party. Only, their party hadn't started yet.

Or had it?

"I said who's there," Russell asked once more. His voice was not as demanding as before and the sound of his voice, along with the uncontrolled shaking of his hand, showed his fear. He was scared shitless, but his determination, and stubbornness, kept him still. He had to see what was there.

Then, there it was, the chain dangling around the turn for the next flight of stairs. Holding the chain was a hand, followed by a man. The flashlights beamed through the specks of dust and simultaneously, both the boys' lights were directed at the face of the man carrying the chains.

They recognized the face to their shock and relief. "You boys better quit messing around in here." It was old man Jake. He was carrying a good-sized link of chain. "It's too dangerous in here to be playing around." Jake stopped and shined his own light down the stairway at the boys. They stood in silence. "What are you boys planning? What's all that for?"

Russell spoke, "We were just gonna have a party up here tonight. It won't hurt nothin'." His nervousness all but stopped once he realized it was only Jake. Everyone knew Jake from his stories about The Mangler. Russell's bravery showed itself again.

"That's not a good idea. The floors upstairs aren't good. You boys leave this chain lying around?" Jake lifted the chain. It looked new and not like it had been there for some time. Jake began walking down towards them. "Get that light out of my face and you boys best be heading home." He walked past them as they moved out of his way.

Russell and Jesse didn't know how to respond. Even at his age, Jake could be intimidating when he wanted. Jake took a step more past them and turned around. "This building is old. Listen to what I tell you." He turned and walked down the stairs towards the second floor. The seriousness of what Jake said settled in their minds for a moment as they heard him work his way down.

They looked at each other. Russell didn't show concern, but Jesse had his confidence shaken. "I don't care what he said. We're still having this party. He just came down from the fourth floor and nothing happened. Everything will be fine," Russell said.

"I know what you're saying, it's just kinda weird. What was he doing in here anyway?" Jesse asked. His question was a good one. One that Russell couldn't answer.

"I don't know. Maybe he has a thing for old buildings. Who knows? All I know is that we're having this party no matter what," Russell said as he turned off his flashlight and grabbed the chairs. He started moving up to the fourth floor as Jesse, his flashlight still in hand, reluctantly followed him.

Jesse's head rang again with the question, What was Jake doing in here?

Doug and Kyle got Brandon to go along with the plan. (A little peer pressure can go a long way) The plan was for each of them to say they were staying at the other's house for the night. That way their parents wouldn't know the difference, and they could actually stay at Doug's older cousin's house. Brandon was the least sure of the idea, but went along, trying to fit in. The noises they heard earlier at the old hospital seemed to be forgotten as the excitement about the party grew.

Old man Jake, the one who all the kids knew as the neighborhood ghost-story-teller, had a secret and special attachment to The Mangler and the old hospital. No one he told the stories to, mostly kids, knew that he worked at the hospital for a short period of time. He had a part-time job there doing odd jobs and delivering the inner-office mail throughout the hospital. On the day after David Henry Coleman was brought in, Jake was working. Jake was working on the fourth floor, but was not allowed in the ICU area unless he was taking mail or documents that needed to be delivered or signed.

He had to walk by Coleman's room to get to the nurses' station that day. As he walked by he glanced at the two officers, or FBI agents, he was not sure which. They stood at the doorway in the typical law enforcement manner, staring straight ahead, hands crossed in front. The FBI agent wore dark shades, even though they were indoors. After dropping the paperwork at the nurse's station, Jake made his way back down the hall. As he got close to Coleman's room he took a look in. Coleman's eyes were closed. He was hooked up to a lot of wires and tubes. He was not on a ventilator, but he didn't look good. Just as he was about to take his eyes off of Coleman and nod to the officers, David Henry Coleman opened his eyes. They opened quickly and stared directly at Jake, as if he knew he was walking by. The stare was so intense and frightening that Jake unknowingly paused. Coleman raised his cuffed hand as far as he could and pointed at Jake. His eyes grew more intense and his hand began to shake. Jake felt like he was saying, I'll get you! Jake broke from the trance imposed on him by Coleman, and he quickly walked away. Just down the hall he heard a nurse scream and the computerized voice went out over the speakers for a patient that was coding.

Jake learned soon after, as rumors quickly spread, that Coleman had died. That one moment that Jake had with the serial killer, no matter how brief, along with him making the call to police, would haunt him and connect the two men years after. This was the secret that Jake held in. This was why he walked the hospital after it was shutdown. He needed to face his fears and not let Coleman take his mind. The experience he had that day scared Jake. He felt he was exercising the demon every time he walked on the old fourth floor of the old hospital. A walk he took once a month. He knew that it was only haunted during the anniversary of its death. He had seen Coleman five times; each time they stood at opposite ends of the hall. Only, it wasn't Coleman anymore; it was The Mangler who stood there, chain in one hand, and sickle in the other. He would stand and laugh down the hall, laughing out loud, as if he knew something no one else knew. The first time Jake saw him he was paralyzed by the same fear that had grabbed him years earlier. He knew it wasn't someone playing around trying to scare him, because each time the killer laughed, he would stop suddenly and point his finger at Jake like he did before. Then as he gave him that same demonic stare, The Mangler would slowly fade away into the darkness like magic . . . dark magic. It was a secret Jake planned to take to his grave. He didn't mind telling the stories to the kids, he knew they were safe, even if they got curious and ventured in the old hospital. But, he made sure no one could get in on the anniversary of his death. He felt that he protected the people and the place, as long as he was able to confront the monster in the hall, and until it disappeared into the mist, like it always did. He held some type of power over Coleman. The power kept the killer in the spirit world. The only time Jake failed to make the anniversary walk was the week the construction worker was killed, or as police say, committed suicide. Now that he knew the kids were planning to have a party there, he had to make sure they could not get in through that door.

Despite Jake's warning, Russell and Jesse continued up to the fourth floor and set up the tables and chairs. They figured that if old man Jake was able to walk alone on the fourth floor, they surely would be safe with a lot of people up there later. After they finished with the things they had, they left and made phone calls to everyone that was invited. They let them know that the party was still happening.

The sun was fading into the western sky and darkness began to take over the town. Kyle and Doug were at his cousin's house and waiting to hear from Brandon. They were getting excited about secretly crashing the party, and finally getting to go up to the famous fourth floor. Kyle was worried that Brandon would screw up their plans.

"Maybe we shouldn't have let Brandon know what we were going to do. He might tell on us and we'll all get in trouble," said Kyle.

"He'll make it. He wants to check it out as much as we do." Doug didn't have faith in Brandon showing up either, but he wasn't going to let Kyle know, or Kyle might back out too.

Brandon sat at home nervous and scared. He didn't want to get in any trouble at home and he had a bad feeling about the party. He was really looking forward to his first year of high school in his new town, something it seemed would never happen. Now, he was just less than a year away and didn't want to ruin it by getting in trouble. But, he didn't want to lose the friends he had in Doug and Kyle. He still had a little time to decide before his mother would ask why he hadn't left for his friend's house to spend the night. He didn't live far from the hospital, maybe a five minute ride on his bike, just in case he wanted to meet them there later.

Jake went back to the hospital a little after dark and picked up the chain he had brought down earlier and used it to secure the door with a padlock. There was no way he was going to let those kids fall into any danger goofing around in the hospital, especially at night. After he locked the door, he had a look around, and didn't see anyone lingering in the area. Jake went home.

Russell and the rest of the party-goers showed up around nine o'clock. Russell and Jesse had already set up a couple of pranks for later. They had a couple of people drop them off and they each had hands full of coolers of food and beer, flashlights, candles and whatever else they felt was needed for the party. The friends that left them there parked their vehicles just down the street at the twenty-four hour grocery store, then walked back.

Jesse made it to the door first and saw it was chained and locked. "Damn!"

Russell walked up soon after. "What's wrong? Door locked?" Russell began to laugh.

"What's so funny? We can't get in now."

"I figured the old man would do something like this. I expected it. But, I know another way in," Russell said with a smile.

"What? Another way?" Jesse had never known of any other way to go in.

"Yeah. Not many know about the entrance in the delivery area. You have to go down some steps to get to the door."

"And you never told me?" Jesse seemed offended.

"There never was a reason to say, as long as we could always get in through here," Russell said as he tapped on the lock with his flashlight. "Besides, my older brother told me about it and made me swear to not tell anyone."

Without another word, they started walking back to the rest of their friends. Jesse wasn't satisfied with the explanation, but it didn't matter right then, it was time to get the party started. As they got back to the group, Russell was all smiles. "Looks like we have to use Plan B." They grabbed their things and headed down the steps to the delivery area on the lower floor.

Doug checked the time on his cell phone, it showed 9:25. "He's not coming. I don't care what he tells you on those text messages," Doug said, "we're gonna have to go alone and hope he doesn't get us in trouble."

"You think we should still go?" Kyle wasn't as into the plan as he was before.

"Yeah, It'll be fun," said Doug as he put his phone back in his pocket.

The boys got some things together and planned to leave at ten o'clock. They didn't plan to or expect to hear from Brandon.

The party was going well. They had made it through the lower entry, just as Russell had told them. Their climb to the fourth floor was a little bit of a walk, but no one complained. They were there to have a good time. The music was loud, but not too loud, and they had enough candles and battery-operated lights to make the hallway of Floor Four a perfect place for their idea of a morbid party. No one could hear them way up on the fourth floor, and with the windows being boarded up, no one could see their lights either. Russell and Jesse overlooked the party in progress and smiled. They were proud they had pulled it off. There were eight kids altogether and some were dressed in black with small chains hanging from their necks as a tribute to The Mangler's anniversary. For most of the eight partying high school kids, believing that the ghost of the famous serial killer actually haunted the halls was just a myth, or they would not be there. One girl, Linda wasn't so sure about the stories being a myth. She had to see for herself, and was glad she got invited as part of the close circle of friends. Russell was waiting for two more people to show up. They were running late and would be there around ten-thirty.

Jake sat on his porch smoking his cigar. He glanced over at the front of the hospital and didn't see anything unusual. Every time he smoked one he thought of his late wife and how she detested him smoking and the awful smell, in her opinion anyway, that a burning cigar makes. He didn't smoke too often when she was alive. He tried to respect her wishes and her genuine concern for his health. As he sat and thought of everything, he planned to take one last walk for the night around ten, and check on the chain and lock he had put on the hospital door.

Doug and Kyle rode their bikes in and out of the soft glow of the street lamps down Memorial Drive on their way to the hospital. Once they made the soft turn west on Memorial, the dark, ominous look of the five-story hospital came into view. They had seen this view many times before, but this time it took on a completely different look and feel. Almost simultaneously they both stopped peddling and let their bikes glide towards the main road. They both knew that this time was different because, if everything worked out, they were going to see the fourth floor for the first time.

When the boys made it to the back of the hospital, they hid their bikes and walked to the door. "Look! It's locked!" Doug said. A look of disappointment came over his face. Kyle walked around Doug and reached out to shake the chain and lock, as if it would make a difference. "There has to be another way in. They had to have found a way in," said Doug as he looked around the building searching for another way in.

They walked a short distance to the side of the building and Doug grabbed at Kyle, holding him still in an effort to keep quiet. He had spotted two high school kids walking down the steps to the secret entrance. The two boys walked down the steps carrying a couple of bags as they laughed and joked. Doug smiled, as he knew they had found their way in.

They waited awhile and then worked their way through the shadows to the stairs that led downward, to a place they had not been before. Kyle reached into his pocket and pulled out his flashlight. Doug looked back at Kyle with a smile and said, "Even if Brandon decides to come he won't be able to get in now, too bad for him." He let out a slight chuckle.

Once they made it to the bottom they peered into the darkness through the half-open door. They listened for the other two kids. The coast was clear.

The feeling of betrayal, even for a thirteen year old kid, was too much to take. Doug and Kyle weren't answering his messages so Brandon decided to sneak out and ride his bike to try and meet them at the hospital. The bike ride to the hospital would only take about ten minutes. He still might be able to catch them before they went in.

Carrying his flashlight, Jake made his way through the fence and into the plaza at the back of the hospital. Lightning lit up the sky to the west; the rain was on the way, it wouldn't be long. He carefully walked through the area leading up to the door. Jake was pleased to see that the lock and chain were still in place. Satisfied, he turned and began to walk towards the fence when he thought he heard music playing. He stopped walking to listen closer. The sound was coming from the side of the building.

Jake walked around the corner and the music grew a little louder. Nothing that could be heard by anyone driving on the main road, but it was just audible enough from where he was. His emotions went from being happy that he had stopped the kids from going inside the building, to anger and fear. He knew what was at stake and he knew that these kids had no idea of the danger they were in. He walked faster to the source of the sound.

Brandon made it to the hospital and parked his bike by a tree. He reached for his flashlight and realized he had forgotten it. Too late now, he thought. At a pace, between walking and running, he got to the door the boys had shown him earlier, but to his shock, it was chained shut. He did the customary, grab-and-pull, but it wasn't budging. Now he really didn't know what to do. Just then, he caught a quick flash of light out of the corner of his eye. At first he was cautious, thinking it might be the police, but his curiosity got the best of him and he quietly walked in the direction that the light came from.

The party had just started, but it was already going good. Everyone that was supposed to be there had made it in, and now it was time for Russell and Jesse to put their little pranks in motion. A total of twelve kids were enjoying the music, food and drinks. Lights and candles were placed in different locations to cast shadows in different ways to give off a creepy look, but also leave enough lighting so everyone could see. The candles were placed on the outer edge of the party area, in the hall, just outside the room where The Mangler had died. The battery-powered lights were placed more towards the middle, creating a darker and eerie edge to the party circle. Russell and Jesse had to slip out, one at a time, to dawn their props for the big scare. They had planned on waiting until midnight, but they really didn't know how long the party would last, or if the police would crash it, so they decided to play there prank now. Russell had placed a good length of chain and a sickle in the ICU room where Coleman had died. He planned to sneak in there and jump out at the party at just the right time. Jesse was to sneak away down the long hall and get his hidden sickle and chain, along with a mask, and walk towards the party group to get their attention, just before Russell jumped out at them from behind.

Doug and Kyle made their way to the third floor without any problem. They could hear the music and good times just above them. They were excited, yet nervous, to finally get to see the famous floor, and also, to be around the older high school kids. That excitement had blocked out all their fear of what might be lurking on the floor above. The door that led to the third floor hall was to their left. It was half open and Doug shined his light into the darkness.

"We better get up to the next floor," said Kyle.

"We will. Don't you want to look around a little bit? We've never been up this far before," Doug said. He pushed the door open to get a better view. "Besides, the party will be going on for awhile," he said, looking back at Kyle. He walked into the pitch black hallway of the third floor. Kyle had no choice but to follow his lead.

Brandon walked around the corner and to where he saw the light. He was standing at the steps that led down to a lower level, but without a flashlight there was no way he was going to go down there. The only thing that kept him from leaving was that he could hear the party's music. He knew that his friends were in there somewhere.

Suddenly a light flashed from behind!

"What are you doing around here this late at night?" The voice scared Brandon and he turned quickly to see who it was. It was Jake.

"I told you boys to stay away from here. It's too dangerous to be in there," Jake said.

Brandon was shaking a little with Jake looming over him and the light shinning in his eyes. He wanted to turn and run to his bike and go back home. "I'm sorry sir. I was just looking for my friends," Brandon said, tears welled in his eyes.

"Look son, you best go home now. I'll find your friends and get them home too. I didn't mean to scare you, but I had to see if you knew the way into the building."

"The only way I know is the way we went in before, but it's locked," said Brandon.

"I know it's locked, I'm the one who did it. Now it sounds like they found another way in." Jake pointed his light to the steps leading down. "You go home. I'll get them out of there before it's too late."

Brandon was scared; he nodded and turned, then walked away towards his bike. Jake shined the light along the path to help him find his way back.

Russell and Jesse moved away from the party and got in position to scare the others. The props of the sickle and chain were just where Jesse had left them. Russell went right to the place where he had left his props, but they weren't there. He anxiously looked around the room, they were gone. He knew exactly where he had left them, and it left him puzzled as to where they could have gone. The only explanation in his mind was that someone at the party had found them and moved them, but it was too late now. They had to go on without them, and he hoped that Jesse's chain and sickle were still there. He quickly sent a text to Jesse to start the plan. Jesse put on the mask and the butcher's apron, splashed with fake blood, and grabbed his sickle and chain.

He was positioned a good way down the hall, and walked out into it, moving towards the unsuspecting party goers. No one noticed him at first. He made it halfway down the hall before a girl at the party saw something moving slowly towards them. The lights from the party gave off an eerie glow from Jesse's view through the mask, as he methodically walked towards the group. The girl who spotted him was frozen at first then turned to the others. "Look! Who is that?!"

Everyone turned and looked in silence at the slow-moving figure as the sound of the chain dragging on the floor could now be heard. The sickle came into clearer view, raised high, as he approached the outer circle of the lights.

"Oh my God!" one girl screamed. The entire group backed up slowly, and as they did, they moved directly in front of the entrance to the room where Russell was poised to scare them from.

"Who are you? What do you want?" Craig said as he stood out in front of the scared group. "Is this some kind of joke?" he demanded.

"Let's get out of here!" another girl shouted.

Just as the screams and shrieks became louder as a group, Russell made his surprise entrance from behind them. He leapt out at them with a scream made for Hollywood, just as Jesse started to run at full speed towards them with his sickle and chain. Russell's leap at them from behind left the group no choice but to run in the darkness down the opposite end of the hall screaming. Craig tried to take one last look at who was scaring them that he saw that one of them was Russell.

"Son of a bitch!" he yelled. What the hell is wrong with you?"

Russell and Jesse began to laugh loudly, and Jesse took his mask off. Craig was furious and walked up to Jesse and pushed him in the chest knocking him back a couple of feet.

"What the hell?" he said again, his eyes on fire.

"It's just a joke man, just a joke," Russell said, "lighten up."

The rest of the party saw what was happening and slowly made their way back down the dark hall. Some laughed, while others were just as upset as Craig.

Once everyone was back at the original party spot, Russell had to make an apology, despite a couple of people clapping in appreciation of the joke.

"Sorry everyone, we didn't mean to scare you. Well, maybe we did, but we didn't want to ruin the party, only to have fun."

Craig and a couple of others were still angry, but were listening.

"He's right," Jesse said, as he stepped forward, "we just wanted to have some fun and figured that the reason we were here was because of The Mangler. That's why we did it."

They slowly let go of their anger in response to what Jesse was saying.

"Really, it was just in fun," said Russell.

Victor, a linebacker on the football team and a friend of Jesse, walked up to him, grabbed the chain from his hand, and raised it. "I'll let you slide, this time, but if you pull some shit like that again, I'll strangle you with this chain myself," he said. He raised the chain to Jesse's neck and looked him in the eye. "Just a joke, right?"

The group was silent; the tension was at a high. Then, Victor smiled. Jesse smiled, and relief set in on him and the party-goers.

No matter how mad some of them were, the party would still go on. Russell was relieved and patted Victor on the shoulder as Victor placed the chain around his neck and walked away.

Russell looked at Jesse. "That was great, but I didn't think they would be so mad."

"Where is your chain?"Jesse asked him.

"I don't know. I thought you grabbed them, or someone at the party found them, but they weren't where I left them."

"Let's go look in there again," Jesse said.

The party continued as if nothing happened. All seemed relieved that it was just a joke, and that made them less fearful of the ghost of The Mangler.

Doug and Kyle walked the third floor hallway shinning their lights in all directions. The dark corridor looked much like the rest of the hospital that they had seen. They heard screaming from up above them. They stopped walking to listen. They were hearing screams. The hairs on the back of their necks stood up and just then they realized that what they had seen in the movies was real. That fact scared them even more. The boys turned and ran at full-speed to the door. Just as they made it there, the door slammed in their face.

Dust and debris flew into the air and floated through the beams of light emitting from their flashlights. They yelled and pounded on the metal door not knowing who, or what, slammed the door closed.

Jake walked into the lower level. He was shocked to find out that there was another way to get in, and he knew that there was trouble for those kids above. He carried his flashlight and crowbar that he brought from the house. Coleman would be waiting for him, he was sure of that. But, he had to get those kids out of there before Coleman had a chance to crossover to the real world and kill again. He heard the faint sound of screams coming from the party. He hurried his pace, climbing the stairs up to the first floor from the lower level. Once he got back up to the main level he went to the stairwell and began making the ascent one step at a time.

Halfway to the second floor he heard the sound of a door slam. He shinned his light upwards, but could not see anything. He hesitated, hoping that the screaming and the door slamming was all part of the kids having their fun at the party. He felt relieved, for the moment.

BAM! BAM! BAM! The banging on the third floor door startled Jake.

"Let us out! Let us out!" Doug and Kyle screamed from behind the door.

Jake made it to the door. "Who's in there? Is that you kids?" Jake asked.

"Yes, it's Doug and Kyle. Is that you Jake?" Doug said.

"What the hell are you boys doing in here? I told you to stay away didn't I?" Jake was angry. He reached for the door handle and twisted the knob, it wouldn't turn. Jake leaned against it and pushed. The door budged a little. "Pull the door!" he yelled.

The boys pulled as he pushed, the door creaked loudly as it opened. The light from the three flashlights intersected between them. The boy's were wide-eyed and scared. Jake's eyes showed anger and fear.

Brandon had fooled Jake. He walked towards his bike, but stopped, once he was out of Jake's view. He quietly followed, making sure he was able to see Jake's light as he walked ahead. Although Brandon was scared, he knew he had to see what was up there, and prove to his friends that he wasn't scared. He had no light but stayed close enough behind Jake that he was able to use Jake's light to guide him up the stairs.

Brandon heard the commotion in the stairwell above him. He stopped, straining his eyes to see what was happening. The only thing he could see were beams of light flashing in all directions. Beyond the commotion, he could hear the sound of music and laughter coming from the party. He continued walking up, doing so as quietly as possible.

"You boys get out of here now. Understand me!?" Jake said, not asking, but telling. Doug and Kyle were scared enough, after being locked in, to gladly get the hell out of there. They ran down the stairs towards the second floor. Brandon was close enough now to hear Jake's demand. He didn't want them to see him, so he ran a few steps down and ducked just inside the second floor hall. He wanted to prove to them that he wasn't afraid, that he was there, but at the same time, he wanted to follow Jake. He wanted to see if he was hiding something. He wanted to see what was on the fourth floor.

The boys ran by, never looking into the second floor hall. Brandon hid behind the door. He didn't realize how much he was shaking until the boys had rumbled down the stairs on their way out to safety. Brandon came out and quickly made his way back up to where Jake was. He needed to stay close to his light, he was scared.

Victor, after making his point to Russell and Jesse, walked down the hall, chain still dangling around his neck, on his way to use the restroom. Although there was no running water, the kids used the actual restroom when they had to go. Victor, feeling brave, walked in with his flashlight and found the toilet stalls, along with the terrible smell. He smiled; yeah -- he was in the right place.

Victor positioned the flashlight so that he could see when he took his piss; it felt as if someone was watching him. His uneasiness and intuition was right on. The chain that dangled around his neck and over his shoulders was grabbed from behind. It startled Victor, he tried to turn. "Hey! What the hell? Don't you see I'm trying to take a piss here?" he said, knowing it had to be Russell or Jesse. The chain tightened around his neck and was pulled back violently, leaving Victor's upper body no choice but to be pulled back with it. He tried to keep his feet planted, as he was taught many times during football practice. Whoever was pulling him was strong . . . very strong. The air was being sucked from him quickly; he tried to turn around, grabbing at the big chain around his neck. "Come on, quit playing!" he tried.

Suddenly he was twisted around and now faced his adversary.

The man he looked at was not one of his friends. He was not anyone he knew personally, but he was someone he knew of . . . the Mangler.

David Henry Coleman struck down on Victor using the sickle, and drove it straight into Victor's chest. The razor sharp point of the blade cut through and lodged in his chest easily. Victor, in shock, never knew what hit him. Coleman stepped away after loosening his grip on the chain and let Victor take his last few steps of his life into the hallway. Victor walked like a zombie into the hall, the only thing keeping him alive was pure adrenaline, but even that could only last for so long. Coleman smiled as he watched Victor try to save himself.

Sarah was the first to see him. She screamed at first, and then thought it was another prank. She walked up to the wide-eyed Victor. "Another joke huh? It won't work anymore. So cut it out!" she said.

Victor's bloody body feel forward in front of her and landed face down on his chest. The sickle was forced up through his chest and partially out his back when he landed hard on the floor.

Sarah screamed, realizing it wasn't a joke. The other kids at the party ran to her. They saw Victor's body and had trouble believing it was all real. The blood was pooling under him. The sickle stuck out of his back like a calling card and warning from The Mangler.

Jake made his way through the fourth floor door just in time to see the kids arriving at Victor's dead body. Sarah, shaking and sobbing, still in utter shock, looked up and saw Jake and screamed loud. Everyone looked at her, then Jake. Jake had come in the only way they could get out. More of the girls screamed and then Jesse realized it was only Jake and the group felt a slight sense of relief.

Russell kneeled at Victor's side doing whatever he thought he could do to save him, or bring him back. Russell was sobbing.

"What the hell are you kids doing!?" He walked closer to the group and saw the dead body on the floor. He paused. "Shit. You kids get out of here," he said softly. Thoughts ran through his head about what he could have done to prevent what happened. Something he knew would happen sooner or later. He finally snapped out of it. "GET THE HELL OUT

OF HERE! NOW!!" he screamed at them. They didn't hesitate. All but Russell and Jesse ran down the hall crying and screaming. Their sounds of terror faded as they hit the stairs going down.

Brandon had just avoided them as he stepped to the side of the door. He was more scared than he had ever been, but he was too close now, he had to see.

"Come on Russ! We gotta get out of here," Jesse pleaded. Russell looked down at his friend, trying to absorb what happened. His hands were full of blood. He cried.

Jesse grabbed at his arm and helped lift him to a standing position.

"Go. You boys need to get going now," Jake told them. "Did you hear me? I said NOW!" he yelled.

Jesse got Russell up and they both ran up the hall and down the stairs.

The thunder and lightning that was in the distance earlier was now over the town and hospital. Not all of the upper floor windows were boarded up, which allowed the lighting to cast its eerie flashes of light down the hallway as Jake stared down at the dead body shaking his head. Anger swept over him, he had enough of The Mangler. No more visits, no more visions, no more secrets. He had to settle this now.

The music was still blaring from the stereo as Brandon carefully peered around the doorway of the entrance to the fourth floor. He saw Jake standing over a body on the floor.

Brandon was scared and shaking and afraid to speak up. Now he knew he should have run down to safety with the others.

Jake found a blanket that was left at the party and used it to cover Victor's body. He walked over to the stereo and turned it off, the hip hop tune that was playing silenced. He knew this would all end now. He felt responsible for the boy's death. There was no way to keep the secret now.

The unmistakable feeling hit him again, one he knew very well. Coleman was with him again. Jake turned to find Coleman standing not more than twenty feet from him. This was the closest that he had ever been to each other, but this time, it was not Coleman, it was The Mangler. This time, he was not a ghost. This time he was real.

He smiled at Jake. Jake tried to hide his fear and use the power, a power which he did not understand; the power that he had used over him before, to make him disappear. "That won't work now old man," Coleman said. "I have been released and tasted blood again. I can smell my victims again. That sweet smell of fear." he laughed, never taking his eyes off of Jake.

Jake had never heard him speak, which proved to him that Coleman was indeed alive. Jake stayed calm, not revealing his fear, outwardly anyway. He studied the killer, who, this time, did not look like a cloud or mist. No . . . this time the thing that stood in front of him was now alive.

Brandon stood in the shadows, in awe and amazement. Was he really seeing the ghost of the Mangler? He wanted to run down the stairs, but the shock held him there. He felt his pee running down his leg. His fear was causing him to lose control of his body. Brandon began to shake so much that his vision became blurry. He was about to go into shock.

"You don't scare me," said Jake. "Dead or alive, you don't scare me." Jake lit a cigar and tried to conceal his shaking hand as he lit it.

Coleman was changing in front of his eyes. Maybe, just maybe, whatever the power is I have, is working, Jake thought. But, Coleman wasn't disappearing into a mist like before. He was growing more human, more real. Jake realized that Coleman was now holding a sickle in one hand and a chain in the other.

Jake knew this meeting with the killer was different. He had just killed an innocent boy and that was giving him the power to come back to this world and murder again. The power he had over Coleman, one that he did not understand, he needed now. The only thing he had done since he began coming up here was standing his ground and looking right into the eyes of the murderer, never wavering. This always worked, and kept Coleman in the spirit world.

Since the day in ICU, when Coleman pointed at him just before he died, the two were connected. Now, it came down to this, but he had no idea how to stop it now.

Jake puffed on his cigar; the smoke swirled and drifted upward in front of him. If this bastard is real now, I should be able to hurt him physically, Jake thought.

Brandon didn't know what to do. With his body shaking so bad he couldn't move. He was far enough away and peeking through the crack in the door that they had no idea he was there, as long as he stayed in the dark.

Jake reached for a small piece of pipe that was lying on a table.

"Go ahead, take it," Coleman told him. "It won't do you any good. Your power over me is gone." Coleman stepped forward raising the sickle and chain. Jake tried to grab the pipe, but it slipped through his fingers and clanked on the cement floor. Coleman quickly stepped within three feet of Jake, sickle raised, about to strike down in his trademark murdering style.

Jake closed his eyes, this was the end.

Brandon watched, mouth wide open, and began to cry.

Jake waited to be struck down behind his closed eyes, but nothing happened. He opened his eyes; the cigar fell from his wide-opened mouth.

Coleman was gone. Jake looked around worriedly, not knowing if he had made him disappear like before, or if he had escaped.

Jake heard a noise behind him coming from the stairwell. He turned quickly, bent, and picked up a piece of pipe. He walked cautiously towards the door, raising the pipe as he did. He heard Brandon crying just inside the doorway. "What the hell are you doing here?" Jake said as he lowered the pipe. "I told you boys to get out of here. I'm not gonna say it again!" Jake was very mad now. Damn kids.

"I'm by myself," Brandon said.

"Here, take this flashlight and get out of here," Jake said, "and don't come back, ever again."

Just as Brandon took the light, he glanced over Jake's shoulder and saw The Mangler looming a few feet behind Jake. Brandon's eyes bulged and body began to shake again. He tried to point to Jake, over his shoulder, but his arm would not rise up. The flashlight in his hand felt like it weighed a hundred pounds. Jake saw the look in Brandon eye's and knew what was waiting for him. He was back.

Brandon turned and ran down the stairs with the shaking, erratic light beam out in front.

Jake reached and closed the old metal door. He was now alone with Coleman. He turned to face his fate.

Coleman, for the first time, looked more threatening to Jake, more like The Mangler. This time was different and Jake knew it. The Mangler stood with a shiny new sickle in one hand, and a brand new chain in the other. He wasn't in a misty state as he had been before. He had transformed into the real world after killing Victor.

Jake reached for a cigar, but the one he had earlier was gone, he smiled. "You know what I just figured out?" The Mangler stood silent listening to Jake. "I don't know why, never have, but I still have power over you. If I die forever, you die forever."

The Mangler raised the sickle again, lifted the chain and took a step towards Jake.

"You're not leaving here without me old friend," Jake said, running with the pipe raised high, towards Coleman. The Mangler's eyes were fixed on his next victim, Jake.

Brandon had made it down to the second floor when he heard a scream from above. The sound of the scream caused him to grab the railing and stop. He looked up into the darkness, knowing it was Jake. He let go of the rail and ran faster than before. He was sure he was running for his life.

Jake's body was found hung from the old piping on the Floor Four. He, like the contract worker, was hung by a chain. But, unlike the worker, Jake's throat was slit, with the sickle lying below him. It was not the trademark killing of The Mangler, with the sickle lodged in the chest.

After a long investigation, the case was considered a homicide, and still unsolved. Everyone from the party was considered a suspect. Interviews were done, but no leads or suspects were found.

Brandon was never interviewed. No one knew he was at the hospital that night. Being young and scared, he never came forward. He was afraid that The Mangler would come after him since he was the last one to see him, and the truth. He knew Jake was murdered.

One Year Later

"We are standing just outside the site of the soon-to-be-demolished, Saint Vincent hospital," the female news reporter from Channel 13 said. "For nearly and year and a half since the double murder of Jake Felder and Victor Ramirez, the old hospital has been secured and boarded up for safety concerns, and for the ongoing murder investigation. Investigators tell us, over that period of time, that all possible evidence and clues have been taken from this location." The reporter talked over old footage that was being shown to viewers. "Despite protests from some members in the community, the sixty-two year old hospital will be demolished tomorrow. Rumors continue to persist that the ghost of serial killer, David Henry Coleman, known as The Mangler, still haunts the building. Even after a year has passed since the last murders, some say that the ghost of Coleman is responsible." The reported paused as a picture of Coleman was shown. "After tomorrow's demolition though, we may never know the truth. On location in Baytown, this is Cynthia Hanson reporting for Channel 13."

The demolition took place the next day. News stations, reporters, citizens and all the kids that were at the party that rainy night watched from behind the safety barricades. Brandon also watched. The hospital went down without a problem in a heap of concrete, steel, and ruble. Most curious onlookers left after it met its fate, but Brandon and few others watched as crews moved in to remove some of the debris. Brandon, being a kid, found many things to keep his mind off what he saw that night, but he had to see the old building go down for himself.

A large truck with a front-end-loader was slowly plowing towards a pile of debris when a ground worker signaled for him to stop. "Stop! Stop!" The worker bent down and began sifting through a portion of the small pile. "What the hell?" he said to himself. "No way."

The big piece of machinery suddenly stopping, and the yelling from the worker, caught Brandon's eye. He watched as the worker bent down and lifted a couple of pieces of metal away and then lifted a thick, shiny, silver chain.

Brandon looked on in horror as he realized what it was. He shouted out loud, to no one in particular. "LOOK!" His eyes wide, he pointed at the worker.

"This looks brand new, no way," the worker said. Then he reached down and lifted the other piece he had found, a sickle. It was as new as the chain. "What the hell is going on? How did this get here?"

Brandon looked on, almost in shock, as the worker lifted both the sickle and chain high over his head.

"Look. I'm The Mangler!" the worker said, as he laughed out loud.

The light from the sun reflected off the blade of the sickle and shined right into Brandon's horrified eyes. The worker turned his head and looked right at Brandon. The sun reflecting off of the sickle was bright, but Brandon saw, not the construction worker holding his tools of murder; he saw was The Mangler.

That night Brandon lay in his bed, unable to sleep. With the hospital now gone, he had been avoiding the latest text messages from Doug and Kyle, not wanting to share what he saw the night of the murders, (that was something he never told them), and what he thought he saw at the demolition. He was thinking, trying to understand his visions of The Mangler when he heard a knock at his window. It has to be them, he thought. He got out of bed and walked in the dark room to the window. The lightning, from outside, briefly lit the room with a flash of light as he stood at the window. Brandon slowly lifted one of the blinds to peak outside. Another flash of lightning hit, but he could not see anyone. Maybe it was the wind. He walked away, but stopped in the middle of the room when he heard the unmistakable sound of something sharp scratching, slowly on the glass. A chill came over him, lighting flashed. The scratching was slow and deliberate. He had two choices; run out his bedroom to his parent's room, or . . . see who was out there.

Despite being young, and with all that had happened, Brandon was still a curious and brave kid. He turned and walked to the window.

Thunder shook the room and as the rain started, the scratching stopped. Brandon took a deep breath, grabbed the string, ready to pull the blinds up. It was time to face what was out there.

He pulled down on the string lifting the blinds, lightning flashed again. No one was there. Then suddenly . . . Jake appeared, the palms of his hands hit flat against the window. He startled Brandon, he took a step back. Jake put his face to the window as rain poured down. He had a terrible look of despair. Brandon began to shake.

"Run boy," Jake pleaded. "Run!"

Tears filled Brandon's eyes, total fear setting in. In a flash, a heavy chain flew over Jakes head and around his neck. It locked tightly as Jake grabbed at it. Jake was flung backward by something more powerful than any living man. His body hit the wet mud and grass, and there stood David Henry Coleman. With his right hand, he lifted the chain, lifting Jake off the ground by a foot. Jake's body shook as he grasped for air. In Coleman's left hand was his sickle. The Mangler stared at the young, terrified Brandon. Thunder and lightning struck again.

"You can't escape me. Anyone who sees me must die," The Mangler said coldly. He dropped Jake's dead body and it landed with a wet thump in the mud. "I'll be coming for you," he told Brandon, who was now crying.

The Mangler burned one last evil look into Brandon's eyes just before he turned and walked towards the woods with Jake's lifeless body being dragged by the chain behind him.

To be continued . . .

(Readers, you get to select how you want the story to continue towards the ending. Details coming soon at: <u>ace-hil-ink.com</u>)

Purgatory

"Do not fear death; only fear not beginning to live."

Imagine your plight. You wake up to complete darkness. Unable to move, trying desperately to comprehend what is happening. Then you hear the sound of something being dropped on the surface above you, dirt and rocks. You realize where you are, but you have no idea how or why? Your mind is racing at the speed of . . . darkness. You scream out and begin to panic. You shake your body trying to free yourself of your grave. Then, claustrophobia sets in. You've always been afraid of tight, closed-in places, afraid of being trapped inside of anything. Now, you are totally confined and helpless to do anything about it but . . . die. Soon your breathing will get harder as the dirt blocks out the oxygen, the thing you take for granted in your everyday life. You scream again as your heart beats faster. Your lungs heave up and down as your body is soaked in sweat. The dirt that seeps through the planks of wood sticks to your wet skin. You cough, and then it sinks in, the air has almost expired. More panic sets in, you begin to cry.

You no longer hear the sound of gravel and dirt covering your death bed. You listen, but hear nothing. Now you and the darkness have a companion; complete silence. Your breathing has even slowed, but more fear sets in. The only one who could help you; no matter, if he has put you there, has gone. The more you think about your dilemma, the more your mind instills terror and uncontrollable fear. You try again to press your body against the walls of your tomb, trying in desperation to free yourself. It is useless. The shortness of breath is becoming more real now, reality is setting in. The only light that is left is the light in your mind. All your memories, all the good times that you have had in your life. The things you should have done! Even that light begins to fade. The air, combined with the dust and dirt, has made breathing almost impossible now. You decide to give one last scream, to waive your last breath in an effort to save yourself, one last time. Your scream is loud and it vibrates your crypt. Still, there is nothing. The light inside you grows darker, and your life's memories flood your mind again. No more air, no more life.

As your light goes black and your memories turn dark, you hear a miracle.

"It's down here! I heard something! It's down here!"

Suddenly the light in your mind glows, if only softly, but it glows. Hope! The power of hope. You are able to catch a breath or two, one last time.

"Start digging! Hurry, there can't be much air left down there. Hey down there, can you hear me!?""

You try to cry out, but the lack of oxygen and the dirt have rendered your voice dry and useless. The digging begins, shovel after shovel. You try to hold on as long as you can. They are getting closer; you can feel the box vibrating. The men's voices are getting louder, but your voice carries no sound. You gasp once more as you breathe in dirt-filled air. Your lungs try to expel it with a cough, but even that is out of the question now.

The sound of a shovel hitting the top of the box is next. You hear boots trampling above.

"There it is!" they holler. "Quick, give me the crowbar."

You hear the sound of a board being ripped apart. You hear it but you don't feel or see it. You try to take another breath, gasping. Nails creak as the coffin is opened.

"There's no one in it!"

"But he said they were buried right here!"

Now you realize that they are not opening your coffin, they are not saving you. They are close; they are right next to you. There must be two bodies buried here. Your lungs burn, the air is gone.

"He lied to us! Let's go get him, the lying bastard!"

You hear the men climbing up and walking off. You scream with your last breath.

"Noooo . . . please help me," your voice barely audible, even to you.

Your plea falls on deaf ears. They can't hear you.

You open your mouth and take your last breath. Your mind's light, which was rekindled just a moment ago, fades and darkens . . . for the last time.

Prized Possession

"You can't take it with you when you die."

"The last item in the will of Mildred Clarice Stone, reads as follows: 'I bequeath my 2009 Cadillac DTS Sedan to David R. Slater of Tucson, Arizona.'"

That's where it all started. One wouldn't think that the last item in a will would cause such a stir or start a chain of events like it did, but this wasn't just any ole last item in a will. This was the Cadillac that belonged to Mildred Clarice Stone, better known as 'Ma'. The Caddy was her most prized possession. The reason I have such interest in it is because, I am David R. Slater.

Let me give you some background of how I got involved in all of this. I first met Ma six years ago. She is my girlfriend Sandra's, grandmother. The first time I was introduced to her, I noticed Ma's strong will and presence. She commanded the room, but did it with class and style, never arrogant. She was one of the kindest women I have ever met. We hit it off right from the start. One thing I noticed about her was that she always looked you in the eye when she spoke. She gave you a mutual respect right from the start. Another thing was that she never wanted to let go of my hand when I went to greet her. She always held on, and after awhile I got used to it, and it always seemed to bring me an inner peace. Kind of like she was saying, 'Everything will be alright'. I didn't see her very often. She lived about an hour away and unless we were heading to that area of the desert for something, Sandra and I only saw her here and there. Sandra always commented on how much Ma liked me. I liked her too, but I didn't really understand how much of an impression I had made on Ma until the reading of the will.

Ma was born in Stone Creek, Arizona, and yes the name of the town is in relation to her last name of Stone. The Stone family history dates back for over a hundred and fifty years. I don't know exactly which came first, the town's name or the family name, but I think you get the point. The Stone name carries clout in and around that town and as time went on Ma ended up as the eldest member and head of the family, but it was not by default or merely by age. Ma was head of the family because it was her will and her strength that set her apart and allowed her to take care of the family business of farming. She was the glue that kept the family together, and was well-liked in town and always carried herself with pride. She expected the same from her family, from her kids on down to her great grandkids.

Ma was 90 when she passed away. Sandra and I were there the day she passed. I saw Ma not too long before she took her last breath. She looked like she was sleeping, but in the hour before she passed away Sandra spoke to her and Ma responded, speaking only one word. I didn't hear what she said, but this proved to me that even though Ma looked like she was sleeping or resting, she could hear, and was watching over her family until her last moment with us.

It was a sad week, starting with her death all the way to the funeral service. As with any funeral, a lot of old photos were found and used in the tribute to her long life. I had only known Ma for six years, but looking at the pictures of her from a young woman, up until the time she passed, one thing was for certain. She never lost her beauty and her hair style never changed. It was part of who she was, and in my mind an example of the consistent way that she lived her life.

The will was read two months after her death. Ma had requested that her will be read aloud. Sandra and I had no idea, and had never thought of a will or anything related to that since she passed. Life continued to move on for us.

Sandra got a call from her mom that the executor of the will wanted to speak with me. We were both very surprised and did not understand. The lawyer met with me at his office in Stone Creek, and I asked if Sandra could attend. I was shocked that I was even mentioned in the will. We sat, and he read to us what you already know. Ma gave me her Cadillac. The lawyer reached across his desk and extended his hand with three sets of keys.

"Mildred was very thorough. She liked an extra set, just in case," he said as he shook them at me to accept. I hesitated before I reached across and took them; still not understanding what was going on. Sandra and I looked at each other.

"Why me?" I asked, as I looked at Sandra, but my question was directed at Mr. Clayton.

"I cannot tell you that Mr. Slater. I do not know. You must have made a fine impression on her. I do know that she loved that car and took great care of it. To her it wasn't a car; it was part of who she was. She asked me to go with her to pick it out, and she insisted on white. I assume she must have felt that you would take great care of it as she did. None-the-less, it is yours now. Do you have any questions?"

"I really don't understand. I guess I could ask a million questions right now," I said as I looked down at the pile of keys and car alarm remotes in my hand.

"Try not to question it Mr. Slater. Take Mildred's kind gift and know she thought you were the right person to have it. My secretary June will take care of the title with you. The car is parked on the side of the building." We shook hands.

Still stunned, Sandra and I went to the lobby to see June.

I drove the car home with Sandra following me. It was very strange driving someone else's car. It didn't feel right to me. The Caddy did drive very nicely, but I knew that it didn't belong to me. The radio had all her preset stations and I didn't touch them. I felt as if I was intruding on Ma's private and special place. When we arrived at home I parked the car on the side of the driveway and didn't plan to drive it for awhile.

Sandra and I talked about it the next day, and I had made up my mind that I wanted to return it to Ma's kids. They all had vehicles and weren't in need of a car, but it wasn't about that. I felt it belonged to the family.

I called ahead to let them know what I was thinking. We met with Leah, John and Beth. I explained to them again what I was thinking. They told me I didn't have to do that because it was what their mom wanted. After awhile of talking, I left them the sets of keys and Sandra and I left.

Almost a month passed before we got a call from Leah asking if we could come back over and talk. I asked her what was wrong and she said she would rather speak in person. Sandra and I thought that maybe something happened to the car, or maybe it had been stolen. We told her we would visit that weekend. Between then and the weekend I really didn't think too much about it.

We got there early in the morning and there it was, shinning in the sun. Ma's Cadillac. Leah was just finishing some coffee and had a worried look on her face. We sat down and she talked to us about the car and what had happened since we left it. Leah didn't really go into details. She basically said that she felt the car belonged to me, like her mom wanted. I could have believed that with no questions, but she had a worried look about her, too much so, to let it pass without asking more questions. Leah began to open up about it all. First she said that the car wouldn't start. It had been that way for a week now. It had been working fine.

"I was the first to drive it. Everything was fine. It drove well and I didn't have any problems. The only thing was that you couldn't change the radio station. It would play the same station no matter which button you pushed. I figured it was because it was a fancy car and all. After a few days of driving it I got used to it, but it started to feel like mom was in there with me. I know you must think that is crazy, but it's the truth. I could feel her there with me," she said shaking her head and taking a drink of water. Sandra glanced at me not knowing what to believe.

"I know it's a hard thing, and with all that has gone on, I'm sure that Ma is still here in some way. It's still early in all of this and those strong feelings will pass in time Leah," I said, trying to give her a different way of looking at it. I was lost on what to say so I took a shot.

"I wish it was that easy David, but I'm not the only one who has experienced it. John only drove it once and he never said anything, but Beth drove it a couple of days and she swears she could smell mama's perfume coming from the backseat and she also couldn't change the radio stations either. She was just as scared as I was." This was getting more bizarre by the minute. "Lately though, my nephew Jacob has been driving it. He said he tried to listen to a CD, and when he put it in the radio turned off. The radio hasn't worked since. He has driven it since then and he says sometimes it stalls at red lights, or runs real rough. The last day that he drove it he said he started it and then ran back inside to get something, and when he came out the radio was playing on mama's favorite station. As soon as he got in, the radio quit playing. When he got home later he looked frightened. He won't say what scared him. Since then, the car hasn't started. We haven't got a mechanic yet. I wanted to call you first."

I was trying to piece all of this together. It almost sounded like she was saying that Ma was haunting the car. In fact, I know that was what she was thinking.

"I don't know what to say Leah. Maybe the car needs a tune up. I can go out and look at it," I said in an effort to comfort her troubled mind.

"Well actually, I have our mechanic Ollie, coming out. I figured you two might be able to find out what's wrong. Either way, the car belongs to you. Mama wanted you to have it," she said, in a way that almost looked like desperation on her face. I had mixed emotions about it, but I knew that I really couldn't argue against it. I knew I would be driving the Cadillac back home, assuming we could start it.

We chatted for another fifteen minutes before Ollie arrived. We went out and raised the hood. He asked me to try and crank it. I sat down in the chair and turned the ignition. It started like a brand new car. The radio played. Leah and Sandra were watching from the doorway of the house. Ollie looked over everything. He even had a portable handheld computer to analyze the motor. He couldn't find anything wrong with it. We drove it around town and up the highway a bit; it ran like a new car.

We both agreed it was running good. Everything, from the radio to the air conditioning, worked fine. I talked to Leah about her keeping the car but she would have nothing of it. I knew then that she wasn't telling us everything. Sandra told me later that when I started the car Leah got tears in her eyes. Almost as if she knew all along it would start when I tried it. Ollie left and we sat and talked with Leah awhile longer. The conversation never went back to the car. When it was time for us to get going I tried once more.

"Are you sure this is what you want?" I asked, referring to the car.

"Yes, it is yours." She gave us a hug and we left.

I had Sandra follow me just in case the Caddy started acting up. We had decided to take the car home and park it on the far side of the driveway, and then get something to eat. As I was driving, I played with the radio and CD player and got Jacob's CD to play. It ran fine, and I never thought anything strange about it. I even sniffed the air in the car, jokingly, to see if I could smell Ma's perfume, nothing.

Sandra and I had lunch and talked about how Leah was acting when we were there. She said she noticed her hand shaking slightly when we were talking. I told Sandra that I didn't know what was going on but the car seemed to run fine. I planned on leaving the car parked and to run it once a week just to keep the battery charged. The car was nice, but I really didn't feel a need to drive it.

The next Thursday night as we were sleeping, I was awakened by the sound of a loud car alarm. I finally got up and looked out of the front window to see the Cadillac's alarm blaring and lights flashing.

"A cat or something must have set it off," I said softly. I grabbed the keys and tried to disarm it from inside, but it wouldn't shut off. I walked outside and got up to the door, pressed the button, and it finally turned off. I walked back to the door and looked back as I armed the alarm again. I was very sleepy, but I swear I saw a shadowy figure in the backseat. I blinked my eyes, I knew it couldn't be, but thought I better have another look. Maybe someone got inside and had set off the alarm. I walked over, slower this time. I came up from behind and looked into the back seat through the back window. The seat was empty. I must have been seeing things. I was very tired.

I decided to take the Cadillac to work the next day and give it get the one day of driving for the week. As I pulled out of my driveway the radio switched to a country and western station. I tried changing it, but it wouldn't switch. When the song was finished the DJ came on and announced the name of the station, it was a station in Stone Creek. That's over sixty miles away. I had never heard a Stone Creek station play in the valley. It was strange because I couldn't change it. I drove on to work listening to a Merle Haggard tune.

After a long day at work I opened the door to the car and as soon as I cracked it open, the smell of a woman's perfume hit me. I opened the door all the way and sure enough, the smell was coming from inside the car. I stepped back. It wasn't like a small mist; it smelled like it was just sprayed on. A very eerie feeling came over me. I looked into the backseat again and didn't see anything. Even though no one was in the car I reluctantly got in and started it up. I rolled the windows down and drove off, headed for home. I caught myself constantly looking in the rearview mirror. I don't know what I thought I might see, but in the back of my mind I didn't want to see anything. Nothing unusual happened as I parked the car and set the alarm.

I waited for Sandra to get home so that I could tell her about the alarm going off and what I thought I saw, and the way the car smelled when I got off of work. I told Sandra what had happened and she thought I was over reacting. She wanted to drive it herself to humor me. I gave her the keys and she took off.

She was gone for about thirty minutes. When she pulled up she unloaded a couple of bags from the grocery store. "I figured I would pick up a couple of things while I was out," she said as she opened the pantry. I was anxious to know if she experienced anything like I did.

"Well? Did anything weird happen?" I asked.

"No, nothing at all. I think you are reading way too much into it."

"Are you sure?" I asked, wanting to believe her.

"David, nothing happened. I drove to the store and then back. The only thing I did notice was the radio played the same station, and it did run a little rough at red lights, like, it was going to turn off."

"What do you mean? It ran rough?" I said in a effort to connect the dots.

"Yes when I would stop it started surging, and then shook some before it smoothed out."

I didn't reply. I just knew that I hadn't had any problems with the motor when I drove it. It ran like a new car. I decided that we would drive it the entire weekend. I had to try and make sense of what I was experiencing, or at least pass it off to my imagination, but I knew I had to confront it.

The weekend was normal. We did things we needed to do and never once did the Cadillac run badly. The only thing that was strange was the radio. It would only play one station. We tried a CD and it wouldn't play. Aside from that it went well and I lost most of my weird feelings about Ma and the car. As a matter of fact, I started gaining a fondness for the car. I felt like it was given to me to be driven and I should drive it. It didn't matter to Sandra if I drove the caddy or my car, so all was good at home. I cleaned it up late Sunday night and was looking forward to going to work the next day in my new car.

I drove it each day and had no strange occurrences or any trouble with the motor. The radio evened started working. I could play CDs and any station I wanted. I was finding my new found joy to be a pleasure to have, and by the weekend I was looking forward to taking Sandra out to dinner and a movie in it. By Friday, Sandra had gotten a full dose from me of everything that I liked or even loved about the car. I think, after awhile, she was tired of hearing about it. I wasn't, I was getting addicted to it in a strange, but excited way.

After a nice Saturday spent with Sandra, I woke up Sunday morning to find her gone. She had taken the

Cadillac. When she got back she was complaining about how the car was running, the radio, and how she got a weird feeling driving it. She had wanted to surprise me, so she had taken it and got it washed and detailed. The caddy really looked nice, but her experience in driving it there and back had ruined it all for her. I felt bad, but I didn't understand how it could have started running so bad all of a sudden, especially after I had driven it for over a week and had no problems at all. She was beside herself, and then started to cry. I went to console her.

"What's wrong? There has to be something else for it to make you cry," I said.

"You were right David. There is something else going on with the car. It's not just about the way it runs or how the radio plays. David, I believe Ma is in the car, it's her spirit or something, but she is part of that car," she said as she wiped her tears. I was floored by her saying that. I had all but gotten past the Ma thing since I had not had any problems for over a week. In the back of my mind I felt there might be something going on, but I was having such a good time that I had forgotten what all the drama was about before. "She is in that car," she said, shaking her head and looking down at the floor.

"What do you mean? What did you see?" I was almost begging for answers now.

"The car running bad wasn't a surprise to me, or the radio. It was when I started smelling perfume. Then…, then I heard her say, 'Best be getting the car back now dear.' I heard her words and her voice as clear as day David. It was Ma!" she said, hammering the point home as if I was not believing her. She looked up at me. "It was her. When I heard it I thought it was something on the radio, but I turned around and got the chills. No one was back there. The only thing was that smell of perfume."

I had to believe her. She had too much conviction in her statement and too much passion in her eyes. Plus, she spoke of the smell of perfume. The one thing no one could discredit. That was real and could not be explained away. It gave me the chills.

"I won't get in that car again. Ma or no Ma. I can't," Sandra said as she got up and walked away.

Everything that I had felt over the last week, the joy and pure happiness of driving and taking care of the car instantly disappeared. I went outside and opened the car. I didn't smell the perfume odor. I started the car and it ran smoothly. The radio and CD player worked perfectly. All of that being normal and working properly gave me the chills even more. I now realized that when I drove the car there never was a problem. It was when someone else drove it that the trouble would start. It all sounded weird and unbelievable, but it was the truth. I went back in to talk to Sandra.

No matter how much joy the Cadillac had brought me before, I knew it had to be sold. There was just too much going on. And the way it scared Sandra was enough for me to part with it. I thought about calling Leah and letting her know, but it was my car now. I didn't have to get approval to do the right thing.

I put the car for sale in a vacant lot close to where we lived. I had it listed for a couple of thousand below the blue-book value and I was hoping to snag a quick buyer. I got a call from a woman who wanted to test drive it. She was very interested and enthusiastic about the car. I met her there and told her to take it for a try. She left as I waited by her car. About ten minutes later she drove up and immediately exited the car, leaving the driver door open. Her face was as white as ghost.

"Is everything okay, ma'am? Did something go wrong?" She shoved her way past me.

"There is something wrong with that car," she said, shaking. As she got in her car she rolled down the window. "There was an old woman in the back seat. She told me to get out of her car!" she hollered, as she drove off, spinning her tires in the gravel. I can't say I didn't believe her. I did believe her, but I couldn't say anything to anyone that might want to buy the car. I had to sell it. I had to get rid of it.

I dropped the price down another five hundred dollars. Everything that was happening was by now, no surprise to me. Although I hadn't seen Ma in the car, I knew her presence was there. It was not something you could tell to just anyone, not without being ridiculed or criticized, or laughed at. I decided to keep the car for sale, determined to rid myself of what had become, my mental torture.

I was leaving the car in the vacant lot over night, choosing not to drive it home each day, but the owner of the lot asked me if I could clear it each night. I had received a call from a potential buyer that afternoon, but he would not be able to see it until the next day so I had to drive it home that evening. As usual, when I started the car it ran fine. I have to admit I was a little on edge and did not want to glance at the backseat. As I pulled down my street, the radio began to blare the Merle Haggard song again. The unmistakable smell of Ma's perfume flooded my nostrils. I felt her in the car with me. My hands gripped the wheel tighter. I avoided looking in the rearview mirror as long as I could, but . . . I had to see! I looked in the mirror, starting at the top and slowly worked my way down. I saw her trademark hairstyle and quickly lowered my eyes. She was there! She was sitting in the back seat, just like the lady said! I was trembling now and almost home, but I pulled over. I got my courage up, put the car in park, and I turned around. Sitting there, smiling at me was Ma. I think I remember my vision blurring for a breath moment. I tried to refocus, thinking I was seeing things again, but I wasn't. Ma was with me.

"Why are you selling my car David? Don't you like the gift I gave you?" she said, as her smile turned sour. I gasped, opened my door, and quickly jumped out. My heart was pounding in my chest and I was sweating like crazy. I looked through the backseat window, and saw that Ma was not looking at me, only looking straight ahead. She slowly faded into a mist, then into nothing. The smell of her perfume was gone just as quick. The radio began to play the rock station I had on earlier and just like that, she was gone. I stood in the street for at least thirty minutes, too afraid to get in and drive the rest of the way home. My eyes rarely left the backseat. I don't know where I found the strength to get home, but I finally got in and took the car home.

The next day I told Sandra of my encounter and she shook her head and waved her hand at me, not wanting to hear any details. She walked away. She had experienced the same, unbelievable vision. I knew her fear and understood her not wanting to know anything, or be involved with the car. But I had to, it was my . . . gift.

I was to meet the man to see the car at the lot, but I called him and asked if he could meet at my house. I did not want to drive the caddy anymore. He agreed and I gave him the directions, he showed up right on time. We talked awhile and I gave him the keys and as he drove off I looked in the backseat, no Ma.

I received a distressing call from the man about ten minutes later. He said he couldn't explain what happened; he just wanted to get his car and go home. He said he left the Cadillac parked on the side of the road near a school and offered no explanation. He didn't need one, I knew what had happened. The car was still running when I got there. Luckily no one jumped in and took it. For all I know, maybe someone had tried and Ma scared them off.

I had two others come see about the White Cadillac and both were scared out of it by what they saw. I assume they saw Ma, but they didn't need to give an explanation as to what happened in their encounter. I knew, and it was becoming all too common-place for me. Ma did not want anyone driving her car, but me.

After the last two attempts to sell it, all I could do was laugh. It wasn't funny at all, but I had numbed myself to what was happening. I took the Caddy off the market. Sandra was not pleased and she asked me to give it away to charity. I told her that no matter who got the car, Ma wasn't going to let them drive it, or have it in peace.

Even though I was becoming numb to the whole thing, and while I truly believed Ma or her spirit was in the car, it gave me a determination to finally confront her.

I decided to drive the Cadillac back to Stone Creek. I left early Saturday morning and if she appeared I would not cower, I was going to confront her. In a way, do my own exorcism of the car. The first thirty minutes of the drive were uneventful. I was getting a little frustrated that I had built up all this courage to do this, and now she decided to not show up. That thought didn't last long. That familiar scent began to omit itself from the backseat. I glanced in the mirror, nothing yet. Not much longer, there she was. Instantly, I got very nervous, but I was very determined and I waited for her to speak, she remained quiet. It was driving me crazy. Speak Ma, speak! Instead, all she did was look out the door window with a pleasant little smile. She's testing me.

About five minutes from town I made up my mind and pulled the car over. I turned and for the first time looked directly into the backseat. Ma looked as real as you or me sitting there. I was scared and angry. As I was about to speak, she turned and looked right at me. I froze. This is what you were waiting for, I thought to myself. Her eyes were just as blue and sparkling as they were when she was alive.

"Why are we stopped dear?" she said to me with a smile. "We better hurry or I might miss my appointment to get my hair and nails done." I had no idea how to respond to that. I was still trying to wrap my head around the last thirty seconds. Imagine if you were me in that situation; looking into the eyes of a dead woman as she speaks to you. In one quick moment, my courage came back to me.

"Ma, I don't understand what is going on or what you want," I said, trying my best to show her I wasn't scared. Am I really talking to a dead person?

"Nothing more than my usual Saturday appointments. I haven't had one in a while. My hair and nails are not up to my standards." I couldn't believe this was happening.

"Ma you are not alive anymore, you are dead. You have to move on." Finally, I said it. I was shaking like crazy, but I said it.

"Do I look that bad dear?" she pulled a mirror from her purse. As soon as she saw herself in the mirror a look of disbelief came over her face. I still did not believe all of this was happening. I rubbed my eyes to clear them. When I looked back at Ma I understood what gave her the look of disbelief. Her face was now unrecognizable. The skin was sunk in and dry. Her hands were bony and her nails were long, curled, and yellow. Her eyes had changed from blue to black. She reached her long bony hand out to me. She grabbed my arm, the nails slightly scrapping on my skin. This was the most scared I have ever been in my life. Ma leaned forward.

"You are right dear. I do look dead," her breath smelled of death. "Now take me to my appointments or I may just rot to death right here in the car." Then she smiled as she patted my arm. Her blackened teeth were chipped and decayed. She bared no resemblance to the Ma that I knew. As she was pulling her hand away she grabbed my arm tighter than before. "One other thing David, don't ever try to sell my car, or let anyone drive it again," she said. Her voice was heavier and much more direct. She put the mirror back into her purse. Her face and hands returned to normal and she continued to stare out the window as she slowly faded away.

The Haggard tune stopped, leaving the car in complete silence.

I didn't realize just how much I was trembling until I looked down at my arm. It was shaking uncontrollably. I turned around quickly, faced forward, and looked out the front glass. It took me a few minutes to get myself together. I had thought I was ready to confront Ma, but realized I was no match for her spirit and will to remain with us. With all the terror and fear raging inside me, an amusing thought popped into my head.

Ma gave me the car so that I could be her, well . . . her chauffeur.

I was fighting a losing battle, and as crazy as it sounds, I began to laugh hysterically.

I drove Ma and the Cadillac to her hair and nail appointments that day and I have done so every other weekend for the last six months.

This had all been too much for my Sandra to take. After three months of that, she called me insane and left me. There was no need to try and explain to her what happened that first Saturday on the road. That was, and remains, between Ma and me.

I did try once, to get rid of the car. I gave it to a charity like Sandra had begged me to do before our breakup. And I actually thought it had worked.

Nearly two weeks had passed since I gave it away, and I thought I might have really been done with it all.

Then . . . I got up on a Saturday. I made myself some coffee and walked over to turn off the garage and porch lights. I strolled over to the window and looked outside. To my shock, the White Cadillac was sitting in my driveway. No one was at the wheel.

I could have panicked and been stricken with fear, but I didn't. I continued looking at the beautiful White Caddy, took a sip of coffee and smiled.

The Crate

"Don't let your curiosity get the best of you."

There have been, and always will be warehouses, buildings or places where a different assortment of items are stored or kept until they are needed. These places each have their own unique stories and history of boxes, crates and items that were mislabeled, lost, or never claimed. So they sit, and over time they are pushed back into a deeper part of the warehouses and buildings that they are stored in. A darker and almost forgotten part of the building is usually where most of these items end up.

Newark, New Jersey, being a port town, has plenty of these warehouses, and this is where security guard, Martin Cranston, works. With almost two years on the job with East Coast Security Company, Martin has been bumped around from location to location, warehouse to warehouse, as part of his "Rookie" classification with the company. Learnin' the ropes is what they tell him. After two years they will designate him to a more permanent location.

At thirty years of age, and pretty much a normal, average guy, Martin was still searching for Ms. Right. He had no wife, no kids, and because of various unsuccessful dates, Martin has had his confidence shaken a bit in the social world, despite his heavy, seemingly confident, east coast accent. It doesn't help that he works mostly nights at his job.

Martin is his job and his job is him. Sometimes he would work a double-shift from evenings to overnight. He didn't mind much and there was nothing wrong with a little overtime pay.

Martin was working evenings and on this night had volunteered for the graveyard shift. "What the hell, I don't have anything special going on tonight," he said to himself. It was the end of the quarterly shipping period and he had to make the rounds in both regular and unclaimed storage. He usually started with the bigger part of the warehouse and when it got close to second shift he would switch to the smaller one. The entire warehouse was so big that there were always two security guards working evenings, but they rarely crossed paths as the building was split in two.

He knew his job well and had a routine and schedule that he kept in his mind and was beginning to like the evening and overnight shifts because he was left to do his job without interference or under any supervisor's watchful eye. He had a desk; he usually stayed at after midnight, located in the 'unclaimed' section. It was quiet there and he could read or listen to the radio in peace and somewhat hidden from the 'early birds' that rolled in around five in the morning.

Around midnight, Martin made his way through the maze of crates and boxes that were there and probably in their final resting place, lost or unclaimed. Nothing was out of ordinary, so he took his seat at his desk near the door. Just as he sat down he noticed a wooden crate, "Crate # 93-82-71", just off the outer fringe of the first row. UK to USA was stamped on the top and bottom. Apparently it had just been put there. It was no more than twenty feet from his desk. It looked out of place, but it wasn't Martin's job to see it was stored properly, so he left it there. He pulled out his cooler and began to eat a sandwich. He looked over the four monitors that had cameras scanning the warehouse and saw the usual, nothing unusual. He logged on to the dating site that he had signed up for a week earlier, hoping to change his luck with women. He knew it was not his style, but he had nothing to lose either. Martin wasn't desperate, and carried pride about himself, but he felt he needed a change to shake things up. Just as he clicked the login button, he heard a noise behind him. It sounded like a box or crate had moved on the floor, like a short, sliding sound. He saw nothing out of place. The nearest box was # 93-82-71, but he couldn't remember exactly which angle it sat before the noise. Curious, Martin walked over to it and tried to nudge it with his foot. It didn't move and the lid was nailed shut. He had a quick look around and decided that it was nothing, and sat back down at his desk.

After finishing his sandwich, Martin picked up his book and read a few pages before dozing off. He was awaked by a thumping sound, again coming from behind him. It scared him out of his impromptu nap. He sat upright and turned around quickly, and the first thing to come into his groggy focus, was the UK crate. He got up and walked towards it. He pulled out his flashlight, even though there was enough light to see. As a security guard he was supposed to keep things secure, but not with a firearm, no, his only weapon was his trusty flashlight. He didn't have it in hand for lighting; he had it to protect himself.

Halfway there he was stopped dead in his tracks by another knocking from inside the crate. It vibrated a little on the floor. "Anyone there?" A voice came from the crate.

Martin couldn't believe his ears and eyes. "What the f. . ." he was interrupted by the voice again.

"I say! Is anyone there?"

The voice sounded British.

"Who's there!?" Martin said, trying to sound in charge. His thought was that someone was hiding behind the crate, not wanting to give thought to someone being inside it. "I said who's there?"

"Just me old chap. Stanley Adams here," the British voice said, sounding happy that he had gotten a response.

What the hell is going on? Martin thought. It sounds like it's coming from inside. "What's going on? I said who is there!? I'm the security guard here. You need to come out now!" Martin said in a louder tone.

"But I can't get out unless you let me out sir," the voice said.

Martin had taken a couple of more cautious steps forward waiting for someone to jump out from behind the boxes, but he was sure now, to his disbelief, that the voice was coming from inside. With his flashlight ready, he walked up to the crate and banged on the side.

"Easy there, that's loud in here."

Shocked, and for certain now, he knew that there was someone inside.

"Wait one second," Martin said as he scurried around looking for something to pry open the top. "I'll be right back."

Many thoughts raced through Martin's head. One of them was. Who was it? Stowaway? Logical thinking took over. The box appears to be three foot by three foot by three foot. Plenty of room for a man to be in there. But how, or why?

He had to get it open. He had to get him out. After looking around the back walls of the room, he found a crowbar. Martin wasn't as nervous as before, but he was still wary. He got back to the box and rapped it on its side.

"You okay in there?"

"Yes, yes I am," the voice replied.

"Hang on, I'm gonna get you out of there."

With that, Martin began to use the crowbar to pry up one end at a time. He had only one nail left and then he would have it open and save the poor man.

"You mustn't open the led unless you are ready sir. Are you sure you are ready?" Stanley said in more of an inviting voice.

Martin stopped prying on the last nail. "What do you mean? If I'm ready?" he said, cautious again and puzzled. He didn't know why, but he knew he better not open it.

"Never mind what I said, please get me out of here." Stanley sounded more desperate now.

Martin stepped back from the crate. He looked it over trying to figure out what to do. He decided to open it, but first he would fasten the small chains to the front of it on each side to allow the lid to open only six inches or so. The backside had two hinges attached which would help keep it in place. He could have a look inside safely this way, using his flashlight. He got the small chains into place.

"What are you doing? What's taking so long?"

"Don't worry, have you out soon enough." That was a lie, for the meantime, but he had to say something.

It was time to open it. Martin was ready and began prying up on the last nail until it popped off, falling and hitting the concrete floor. There was no sound from inside. He slowly, using the crowbar, began to lift the lid. He had his flashlight in his other hand and shined it through the opening as it widened until it hit the length of the chains he had fastened.

"Hello, Stanley?"

"Yes I'm here. If you could open it a little more, I won't be able to get out through there."

Martin leaned forward, using the bar as a prop for leverage, and peered deeper into the darkness. The beam from his flashlight tried its best to show him what was inside, but it only lit up a four inch circular spot at a time. He moved the light slowly across the dark area until he saw . . . him or it. Staring up at him were two red eyes, deep from within the sockets a skull.

Its jaw moved.

"Please open it all the way."

Martin jumped back, his flashlight fell from his hand; his eyes must have deceived him. The crowbar was still lodged between the lid and the crate wall, leaving open a one inch gap. The crate rattled and Martin grabbed the crowbar. The lid popped up as far as it could go, the chains held tight.

He pulled the crowbar out and grabbed his light. Shinning it inside he thought he saw a bony hand holding the lid up.

"What did ya go and put chains on it for?" The British accent was as strong as ever. "I just wanted to get out and stretch the ole legs."

"What the hell is going on? Who are you?" Martin held the crowbar up high, ready to strike down on anything that made its way out.

"I told you, I'm Stanley Adams, Edinborough, U.K."

"This has to be some kind of joke. Who put you up to this? Did the guys do this?" He lowered his eye level so he could look straight into the darkness. His light shinned directly into the red-burning eyes. A skeletal hand reached out suddenly trying to grab at Martin. His instincts took over and he stood and slammed the lid down on the bony hand. A painful cry shrieked from inside as the hand withdrew in pain.

Martin didn't know what to do. He wanted to get a hammer so he could drive the nails back into it, but he didn't want to leave the top without weight on it so the thing or whatever it was couldn't reach out again. He decided to use the crowbar to nail the top shut.

As he pounded a couple of nails down he listened, curious to hear the voice again, still not believing that his was real. Nothing but silence filled the room. He looked around the room halfway expecting his coworkers to burst in and revel in their practical joke. Again, the room was silent.

BAM! BAM! BAM! The crate shook. "What did you close it for? Why did you lock me in here? Please let me out of here," it said.

If this was a joke, then it was a pretty good one in Martin's mind. He hoped it was, but something was telling him it wasn't.

But, what is it?

"I'm gonna ask you one more time, who put you up to this?" Martin said, standing over the wooden box.

"I told you, no one did. I've been in this thing for a long time now, all the way over from the Queen's land."

"Yeah right, I'm gonna have the Chief Shipping Inspector check all this out. He'll be here in just a few minutes," he said, in hopes of scarring the jokesters.

"Yes yes. Anything to help get me out of here," the voice called out.

That seemed strange to him. Martin hadn't realized that it was already four in the morning. The day shift would be arriving soon. He had to make a decision. Wait until the guys came in on days and see who would take responsibility for the joke, tell someone higher up and have them look into it, or not tell anyone and come back in on his shift later in the evening and see if the joke was still on. Martin decided on the third option. He would play along with the joke, if indeed that's what it was, and push the crate back into the mix of wooden boxes and check on it when he came in later. By then the joke would be up or someone would tell him.

"Where are you taking me? Are you going to let me out?"

"Fat chance buddy. I'll check on you later," he said with a laugh.

Martin mixed the crate in with the other boxes and lost items and propped a broom up against it so he could tell if it was moved or opened.

The morning shift arrived and nothing was said to Martin about the prank. No one looked suspicious. He went home and slept before waking and getting ready for his evening shift. He had a quick lunch and headed out.

His thought was that they were really playing the joke up and carrying it on for a long time. He was certain that whoever it was would admit to their joke and would get a laugh out of it.

Nothing was unusual after he arrived at work. The normal banter between fellow employees and the normal changing of shifts were all that he experienced, but not what he expected. He made his rounds and took notes, logging them in as required. He couldn't wait to get back to the storage room where his desk was. He wanted to see if the joke was still on.

He opened the doors to the storage room and flipped on the lights. Immediately he noticed that the broom was no longer propped up on the crate. He logged into the computer and looked to see if anything had been claimed or moved. There was no activity.

"So it was a joke," he said out loud. He walked over to the crate and saw that the broom was lying on the ground. He gave the carte a quick kick.

"Easy chap. Not so rough."

Martin was startled. He took a quick step back.

"Are you guys kidding me or what? Come on, enough of this already."

He stepped forward and tried to pry the lid off. It was still nailed down exactly like he had left it. It hadn't been touched. That's' strange, he thought. If this was a joke, how could he still be in there all this time? He ran over to where he left the crowbar and brought it back to the crate and began to pry the nails out. He was determined to see who was in there and end this little prank. He left the little chains attached to the sides, just in case.

After the last nail was pried out, he lifted the top as high as it would go against the chains. "Who's in there? Show your face!" he demanded. He shined his flashlight into the darkness, but couldn't see anything. From the angle he had, he couldn't see to the bottom of the crate. He would have to undo the chains to look in deeper. He undid the right one and started on the left.

"My, you have a heavy New York accent."

Martin stopped working on the chain, surprised by the voice. Then it dawned on him. There was no one in there. They probably used a speaker or a recorded voice to mess with him. That's why he couldn't see anyone in there.

With this newly acquired thought he smiled and undid the second chain. He was about to lift the top.

"Please, DO NOT open it, unless you are truly ready."

The words made Martin pause. He was still thinking it was a joke, but something about the way it was said made him hesitate. It scared him a little. He held the top steady, not opening it all the way.

"What do you mean? Truly ready?"

"I can't explain, I can only warn. I'm not at liberty to say. Only that, whoever opens the crate must be prepared for the consequences."

"Oh yeah? So Stanley, or whatever your name is, how long have you been in there?" He was trying to sound brave, but he held the lid down tightly against the crowbar, just in case.

"I would say, about forty years or so. I was punished you see. I am stuck here forever unless . . ."

His speech stopped.

"Unless what?" Martin asked in an attempt to humor the pranksters. It has to be a live interactive speaker system of some kind. "Wait one second; I got to hear this in comfort." With that, he attached the chains again and slid the desk chair over to the crate. The six-inch opening was held up by a scrap piece of wood.

"Okay Stanley, continue," he said as he took his seat, content on playing this thing out.

"Well sir, I was put in here forty years ago as a punishment for something I did. I am forbid to speak of it."

"And you say you can't get out unless?"

"Yes, unless the person who opens it trades places with me of their own free will."

This got a loud east-coast laugh from Martin. "You mean to tell me that if someone opens this box, you will be free, and whoever opens it will be stuck in there like you?"

"Yes, it is the truth."

"Ha ha ha, that's the best one I've heard in awhile Stanley."

"No one ever believes me. Either that or they get scared and box me up and send me off."

"That reminds me, I need to see exactly where this shipped from. I'll be right back." Martin took the chair over to the computer and logged in the crate's number and I.D. tag. He found it, originally shipped from the U.K. three months ago, unclaimed for two months. "So that part is true, but what were the contents?" He did some more searching, but found nothing in the database naming what was in it. That was strange. It was like it was erased or overlooked. He glanced over at the box. He had a mind to just go over and rip the lid off and get down to what was going on. But, he decided to go a little further.

He walked back over to the box and drug it to the center of the room and sat in the chair. "Do you know what was in this crate originally?"

"I don't know what you mean? Only me, that I'm aware of."

"Okay Stanley, if you have really been in there for forty years, how have you survived all this time without food or water?" Martin asked the question as he leaned back in his chair. If it wasn't some kind of speaker system, and someone was really in there, they had to give in sooner or later. He planned to wait it out.

"Well, I don't need food or water sir; I am not of this earth anymore. Each year I deteriorate more and more. At the moment, I am down to bones. My eyes have not been affected and I am glad, as it is good to be able to see the light from time to time."

Martin couldn't believe the lengths that they were going to. In his mind though, he felt a little uneasy. Something just wasn't right, but he couldn't let them know, just in case they were watching.

"So you say you can't tell me what you did to get yourself put in there?"

"No sir I can't."

"And the only way for you to get out of there is to have someone willingly take your place? Is this right?"

"Yes, it is very simple really, but no one has wanted to do that."

"What will happen to you outside of there if you are nothing but a skeleton?"

"Well, I can tell you that as soon as I am out of here I will slowly transform into my old self. This is what I have learned in all these years."

"Who told you that?" Martin said, getting more into the question and answer session by the minute. He was beginning to enjoy playing along with the joke.

"Them," he said softly, and then paused. "Those who dwell beneath."

"I see. Are they there now?"

"Not right here at the present, no sir, but they are down there."

"Do they speak to you? Or how do they tell you these things?"

"They speak within my mind, but they can be heard by anyone, even you, if you really listen."

"When you say beneath or down there, what do you mean? The box is only three feet deep."

"Well sir, in your world the bottom of this prison is only three feet deep. But in my world, it goes to a place that is full of unspeakable horrors and evil deeds. Don't let your eyes deceive you."

Martin shined his flashlight through the opening trying to see if someone was really in there. The prank was very good, he had to admit. "What would happen if someone opened the lid and didn't know about you or trading places like you say?" Martin was getting more to the point. He was trying to trip up the pranksters.

"This is why I said do not open it unless you are ready. If the person is not ready to accept the terms then they will burn in the fire below, and I will still be stuck here."

"If that's the case, and someone knew these facts, why would anyone even consider opening the box? If they knew they were going to burn in fire or be stuck in there like you are, there is no way ever, anyone in their right mind would do it. So, in my mind, it doesn't make sense that you would ask me if I was ready."

"All they have to say is yes. If they say yes to my question and then they open it. I will be free. There is much more at work here than just a wooden box. The power below is unimaginable."

"So why have they granted you this chance? Why are you not burning down there?" Martin was growing more irritated with the length of the joke.

"My punishment has been to sit in here for all this time. Yes, I do have a chance to get out of here, but as you can see I have been here for four decades. Imagine being in my position. Confined, not able to stand up and stretch your legs and living in the dark. No one will listen to you. Maybe this is why I am here. I'm being used as an avenue to send people to hell."

"Hell? Did you say hell?"

"Yes."

"Now it sounds like this is a life or death, heaven or hell thing. Is that what this is about?" Martin asked. He felt he was finally getting to the answer of it all.

"Some people call it heaven and hell. Some people call it purgatory, but if they do not repent and say yes to God, they burn in hell." Stanley finally let Martin know the truth.

"That's pretty deep shit if you ask me." Martin said, dismissing Stanley's last statement. "Well I will say that this box is marked with **Do Not Open** all over it. There is an attachment here in plastic that says, 'Only, the rightful owner may open this box, and only then, under extreme caution.' This has terrorist threat written all over it. I can't believe this made it through security and customs. They must have x-rayed it. Has anyone besides me tried to open it?" He was growing more curious.

"Yes, many have. They just weren't prepared and did not say yes to my question."

"What happened to them?"

"They were pulled down and burned in the fires below. This is why I cannot trick anyone into opening it. It doesn't do me any good. They are sent to the fire and I stay here."

"I think I would go crazy being trapped in there all that time," he said, going along further with the joke. "I might have to consider killing myself at some point."

"Oh yes, I have gone quite mad many times and I have tried suicide. I succeeded once, using a broken piece of wood from this coffin of mine. I sharpened it the best I could, placed it to my neck and against my carotid artery and pushed it in. I don't remember dying, but I remember waking up, still inside this box. No remnants of me dying, no blood and no hole in my neck. I knew then that I was stuck here forever. Unless, like I said, someone agrees and says, yes."

At this point Martin had the urge to just end the joke and rip the top off and looking inside. He truly believed it to be a joke, but, there was just something that made him a bit more curious. Plus, he was killing time on his work shift by playing along. He leaned back and propped his feet up on top of the crate.

"Okay Stanley, one more question. Who shipped you and this box to New Jersey? I mean, I've checked all the shipping manifests and traced it down in the computer and there is no listing to the person who sent it. Can you explain that one buddy?"

"I do not control how or where I am moved around to. I am glad to be in a new place, as I have traveled from England to Italy and through Europe. Then finally I ended back in my homeland. Now I have landed here. I wish I could explain more to you, but I truly do not know all of the details in my predicament. You do not believe me do you?"

Martin started laughing. "Do I believe you? Well, let me say, you are very good at what you are doing, you and whoever else is involved. But I figure I'm gonna find out here very shortly. It's almost time for me to get off work and I want to end this by then."

"So you will agree and open the lid then?" Stanley said, sounding more upbeat and began stirring around inside the box more.

"I might agree if you can prove to me that you are real," he said, knowing that all he had to do was open the lid to see for himself, but he wanted to break the pranksters at their own game.

"What type of proof do you need sir? Haven't you already seen me when you looked inside?"

Martin did remember what he had seen, but as real as it looked he knew it was some type of prop from a costume store or somewhere. It was a great joke he had to admit, but he wouldn't give them credit.

"Shine your light in here again please, you can see my sad state," Stanley said, sounding more British than ever.

"I think I'll wait awhile longer. I still have a few minutes before I need to make my last rounds."

"Please Martin, open the crate and say yes, please?"

Martin sat up in his chair, excited and animated. "Aha! Got you! I never told you my name. Only the people I work here with would know my name," Martin said. He began to laugh loudly figuring he had finally made them slip up.

"Why do you laugh sir? Because I know your name? I know who everyone is who talks to me. I know that from the highest authorities down below. They tell me things all the time. Things like a person's name, to some very evil and unimaginable things that I'd rather not hear of."

"Oh, is that right? Another burst of laughter bellowed from deep within Martin. He was really enjoying himself now, but time was getting short. He had to end the joke or let it ride for another night. "Well, I think it's time for me to go."

"Please don't go. Martin, will you please say yes and open the box?"

"Like I said buddy, I got the power to agree or not, and right now, I say, no"

Just as he ended his statement, Stanley, or what remained of him, raised himself to the opening and grabbed the edge with both of his skeletal hands. "Nooooo!" he shouted. "Open it now!"

He peered out at Martin. The sudden movement and the bony hands sticking out of the crate scared Martin at first. He slid back in his chair a bit before he got his composure. He grabbed his flashlight and shined it in the darkness, just past the long bony fingers that flicked nervously on the top edge of the crate. His light hit Stanley's eyes head on. The red, fire-like eyeballs were like lasers zeroing in on their target.

The vision of the eyes and the shiny skull startled Martin again.

"Screw this!" Martin jumped up, angry and scared, and grabbed the crowbar. He pushed it through the opening. The skeleton's hands withdrew inside. Martin pried up hard on the lid until the small chins snapped from their metal clips.

He fell forward on top of the crate, reclosing it. The crowbar rattled on the floor as Martin stood up straight.

Do or die time.

He listened one last time, but heard nothing. Lifting the lid fast and flipping it backwards in a fit of anger and fear, he watched it fall to the ground as he leaned forward and looked into the crate.

Darkness.

Grabbing his flashlight, he shined it inside. The light seemed to disappear into the darkness. His arm was grabbed by the skeletal hands and was pulled halfway over. His feet left the floor as he teetered on the edge. He tried to pull back but it had him. The flashlight dropped from his hand, and to his shock it disappeared into the darkness, never hitting the bottom.

"You opened it, but you have not said yes, you have not agreed!" Martin was pulled down further, his feet were the only things left hanging on the edge. The skull of Stanley Adams met him face-to-face, its eyes burned with anger. "Do you agree to take my place, Martin?"

The bones squeezed tighter on Martin's arm. He began to scream.

"We have little time. Decide now! It's the only way to save you." It pulled Martin in head-first, dropped him further into the blackness and held him by his ankles. "Look! This is what you will get if you do not agree."

Martin's screams stopped as the darkness lit up below. At first, it was a small amount of light, but it grew brighter and brighter. He realized that it was not a light, it was fire. The gateway to hell was opening. A red, orange, and black cloud of fire was ascending towards him. In shock, Martin could only watch. It grew closer and the temperature became unbearable. He felt a terrible pressure in his chest. The cloud of flames began to part and emerging from it was, The One Who Dwells Below. The demon's eyes were made of fire and two, thick black horns rose from its head. Martin screamed as it grew closer. Its mouth opened, reveling its razor-sharp teeth, and snake-like tongue. As it opened wider Martin could see more fire inside. The heat increased and he could hear screams. To his horror, he saw bodies burning in the fire within. The devil's mouth surrounded Martin, and just as it was about to swallow him.

"Yes! Yes! I agree to your terms! Get me out of here! Hurry! Please!" Martin yelled.

"Do you repent Martin!? Do you say yes to that?" Stanley shouted down.

"Yes! I repent!"

Martin felt his body being lifted. The demon's mouth closed and it began to descend, the fire grew dimmer. He felt the demon's laughter rumble in his chest.

The morning janitor found Martin unconscious, unresponsive, and slumped over his desk. He called 911.

When the paramedics arrived, Martin went into cardiac arrest. They performed CPR as they loaded him into the ambulance.

Martin survived the heart attack, but had six weeks of recovery after his by-pass surgery. He told his story numerous times and had the company look up Crate # 93-82-71. After an extensive search the crate was never found and had never been there, according to their database. Most people there assumed that his story of the crate was a by-product of his traumatic experience. Martin knew better, but gave up trying to convince them. His near-death experience had changed his life and had made him a much nicer, more religious, man. That was all that mattered to him.

On his first day back at work he was met by Mr. Davenport, his supervisor.

"I am very happy your recovery has gone well Martin. You're a good man, welcome back," he said, shaking Martin's hand.

"Thank you Mr. Davenport."

They walked into Davenport's office.

"Martin, since this is your first day back, I want someone to work with you for a couple of weeks. You know, until you get back into the swing of things again. He's fairly new here. Maybe you can show him how things work around here"

They walked over to a man sitting at the desk.

"And here he is. Martin, this is . . ."

The man stood up, interrupting Davenport's introduction.

"Pleasure to meet you Martin." The man spoke with a British accent. He smiled and shook Martin's hand. "Name's Stanley, Stanley Adams."

Ritter House

"Shadows of deceased ghosts do haunt the houses and the graves about, whose life's lamp went untimely out."

"Test, test. I am going to record the next twelve hours or so, for my research project for my next novel, yet to be named. It is 5:30 p.m. Friday, July 22, 2011. I am horror author, Peter Keller. I am labeled as a horror author in the sense that I tend to write about such things, and in turn, it allows my fans and critics alike, to find a starting point to attach themselves to me and my style. I'm not big on labels, but in fairness to everyone, I do tend to dabble in the horror and macabre. I can't complain, and my next novel will be much enhanced by my visit to the famed and notorious,

Ritter House. I am staying a night and making this recording in audio form and with pen and paper only. The owner and proprietor of the house, and a very kind gentleman if I may say, Daniel Ritter, asked that there be no video recordings done while I am inside. I had no issues and will respect that. After all, I am going there for my research, to absorb the elements of the home and take in the true feel of the energy that is supposed to haunt the place. I am not a paranormal investigator or scientist in any form, as my wife can attest to that. I am just a man who prefers to research the material that I will deliver to your mind's eye. My intention is to go in without any direct plan or agenda other than to experience the house for what it is. And yes, I am aware of the history and things that have gone on there, and of what people have said they have experienced. I am not blind to that fact at all, but I do go in open-minded. I will go into the detail of the history of the house when I arrive there in an hour or so."

"It is now 7:00 p.m. and I have been let in the house by Mr. Ritter. I plan on staying here for twelve hours and take notes accordingly. I asked Mr. Ritter to shutdown the electricity, but he insisted on leaving on the breaker, that controls the first floor bathroom. As I think of it, I can't say I disagree. Running water will be available if I need. In my possession, I will have a flashlight, a digital audio recorder, a pad of paper and pen, a cell phone, for emergencies only mind you, and my laptop computer with an extra battery – I plan to write as the mood hits me. I have also brought a snack and water. I will make my next recording after nightfall draws on the old house."

"The night has spoken; it is now completely dark in the house. In the past two hours I have walked around the downstairs of the house so I could get my bearings. It is a nice house really, full of furniture and ready for someone to move right in. But, I believe that is easier said than done, as Ritter House has not had a tenant, according to Mr. Ritter, in ten years. I must say, he really keeps the place up quite well. The place is very clean and not dusty at all, although I am looking through this place through the light of my flashlight. I have set up shop, so to speak, in the living room at a rather nice desk. The desk is made of solid wood and as far as I can tell, no expense has been spared in the décor of this place. I'll take a seat there and go over my notes."

"A few notes about the Ritter House. It is located, as most that follow haunted houses know, in a small neighborhood just south of Cicero, Illinois, not far from my home in Chicago. The house is a three-bedroom, two-bath, two-story home. It was built in 1948 making it at least sixty-three years old, by my math. The house was built and owned by Nicholas and Debra Blakely, and that is why the house is sometimes referred to as Blakely House. In 1951 Debra Blakely had dinner with her husband, washed the dishes and walked outside to the backyard shed. She brought back with her an axe and hacksaw. As her husband Nicholas slept in his living room chair, she raised the axe above her from behind him and brought it down on his head. The axe slicing through his skull killed him instantly. After a couple of more blows he had fallen out of the chair to the floor. Thank God for him that he died on the first blow rather than endure his lovely wife taking the hacksaw and cutting him into six pieces; two legs, two arms, his torso and his head. Debra was found wandering the streets that night covered in blood, and in the state of mind of a lost soul. Her words were to no one in particular, but those words set the tone for reputation and history of the house."

"'The devil made me do it. The devil made me do it.' These were the words that Debra Blakely spoke when authorities questioned her. The pieces of Nicholas' bloody body were found that night, July 22, 1951, in the exact spot that I am sitting now. Debra committed suicide while in jail four months later with authorities never getting an explanation of why. Yes, tonight is the sixty year anniversary of the murder. Debra's claim was that he devil made her do it . . . noted. But, there is more to the story of Ritter House, it seems. First I must take a quick break."

"I guess I am getting old or tired. I went to the bathroom and as I came out I thought I heard a door close down the hall. The doors to the two downstairs rooms were open, so I thought it could be the closet doors. I walked to each room, and in the second room the closet door was closed. I do not scare easily, but I must admit that with only my flashlight to guide me, the room did take on a dark, gloomy look. I reached for the door knob and turned. As I pulled the door open, I shined the light inside the closet. It was empty, with only a few hangers and a shelf looking back at me. I did smile over the little incident. I do not know what the sound was, but I can report that I found nothing."

"Now, I'll finish off what I know about the history of this house. The house remained vacant for three years after the Blakely murder, and rumors of the place being haunted by either the ghost of Nicholas Blakely or worse, by a demon, quickly spread through town until new owners were found. Let's see here, William and Mary Ritter bought the house for the low price of $8,000.00. Considering what had happened, I'm surprised that they didn't just give it away. According to some of the old-timers around here, there were no odd or strange reports about the house after the Ritters moved in. That was until two years later in 1956. Again according to reports, while the Ritter children were away with relatives, William Ritter took a shotgun and shot his wife Mary three times while she slept. It is agreed by investigators, that he then walked into the hallway just outside their bedroom, where he turned the gun on himself. No one reported hearing any gunshots, probably due to the thunderstorms that night. From that time, the Ritter family has owned the house. The kind young man Daniel, who let me in and agreed to me being here, is the nephew of William and Mary. Apparently, no one has lived here for more than a month before they moved out claiming this place to be haunted or possessed. Daniel has had ownership of the house since 1994. He hasn't changed much about the place. He doesn't even list it as rental property, and from what he says, he holds on to the place in memory of his family, despite the tragedy. I asked him if he had experienced anything paranormal here. He didn't answer me."

"The old pendulum clock on the wall, that I set the time on when I arrived, now says the time is midnight. I was pleasantly surprised that it still worked. After taking a short break to write down some notes and write a little on the computer, I am ready to explore the upstairs thoroughly. Just a side note, before I made my trek here, I looked up the history of the land before houses were built here. I could not find any information, through several resources, that there was anything unusual here, other than just a piece of land on a hill. I did talk to one older gentleman who said his father told him that the land on the hill here was tainted, that it was cursed. He recalled his father telling him that long ago, before the houses, murdered bodies were buried here on the hill. His father forbid him from playing in this area. I have found no proof, nor have I heard of anything like that in my research. I'll grab my flashlight and head upstairs."

"I plan to look around further downstairs after I finish looking around upstairs. So far I have not encountered anything unusual, other than the sound a door slamming. I carry with me, a flashlight, a digital audio recorder and in my pocket, my cell phone, which my wife insisted that I bring. The stairs are wooden and old, and creak with each step I take. As I look around, again I notice, even with the limited view of my flashlight, that the place is very well kept. There are pictures on the wall here as I ascend the stairs. No recent pictures, only older ones. Here is a picture of The Ritter family, William, Mary and kids. They are similar to the pictures I have seen of them in my research. It is very dark up here. The smell is musty and that of old carpet. The upstairs is a bit smaller than below, and as I stand at the top of the stairs, to my left is a small office that I will venture in first."

"The office is the typical setup of a desk, a chair, and a lamp. A small bookshelf accompanies it on the west wall and a nice window view of the backyard makes me think that this would be a nice place to write a novel. Of course that's the writer in me speaking there. I think I'll sit at the desk and soak in the atmosphere of the room for a moment."

"I have sat here for roughly ten minutes, concentrating and listening, trying to absorb the dark vibe that must associate this place, considering the murders that have taken place here. Sitting in a dark room and closing the eyes is the best way take in the visually hidden vibe of a evil place. In my warped way of thinking, it helps me later in my writing, when I recall the feelings or chills I might experience from a place like this. It's time to visit the scene of the murder-suicide."

"The hallway is lined with very nice wood paneling from one end to the other. I am at the doorway of the office, looking down the hallway. My flashlight is strong and the light is bearing down on the door to the bathroom directly at the end of the hall. Knowing that William Ritter committed suicide in this hall, right outside the door of the adjacent bedroom, does give me a little pause before I walk down there. I don't see anything other than what is supposed to be there, but for the first time I do feel apprehensive. The hall is not long and I can see the light reflecting off of the mirror in the bathroom as I get closer."

"I am now standing in the spot where William ended his life, just outside the bedroom and against the hallway wall. I feel a bit of a chill standing here I must admit. As I stated prior, I am not a paranormal investigator, and I do not relate chills or anything other than an actual visual experience, to anything more that what it is. But, it is a bit colder here. As it is very dark in here I can see how many people, if put in this situation, could be scared and let their imagination run wild. This house is not the most uplifting place for a wayward soul. I am now shinning the light into the bedroom of William and Mary. The bed is clearly visible from here. I can only imagine what was going through William's mind just before he ended his life. From this spot he could clearly see his wife's dead body and blood-splattered white sheets. For me, it is the unthinkable."

"Upon entering the bedroom, it appears that the furnishings here are not modern, nor are they from the last two decades to be sure, and it is just as Daniel told me it would be. I am assuming that this is how the room was that terrible, stormy night. The four-post bed is of beautiful construction. The wooden frame is stained in a dark, cherry wood. Looking around the room I can see that all of the furniture in here is a matching set with the bed, very nice indeed. The view from the window looks out over the front yard and street. This house has a slightly higher post than the others on the street as it sits at the highest point of a small hill. Not much stirring outside and not much stirring in here. I must check out the closet. Closets can tell a lot of a person, and I am curious as to the state of this one. The door creaked loudly, almost as if it was singing, or telling the story of what it witnessed that night. I like that line; I may just use it in my next novel. The closet is full of dresses and suits. All of the dresses are white, strange. It looks as if nothing has been disturbed here for years. I will not disturb it now. The closet door has a full-length mirror attached to it and as you close it, from this point of view, you can see the bed. I am sure that this mirror has its own story of the murder it witnessed as well."

The sound of the wooden floor creaking behind Peter causes him to be silent and listen. He turns quickly.

"I just heard a noise behind me, but nothing is there. The floor creaked as if someone was walking slowly across it. Maybe the wind or maybe, my imagination is running wild as have others here. Now I will go take a look around in the bathroom across the hall."

"The hall is quite cold, much colder than it should be. Maybe there is a draft coming in here from the attic. The bathroom is similar to the one downstairs except it is bigger and has an oval-shaped window. The bathroom is completely white, even the faucets and knobs for the drawers and cabinets are white. Someone definitely had an obsession with white."

"The only place I have not seen in this house is the attic. Mr. Ritter would not grant me access to it for safety concerns. I will head back downstairs only to return here at 2:45 a.m., the approximate time of the murder-suicide, when at that time I will lay in the Mary's bed."

As Peter is about to descend the stairs he hears a slow, thump…thump…thump, of what sounds like someone walking down the hall towards him. He shines the light down the hall quickly, the noise stops.

"I just thought I heard someone walking towards me in the hall here. No one is there, but I will replay this audio later to see if it picked up that sound. I am here to take in the feel of this house and so far, that has been the only thing to give me pause. What I just heard sounded very real to me."

He finally takes the light from down the hall and shines it down the stairs so he can see his way down.

"I am sitting back at the desk making notes. It is nearly 1 a.m. and I find myself very much awake. I will not play back any audio until tomorrow morning when I leave here. I am taking a break and reflecting on what I have experienced so far. Practically nothing, but I can say I have been a little on edge a couple of times. This house has a terrible history and reputation as one of the most haunted, and no matter what has or hasn't happened so far, I will say that this is not a pleasant place to be. The feeling you get when you . . ."

He cuts his words short when the chair next to him slides a few feet to his left, on its own. He turns to his left, startled, and sits up straight to look at the chair.

"I'm not sure if you could hear that, but the chair next to me just slid at least three feet to my left. Hello? Is anyone here with me? I am calling out, not to any demon or spirit, but to whoever may be in here. Someone has to be here."

Peter shines the light in all directions and sees no one. He stands to walk around.

"I said, is anyone here? If this is some kind of prank I will be very upset with Ritter and whoever may be involved."

Not admitting it, but this scares him. He walks into the kitchen and looks around, then down to the bathroom and turns on the light. He is determined to find out who is playing this joke on him. He doesn't want to admit that this could be the work of something beyond our world.

"Alright, enough of this. I came here to experience this place and be objective about what I see and hear. If there is no other living person here with me, and I am truly alone, then I must be open-minded to what just occurred. I will take my seat again at the desk and make notes of what just happened, and of my feelings of what was going through my mind at the time. After all, this is in the name of research!"

Peter writes down his experiences, and notes all that has happened. He fires up his laptop and does some writing, while in the mood of the moment. This is what he had hoped for.

"It's not the most normal environment to write in, but it is highly appropriate and perfect for what I am writing."

As the pendulum clock on the far wall swings to 2:30 a.m. Peter closes the lid on his computer and leaves his note pad and pen on the desk. He gathers his recorder and flashlight just as his phone buzzes in his pocket. He pulls it out and sees that his wife has sent him a text message, asking if he is alright.

"Damn. I asked her not to disturb me so I can focus on this, but I know she is worried."

He types on his phone: 'I am ok…talk soon'.

"That should hold her until I get out of here in a few hours. My plan now is to go to the Ritter's room and, as someone involved in the paranormal would do, go to a murder location in the house at the same time when the murder took place, the murder of Mary Ritter. That's this author's idea of investigating the possibility of spirits or demons here. I can feel, as I get closer to the top of the stairs, that the air is much colder. This is the second time that I have experienced this."

He walks down the hall towards the bedroom shinning his light straight ahead and along the walls. Arriving at the doorway of the Ritter's bedroom, and just as he pauses to speak, the door to the room slams in his face. The shocked author jumps back a step.

"My God, the door to the bedroom just slammed shut right in front of me. Someone must be in there. Who's there! I'm tired of the pranks."

Peter reaches for the knob and tries to turn it. It will not turn. He now leans on the door and it begins to rumble wildly on its hinges. Startled, Keller steps back. The rumbling stops and the door slowly opens.

"What the hell? As I must describe what is happening, the door shook wildly as I tried to open it. I leaned on it and tried to turn the knob to no avail. Then the shaking stopped and the door opened on its own. Either this is a very good prank, or there is something very, very dreadful going on here. No, no it must a prank."

Keller charges into the room shining the light in all directions.

"Whoever is here, show yourself."

"You better leave before it gets you too."

The voice comes from behind Keller. He turns and sees the bloody body of Mary Ritter lying in bed, looking at him.

"Who? What the . . .?

Mary throws her head back and laughs crazily, then slowly disappears in front of Keller's eyes. The stunned and disbelieving author stares at the now empty bed.

"I . . . I . . . I am not sure what I just heard and saw. I don't know if it's my imagination, or that I'm tired, but I just saw the ghost of Mary Ritter in her bed."

Keller paces the room, keeping his flashlight shining on the bed.

"She spoke and in my disbelief, I am not exactly sure what she said. It was something to the effect of: 'They will get you too.' I can't believe I'm even saying all this, but that is what I saw. It's freezing in here now."

Peter cautiously moves closer to the bed to have a better look.

"The bed looks undisturbed and I just saw her lying there and . . ."

The closet door behind him opens and closes then slowly creaks half open.

"Leave this house. Leave this house now!"

A dark, demonic voice comes from the closet. Keller stands quiet, not wanting to turn and see who, or what spoke those words. The voice recorder drops from his hand as he builds the courage to turn. Turning slowly, his eyes come into view of the closet door and it slams shut. He is torn between running from the room, or keeping his bravado, and opening the closet door. With his nerves rattled and feeling total distress, he decides to take a step towards the closet. The door rattles in front of him as he reaches out. The white, porcelain knob feels cold to the touch, and in one swift motion, he turns it and opens the door.

"I have gathered myself and am going back downstairs. I lost my composure for a few moments and dropped my audio recorder. I have experienced something I cannot dispute. I have witnessed paranormal events in this house. They include visions, voices, and movement of solid objects that have no explanation. The time is now 3:30 a.m. and I will gather my thoughts at my desk and note all that has just happened."

"At approximately 3:00 a.m. the ghost or what appeared to be the ghost, of Mary Ritter spoke to me as she lay, bloody, in her bed. I played back the audio and she can clearly be heard telling me to leave before it gets me too. I must say that even I cannot pass this off in some skeptical, scientific way. I saw and heard this very clearly, and now I have it recorded. She slowly dissolved into nothing after her warning to me. Soon after that, the closet door behind me opened and closed and a completely different voice, a very evil voice, told me to leave the house. I walked to the door, and will admit, that I was very scared. The door began to shake violently and when I grabbed the knob, the shaking stopped. I flung the door open and found no one or nothing inside. I have tried to pull the voice up on my recorder, which I had dropped just a moment before, but I have not been able to hear it. I will get this to the proper audio experts for analysis later today. I will take a moment now."

"I speak to you now from the kitchen; it is almost 4:00 a.m. I have scribbled on paper, the best I could, my account of my night thus far. Mostly, I have sat in a numbed state of mind and in thought. Nothing more has happened in the last hour or more. Before I came here I was not a skeptic to these types of things happening, but I wasn't a believer either. I wanted to come here, as I have stated before, to soak up, for my next novel, this so-called evil environment, based on the reputation of this place and because of the violent acts that have happened here. It does not matter if what I tell you is believable to you or not. What matters is that I know what I have experienced, and with that I know that this place is indeed evil and persuasive. The evil that dwells here, in my opinion, is responsible for every violent murder that has occurred in this horrid place. Debra Blakely, sixty years ago, told all, that the devil made her do it, I believe her. My thoughts are this way, not only because of the things I have experienced physically, it's more than that. In the last hour I have been experiencing a mental weight or anguish. It comes from within, like a dark force driving at the mind and spirit. It is a pressure that is hard to describe, almost, if I dare say, like possession. I know I should leave this place now, as I was warned, but I am drawn to learn more, to see if I can bring out more visions of the past. I plan to leave here at

7:00 a.m., so I have roughly three hours to complete my stay and learn as much as I can."

"I now sit at the desk, but am about to go upstairs and can again hear the loud thumping, or stepping. The steps are slow, but grow louder with each one. They are coming from beyond the kitchen, now moving closer. Whatever is making these sounds is clearly in this room."

Peter's voice is now shaky and for the first time sounds frightened.

"I see no one or nothing with my light. I have chills, but I am sweating, I sense the dread and overpowering feeling of this evil entity. I know it is here with me, very close. The last step shook this wooden floor underneath me."

The walls begin shaking, the floor vibrates, and the desk begins to rattle. A scared and shaking Peter Keller stumbles backwards and trips over a stool. He loses the recorder and light. The house, from the windows, to the walls, begins to shake violently. Cries and screams rain down on him from all directions. The piercing cries of pain and suffering ring in his ears. Keller feels around for his only companion, his flashlight. He is almost in tears when he feels the light. He grabs it and shines it all around the chaotic room.

The demons speak to Peter. "Kill her. Kill her. Kill the bitch!" He is shaking and sobbing, and covering his ears. Suddenly the house goes calm. The noises and the horrible screaming stop. The house goes deafly quiet. The only sound he can hear is his heart rapidly beating in his chest . . .

until he hears the sound of a woman laughing from a distance. The laugh is not a normal laugh, it sounds crazy and deranged. He tries to gather himself from the shaking and shines the light towards the staircase. Peter's eyes grow wide as his light shines directly on a woman walking down the stairs. She carries an axe over her shoulder. She turns her head to him and he sees that her eyes are completely white. He is unable to move, frozen in place. She is standing over him in a split second and raising the axe above her to strike down on him. He recognizes her instantly from the pictures. Debra Blakely!

"Kill her!" Debra commands. It's all too much for the author to take in. He passes out.

After waking up in a daze, a couple of hours later, Peter gathered his things and left the Ritter House behind. He arrived home carrying his duffel bag over his shoulder. His wife Katherine was very much relieved. After a very brief hello, Peter went to his bed to lie down. Katherine, feeling somewhat disappointed in not getting to hear about his night right away, decided to run some hot water for a bath.

A few minutes later, as Katherine lay in the tub with a warm rag over her eyes; Peter pushed the bathroom door open and walked in. He was carrying an axe. Katherine barely had time to remove the rag from her eyes before the first blow struck down on her chest. With the power and intensity of the blow, the axe easily cut into her chest and logged deep inside. She didn't even have time to scream.

The tub's soapy water began to turn a shade of crimson as the second blow from the axe landed with the same force and splattered blood all over the walls, mirrors, and floor of the once peaceful bathroom.

Peter left the axe wedged in Katherine's neck and calmly walked down the hall and into his room, picked up his phone, and dialed 911.

"911, what's your emergency?" the operator asked.

"I . . . I just killed my . . ." The 911 operator then heard him begin to weep.

"Sir? Are you there?" she asked. She got no answer, only the sound of his weeping. She tried to get him to respond, and after a few seconds the operator listened as his cries turned into laughter, hysterical laughter. The laughter became louder and louder and more uncontrolled.

Police were dispatched, and when they arrived they got no answer. They broke into the home of the world-famous horror author, Peter Keller. He was nowhere to be found. Katherine's body was found in the blood-filled tub, the axe still lodged deeply in her neck.

Upon searching the house, police heard voices coming from Peter's room. After carefully entering, they found the audio recorder on his bed. The recording device was looping, playing a portion of what had been recorded at the Ritter House.

"Kill her. Kill her. Kill the bitch! Kill her. Kill her. Kill the . . ."

Santa Claws

"Do not be deceived: God is not mocked, For whatsoever a man soweth, that shall he also reap."

When I think back on Christmas I can remember back to when I was around four years old. I remember the excitement and anticipation of the season's festivities building in me, even since Thanksgiving. It was a fun time. I was the youngest of three kids. I had two sisters, Claire and Becky. I was the youngest and the only boy, so I got special attention from my parents through the years, and at times, my sisters hated my guts. It came and went depending on their moods.

"It's always Jimmy this or Jimmy that!" they would say. They could be mean to me sometimes, but nothing ever ruined Christmas for me, nothing. I always acted good and never got out of line. From around four to the time I was eight I can recall every Christmas and the fun that lead up to it, especially Santa Claus. At that age I truly believed in Santa. I had proof. I snuck downstairs every Christmas eve in the middle of the night to try and get a peek of him. I was never disappointed. I would only creep about halfway down the stairs and stop once I saw him. There he would be in his bright red suit and huge sack full of presents. He never saw me but I enjoyed every second watching him work. When I saw him begin to eat the cookies and drink the milk, I left knowing he was done and it was time for me to get back to my room. Whether or not it was my dad, it didn't matter. I believed it was Santa! Great times!

That was until the summer of 1984 when I was nine.

My two best friends were Mark and Drew, we always played along the outskirts of town in the summers, just outside of Austin, Texas. We would go to the lake or fish in a pond. You know just normal kid's stuff. Well that summer we cut through the Finley Farm like always only, we didn't know that it had been bought by some other people a couple of weeks earlier. As we were walking through, an old man started yelling at us from behind the barn. We didn't recognize him and we were kind of frozen not knowing what to do as we stood there. He was shaking a hay fork in his hand and yelling at us.

"Get off my property you damn kids! No trespassing here. That's why I moved away from the city!" he was angry. We didn't get scared until his big German shepherd came around the corner of the barn running directly at us. We ran as fast as we could to the other end of the property. The dog was barking louder as it closed in on us. We all ran together, but I can tell you, it was not one for all as they say. We got to the fence line and slid between the barbed wire and turned to see the dog retreating as the old man called him back. All of a sudden our bravado came back. It's funny how it works that way when you are a kid and don't know any better. With the big dog almost out of sight, we all acted like we were never scared, but the truth is we were scared shitless.

Later we found out old man Finley had sold the place to Mr. Mitchell. We knew now that our shortest path to get to the lake was gone. We would have to walk an extra half a mile now. It really wasn't that big of a deal to me but Mark and Drew wanted to test the old man and the dog. For the rest of the summer they plotted and plotted, trying to figure out a way to sneak on the farm and scare Mr. Mitchell. I admit I was part of the plan, but I wasn't into it like they were.

The plan never unfolded, so the summer came and went. The next thing we knew, we were back in school. About midway into October Mark and Drew were back at it in their plan to scare the old man, and what better time to do it than Halloween. They kept saying: "It's not that big of a deal. We just want to give him a little scare."

The plan was to sneak up there on Halloween night and knock on his door as trick or treating kids. After we knocked we were supposed to hide and then scare him. The only problem was that dog, but Drew had a plan for him.

Halloween arrived and we all knew what we were going to do. Just after dark we headed up the road to the old man's place. It was a lot darker out there than in town, but we had flashlights and were all dressed up in our costumes, or as Mark called them, disguises. As we approached the road in front of the main entrance to the house we all got an eerie feeling. The house was dark and the only light that was on was the porch light. We made our way down the driveway to just outside the porch. The plan was to knock, and yell 'Trick or Treat!', then run to the bushes and watch him. Drew pulled out a steak, and set it on the top step of the porch. That's his plan to keep the dog from chasing us? I thought.

We each had a werewolf mask on along with our black sheets. Aside from our flashlights, we each had smoke bombs and firecrackers. Mark had an old Halloween prop of a decapitated head with fake blood, and eyes bulging out of its skull. I was nervous as Drew went to knock on the door. Mark and I waited.

Knock Knock Knock

Drew pounded the door and ran back. We heard a voice from inside.

"Who is it?"

"Trick or treat!" we yelled. We heard a mumbling form Mr. Mitchell, and the door opened. We lit our smoke bombs and dropped them in front of the bushes to make a cloud for us to jump out from. Then we lit our small packs of firecrackers, and as they started popping, we ran out from the cloud of smoke and towards him. We all howled like wolves with Mark leading the way. He was running and holding the fake head to his mouth, as if he had chewed it off of someone. Mr. Mitchell yelled, and started falling back, but the wall caught him and as we got closer I could see how terrified he was and I immediately felt bad. He caught himself before falling and slid inwards, towards the front door. He made it in and slammed the door just as we hit the steps.

We kept howling for a second and started laughing, and then decided to get out of there fast. The prank was over. As we turned we could hear his dog barking from out back. Then we heard it getting closer. We took off running towards the road knowing that big dog was coming and we heard Mr. Mitchell holler at the dog.

"Get 'em boy! Get 'em!"

I don't know if the steak slowed the dog down or not, but we made it to the road just as the dog closed in on us. We cut across the road in an angle to try and get away. The headlights of a truck were bearing down on us as we crossed. As it passed us, we heard the unmistakable sound of the high-pitched bark and squeal that a dog makes when it is hurt. The barking stopped as the truck skidded to a stop. We knew then that the truck had run over Mr. Mitchell's dog. We stopped running and looked back in horror as the mangled body of the German shepherd lay twisted in the road. I could see Mr. Mitchell walking fast to the road. We ran and ran and ran as fast as we could, never looking back again. We made it back into town, and after we threw our costumes in a dumpster, we went to Drew's house. The three of us made a promise to not to ever say anything to anyone, and we never talked about it again.

The word about what happened got around fast, and from what I can remember, there was sympathy for Mr. Mitchell. We came to find out that his dog, Jessie, was over eight years old and was his most cherished thing in the world, since his wife had passed on. None of that made me or my friends feel any better, but there was nothing we could do. People wondered who the three costumed pranksters were, but we were never found out. After time the story faded, and with Mr. Mitchell being new to town, it slowly drifted into the back of everyone's mind, except for me.

We were nine year old kids, and although we had caused something terrible, we sort of went on with our lives. Thanksgiving came and things went back to normal.

Christmas was right around the corner, and I was looking forward to my private visit with Santa.

On the Sunday after Thanksgiving, my mom was watching a church program on TV. I remember just how true, part of the sermon was that day.

"You know, God forgives us of all our sins no matter what they are. Some of us live up to our sins and confess them. Others have to be reminded in other ways. It's not such a good thing, but sometimes the only way person feel shame for, or admit their sins, is when they feel the same pain that they may have caused someone else. We all reap what we sow."

I remember those words vividly. I really didn't understand them until my mom explained what the preacher was saying. Then it hit me like a ton of bricks. I immediately felt guilty. Mark, Drew, and I had promised to never talk about it again so we were each left to deal with it on our own. They seemed okay about everything, it was an accident, after all. Maybe it was just a dog, an old dog, but I felt so bad for Mr. Mitchell. Now he was alone.

Time passed and before I knew it, the Christmas holidays were here. My excitement was building. Christmas was on a Tuesday that year, so we had almost a week until then.

Here's where it gets crazy.

We got out of school on a Thursday, and that night things began to get weird. Mark had a little Shetland pony,

Buster, that his parents had given him a couple of years earlier. He loved that little horse and always talked about it. He even did a report in class about it. That day, his parents sold the pony while we were at school. They were in financial trouble and needed to get money as fast as they could. Mark said they planned to buy it back for him, but he was devastated. He was angry at his parents, but mostly just sad. I have never seen him that sad.

Drew called me two days later telling me his dog was missing. I didn't think his parents had sold it like Mark's parents did, so it had probably been stolen or was lost. Drew, like Mark, was very down and was constantly looking for his dog. He cried a lot over the weekend.

I woke up Monday morning and it hit me. I remembered what the preacher said on TV, 'We all reap what we sow,' rang in my head.

It couldn't be? Could it? I thought.

Mr. Mitchell lost the thing he loved the most, his dog. Mark and Drew each had lost their most prized pets. Could it be just like the preacher said? But I didn't have a pet. It wasn't making sense when I thought of it that way.

We were kids and I knew Mark and Drew weren't looking at it like I was. I was only nine at that time, but I was pretty smart. On top of that, I never stopped feeling bad for what we did to Mr. Mitchell.

I worried and thought about it all day, but soon it was Christmas Eve night. My excitement for seeing Santa, no matter if it was dad or not, overrode everything else.

That night I set the cookies and milk out in the same place I had for the past five years and like clockwork, I left my room and tiptoed across the hall to the staircase. I stopped and listened, I could hear some movement downstairs. I smiled big, knowing Santa was back. Slowly, I walked down the steps, one by one. I didn't want to make any noise. It was cold in the house, a lot colder than last Christmas for sure. Suddenly, there he was! Santa! I stopped where I was and watched. He had his back to me as usual, working with his big bag of presents. The tree was lit up and the cookies and milk where there and ready for Santa when he was done. He must have just started because there weren't many presents scattered out. He looked taller than before, and not as fat. I watched him with his bag, and bright red suit, and noticed that he wasn't pulling any presents out, he was putting them in. I rubbed my eyes to make sure of what I was seeing. One after another, he was putting them in his bag. I was shocked and didn't understand. I decided to ease down a few more steps to get a better look. He picked up a large box and shoved it in his bag. I wanted to say something, to ask why, but I was frozen in place. It was a lot colder now and I had not realized it, but I was now only three steps from the bottom. I still could not see his face as he worked with his back to me. Then I saw his hand as it reached for a present, it was hideous. It looked more like a claw, old, bony, and dark and black. I put my hand up to my mouth in shock as my eyes widened in fear. The old-looking claw moved to drop the present in the bag. This thing was now only a few feet from me. I wanted to scream or run, but I was couldn't do either. I heard an evil-sounding laugh as it stood up straight, dropping the huge bag. Whatever this was, it slowly began turning around. I was trembling, and as it was turning, it began to softly sing.

"You better watch out, you better not cry, you better not pout I'm telling you why, because I'M coming to town!" it said as it turned all the way around, and like magic, it was standing right in front of me.

It wasn't Santa. It was the most sinister, evil-looking thing I had ever seen in my life. It bent down and moved its face only inches from mine. Its eyes were fire red, as if they were burning. Its teeth were black and very shiny. They looked razor sharp. I was shaking in place.

"I see you when you're sleeping. I know when you're awake. I know if you've been bad or good." He put his long claws around my neck. I had tears in my eyes now. The tone in his voice had changed.

"Do you know why I'm here boy?" it asked me. All I could do was nod no. I wanted to scream out for my parents or sisters to help me, but I couldn't. "I'm here to take something from you as you have taken something from someone else."

His grip around my neck tightened. He began to lift me off my feet and brought me level with his face, as he stood up straight.

"You and your friends must face what you have done and must receive punishment for your sins," he spoke in a slow, demonic voice. I knew then why those things happened to Mark and Drew's pets. Tears welled in my eyes to the point where I could barely see him now.

"Your most favorite thing is Christmas little Jimmy. To pay for your sin, you will no longer get to appreciate your precious Santa Claus anymore. Your Christmases from now on belong to ME!" he said with anger. Then he laughed as he looked up at the ceiling. The lights from the Christmas tree reflected and shined perfectly, off of his black teeth.

He lowered me down. I was crying out loud now but I could not hear myself. It was the strangest feeling. He let go of me and all I wanted to do was run upstairs to the safety of my parent's room, but my feet were unmoving.

"Yes boy, your punishment will be no more Christmas, no more Santa. To help you remember, and to remove all doubt from your mind that I am real, I will leave you with something."

He reached into the bag full of presents and pulled out a long knife. I sobbed, thinking he was going to kill me. He put his hand on the stairway railing with only his index finger pointing outward. He then slammed the knife down and chopped his finger off. I was beyond scared, and to this day I don't know how I didn't pass out. The finger remained on the railing with its nail dug into the wood. He put the knife back in his bag and turned to me one more time.

"You now have part of me with you. You will never forget boy. I will remind you every year until you die," he said as his stare burned into my eyes permanently. He grabbed the finger from the railing and grabbed my hand. He opened my trembling, shaking hand and used the black, claw-like finger nail to cut the palm of my hand on the surface, until I bled. He then closed my hand around his finger.

Like magic, the lights went off and I was standing in complete darkness. I could feel my heart beating in my chest, my hand still clenched around the finger. After a moment, the lights came back on, and he was gone. All of my presents were gone. I looked down hoping the bloody finger was gone, but it was still there. I ran up the stairs to my room and locked my door. I threw the clawed finger into the garbage and didn't sleep the rest of the night. Every time I felt like I was falling asleep, I could hear his evil laugh.

Twenty-five years later I still have the scar on the palm of my hand as a reminder. Every time I visit my parent's house, I can still see the mark that the knife left in the wood on the railing. It's not deep, but I can still see it. I got rid of the finger that next day and have not celebrated Christmas with Santa again since. As if the scar in my hand, and the notched wood on the railing weren't enough, I have been reminded of what happened every Christmas eve, for the last twenty-five years, by waking up to find the black-nailed, bony-clawed finger, waiting for me at my bedside. You could say I've gotten used to it over the years, but one thing I will never get used to, and sends a chill down my spine, is when I awake to see the finger, I hear that evil laughter, and I can smell his terrible stench, as if he's standing right next to me.

Just as he told me that day, he will be a part of me, until the day I die.

Strangers

"Step right up, test your luck. Pick a card."

Trevor Hammond wasn't having a good start to his Saturday. He had just left his house in a rush, after another stupid argument with his wife. The arguments never made sense to Trevor. They always seemed to start in the most innocent of ways, and then usually escalated to an absolute disagreement and then on to screaming and yelling. Trevor wasn't the fighting type and it always bothered him to argue and fight with the woman he loved. But this was life, and life is hard to figure out sometimes --all the time. He would have to figure out what to do with his marriage and try to bring it back to what it once was. When the fights occurred he would begin to argue, but would catch himself and leave. Better to let things cool off than to let it get to a point where things could be said that can't be taken back, then suffer with regret. He had never, and would never; hit a woman, so he knew he wouldn't get to that stage in his marriage. He just wanted it to go back to the way it was before.

As he drove down the road with all of these thoughts banging around in his head, he decided to pull in to the Country Buffet to get something to eat. There he could sit awhile and relax. He and Stacy ate there once or twice a month. The food was very good there and he knew the routine. He paid, grabbed his orange juice, picked out a corner booth, and headed to the buffet tables.

The restaurant was more crowded than he thought it would be. The smell of eggs and bacon cooking in the kitchen spilled over into the eating area, and the clinging of plates and utensils banging together filled the room with the typical sounds of a restaurant.

He grabbed a plate and looked over his choices. His mood was changing and the food was taking his mind off of his situation at home, even if it was just for the moment. Trevor loaded up on some scrambled eggs and turned to go around to the bacon when he bumped into a man heading in the same direction. Trevor backed away, making sure his eggs didn't fly all over. The younger man gave him a go-to-hell look.

"Excuse me buddy," the man said in a condescending way, as if blaming Trevor for the bump. Trevor took offense.

"How about excuse you?" The anger that Trevor felt earlier, boiled up inside him. They stood face to face, both holding their half-empty plates. The stared into each other's eyes and Trevor could tell that the man was upset about more than their little bump into each other. An older couple sensed the friction and moved away. Trevor walked away without saying more. The man stayed and stared at him as he rounded the corner. A look of satisfaction came over his face.

Trevor finished loading down his plate and went back to his booth. The food smelled good and he was hungry. He wondered, in a funny way, if the man was having a bad day like he was.

The man, Josh Evans, was sitting on the other side of the restaurant and was also alone. He was in his upper-twenties and going through his own personal turmoil. His problems didn't involve a woman. His problems involved the law and his dead-end job at the factory. Josh was younger and cockier than Trevor which made him prone to get into altercations in the past that led to run-ins with the law. His temper was not his friend.

Trevor ate fast, and as time went on, forgot about the incident, and his mind turned towards Stacy. Usually she would wait an hour or two before texting him. He had not received any messages from her after an hour and a half.

That bothered him. He loved her and he just wanted peace and happiness at home.

He had a couple of more plates of food and a little dessert before leaving. He saw the man, Josh, he had bumped into earlier, but they never crossed paths. Trevor pulled out three, wrinkled, one-dollar bills for a tip, and left them on the table.

The temperature was already building outside and the heat hit his face as soon as he opened the door to leave. Trevor couldn't take it anymore; he sent Stacy a text message. He felt the heat on the door handle as he got into his pickup. Hoping that she would reply right away, Trevor turned the air conditioner on and sat back in the seat. His phone rang, it was Stacy. A sense of relief came over him and at the same time so did his apprehension.

"Hello," he answered, as if he didn't know who was calling.

"I got your text. I'm fine Trevor. You're the one who stormed out of here. Where are you?" Stacy wasn't letting up; the tone in her voice told it all. There wouldn't be a quick ending to this disagreement.

"I'm just sitting and thinking. I left because I didn't want to argue or talk about it while we were both mad. I was hoping things would cool down."

"It's just so immature for you to leave every time we get in an argument. We should act like adults and talk it out. But you always leave, and avoid it. Just stay wherever you are until you can act like an adult!" She hung up on him.

Trevor was stunned. Why was she still so upset over something so minor? She is really mad at me. "Screw it! I didn't do anything wrong. She can stay mad if she wants to!" Trevor said aloud. He put on his seat belt and left, planning to take a ride and kill some time.

Josh had long forgotten his little stare-down at the restaurant and was headed to pick up his girlfriend, Sharon, from work. She worked at the Circle K and had the early shift. Aside from the run-in with Trevor at the restaurant, Josh was in a better mood since he had eaten. Sharon came out and got in his black Nissan truck and kissed Josh.

"Good morning. How was breakfast?" she asked. Her question reminded him of the run-in he had.

"It was good. I had some dipshit bump into me and then act like it was my fault. I should have met him outside."

"That wouldn't have solved anything Josh. It would only have got you into more trouble. You don't need that." She said trying to sound sympathetic but also giving some advice.

"I know, and that's why I didn't do that. I'm not stupid."

"No one is saying you are stupid. Tell you what, how about we see a movie?"

Josh smiled. That sounded good to him. "Sure. A comedy might be best," he said jokingly as he pulled through the intersection.

Trevor drove aimlessly through town with Stacy heavy on his mind. He was mad, but at the same time, very sad. Those were emotions that he found the hardest to understand. Before he knew it, he had driven on the other side of town. He pulled into a shopping center and noticed a movie theatre in the far corner. Stacy will be mad at me all day, he thought. So, why not go watch a movie? Something upbeat, maybe a comedy.

Little did Trevor and Josh know, they were destined to meet again.

Josh and Sharon shielded their eyes from the bright, high-noon sun and looked up at the marquee displaying the show times. They decided on a newly-released comedy. After getting their tickets they disappeared into the darkened movie theatre.

Trevor unknowingly pulled into an empty spot next to Josh's black Nissan truck.

The line was long for buying tickets to the matinee, so Trevor went to the automated ticket machine. After grabbing his tickets, he made his way to the ticket-takers booth.

"Welcome, Mr. Hammond," the theatre worker said as he took his ticket. Trevor looked up at him; the man was smiling at him in a strange way that made Trevor feel uneasy. How does he know my name?

"How do you know my name?" he asked the man in a restrained, but yet, demanding way.

"Well Mr. Hammond, it's on your receipt." The man smiled again, pointing at the receipt in his hand, and handed him the ticket stub. "Your movie is on the right, theatre nine. Enjoy the show."

Trevor was sort of frozen, and caught up in the stare of the older man. He finally pulled his ticket away from the man's grasp and walked in. He glanced back at the man who was taking the next person's tickets. He still felt an uneasiness about the man.

A good-sized crowd, accompanied by the usual noise and excitement of movie-goers, and the smell of freshly-popped popcorn floated in the air. Trevor couldn't resist and headed straight to the snack bar. Looking around, he noticed that everyone seemed to be in a good mood, enjoying a Saturday at the movies. He grabbed his popcorn and drink and began to walk towards his movie when he saw the man he had run into at breakfast. He couldn't believe it and stopped to see where he was headed. Josh turned, after getting his snacks, and walked in the direction of his theater. "Shit! He's going to the same movie I am," he said in almost comical disbelief.

"Excuse me?" A woman overheard him. She looked at him with disdain.

"I'm sorry. It slipped out."

She walked away, never acknowledging his apology.

He's not going to ruin my movie. I don't care if he's here or not, he thought to himself and then walked into the darkened theater. He casually looked around to try and locate Josh but could not pick him out of the crowd so he took a seat about halfway up, near the isle.

The previews for upcoming movies were showing, so the theater was dark enough for Trevor to feel comfortable that Josh hadn't seen him.

Soon the movie started, and was going along at a good pace for a comedy, when about halfway through a man began making his way through the seats towards Trevor. He moved his legs to the side, as everyone does when someone barrels through during a movie, and just as the man was in front of him they locked eyes. Even in the dark they recognized each other instantly.

The run-in they had earlier really wasn't that big of a thing, but with both of them being in the moods they were in at the time, and both leaving there with a feeling of unfinished business, the contempt for each other rose to the surface once again. Something about the male ego just won't let things go.

"You!" Josh said. Trevor was not in a position to argue or say anything as Josh stood over him. "I should have kicked your ass back at the restaurant."

"Hey man, I don't want any trouble. We're in the movies." Trevor said, trying to defuse the situation.

"I don't give a shit," Josh told him, "but you're not worth it." He finally moved through as people began to ask him to sit down. As he moved into the isle, he gave Trevor's leg a little kick. Trevor flexed his leg back at his to give him the same kick.

"Asshole." Trevor said as Josh walked down the dimly-lit aisle.

Trevor debated on changing seats, but the theater was already too crowded. He decided to stay and try to enjoy the movie he had spent his ten dollars on. The movie was very funny, but now it was partially ruined by Josh and his macho attitude. He noticed Josh was with a woman and it immediately reminded him of Stacy. It made him sad, but that feeling quickly faded when he spotted Josh making his was back up the aisle. He had a soda and a bag of popcorn, he was looking right at Trevor. As he neared Trevor was getting up to let him in without any conflict, but Josh was quicker and forced his way into the row intentionally banging Trevor's legs against the sides of the seat.

"Excuse me asshole." Josh said with a smile, and tipped the bag of his, oily-buttered popcorn just enough, causing some to spill out onto Trevor's lap.

Trevor jumped up, full of anger. "What's your problem?!"

They stood face-to-face in the small row of seats.

"You want some of me? Do something dickhead!" Josh wanted to fight. All the tension that had built up in him from earlier was showing on his face. Trevor could see the rage in Josh's eyes.

"Fuck off," he said, and backed away. He walked out of the theater not wanting to deal with it. Josh just stared and felt his arm being pulled by Sharon and he focused in on her and now could hear the crowd telling him to sit down or get out. He sat down next to an embarrassed Sharon.

"What the hell is wrong with you? Who is that guy?" Sharon said angrily, but quietly, knowing all eyes were on them. She expected theater personnel to come in at anytime and run them out.

"He's just this asshole I ran into at breakfast. Don't worry, I took care of it."

No one came in to escort them out. The movie continued with a few disgruntled moviegoers, but in the end, the movie ended on a good note.

Trevor never went back in. He stayed in the lobby near the game room, trying to clear his head.

Josh and Sharon made their way out of the theater after most of the people had cleared out. She had calmed Josh down enough to enjoy the rest of the movie and was actually having a good time. They walked out of the dark theater and into the entrance hall where theater employees, armed with trash cans and brooms, were waiting to get in and get the theater ready for the next show.

"Hope you enjoyed the show. Come back and see us again soon." The customary greeting you get after a movie. They walked into the lobby and towards the exit. Josh dropped his greasy popcorn bag in a garbage can and took a sip of his soda as they made their way towards the parking lot.

Josh never saw the blow coming. He was blind-sided and knocked across the sidewalk, dropping his soda. Trevor's anger took over his easy-going self, he had enough. He had been waiting in the lobby. He followed them as they got close to the parking lot, where he sprinted from, at full speed, until he ran into Josh knocking him straight into the landscaped area in front of the theater. Sharon, who was talking on her cell phone, barely missed being knocked down herself. Trevor stood over a confused Josh and had both fists balled, ready to fight.

"What the hell is wrong with you!?" Sharon screamed at Trevor. He paid her no mind.

"Come on asshole! You think you're so tough." Trevor shouted as people looked on curiously, but kept their distance. Most were there with their families.

After Josh got over the initial shock of being knocked down, he looked up and saw a very angry Trevor. Josh was younger and bigger than Trevor, but sometimes anger and rage can even a fight, so Josh stood up cautiously, his face had turned a fiery red. Once he stood, his own anger and rage took over. Sharon tried to intervene, but Josh pushed her aside, his eyes fixed on Trevor.

"You fucked with the wrong man now." Josh said to Trevor, and stepped forward without fear. Josh balled his right fist and took a hard swing. Trevor saw it coming, but

Josh was faster than he thought, and as Trevor tried to duck, the blow landed at the top of his head. The punch dazed him for a split-second, but he recovered enough to send a punch to Josh's stomach. The blow knocked the air out of him and doubled him over. Sharon jumped in between the two and screamed at Trevor as the crowd gathered around. A few nervous bystanders made 911 calls on their phones, others, with their families, ushered them along to safety.

In the confusion of the scuffle, and from Sharon jumping in the middle, Josh found one more opportunity to sneak in another punch, this time to the side of Trevor's face. The punch caused everything to go white for a brief moment in Trevor's head, almost knocking him out and sent him to one knee, his head hung down. The result of the punch almost knocked Sharon down.

"Get up punk! Come get some more!" Josh yelled at Trevor.

Security from the theater stepped in and pushed Josh back against the wall. He offered no resistance. A police car drove up and both officers jumped out, one went to Josh the other to Trevor.

"He started it officers," Sharon said, "he came up and pushed my husband for no reason."

"That's right, he started it all. I was just defending myself." Josh told them with a smug look on his face.

Trevor, groggy, and still feeling the effects of the blow to the head, was helped up by the officer. They pulled all of them to the side and took their identification, trying to sort it out. Josh became anxious when the officers didn't believe his side of the story. He was cuffed and put in the back of the police car until they decided what to do. Sharon was getting louder and louder siding with Josh.

The police turned their attention to Trevor. "What's your story Mr. Hammond?"

Trevor's head had cleared enough to tell his side. He thought about telling the truth, that he had started it, but with Josh taking that last cheap shot, he decided to play dumb. "Basically that guy started it all. He started it all in the theater; he kicked me and dumped greasy popcorn in my lap."

"That's a lie!" Sharon protested. "He ran from behind and knocked Josh to the ground!"

"Miss, if you don't calm down I will have to put you in the car with him." The officer moved her a few feet away to separate the two.

"Mr. Hammond, the witnesses we have talked to said you pushed Mr. Evans. Is this true?"

"Look, to be honest, this whole thing started this morning at breakfast."Trevor's honest side came out and he told the officer everything, exactly as it happened. The theater manager was involved now and wanted them escorted off of the property. Josh wanted charges filed on Trevor, so Trevor decided to file charges on Josh. The officers cuffed Trevor and took them both into custody. As the car holding Trevor passed in front of the theater, he glanced at the curious crowd and only recognized one face. It was the man who had taken his ticket and given him the uneasy feeling. The man was looking right at him and winked. The wink made the hairs on the back of his neck stand up. He didn't know why, but the man scared him.

It wasn't the first time for Josh to be in jail. He had a DUI on his record several years back and had been involved in another fight a couple of years before. He had a bit of con-man in him, but had not been busted for anything involving that yet. His other problem was gambling. He owed money to two different bookies and that was part of the problems he was having. Until he got those paid he couldn't concentrate at work, or live in peace. He had a fear that after awhile the ones he owed the debts to wouldn't be so forgiving and come looking for him.

Trevor had never been in jail. This was his first time, and it was all behind some nonsense. He couldn't believe his luck. His day started shitty and now it was going to end the same way. He couldn't believe how stupid he was, pushing Josh like he did, he should have just walked away. The time to make the right choices had long since passed and the reality set in, as he was being escorted to a jail cell.

This particular sub-station was the oldest in Mesa. The old, decaying station, smelled like urine and was due to be replaced, but budget-constraints kept it alive for now. The two cells in the basement were separated by only one set of bars, probably in an effort to save space. There were two men, one in each cell. The cell door opened with a rusty creak and the officer escorted Trevor to the entrance. The sound of the door slamming behind him made him feel the reality of it all and put an exclamation point on the events of the day. The man in Trevor's cell was sitting in the corner. He looked younger and had his shirt pulled up over his head and looked as if he were wearing a hoodie. Trevor turned around to examine his temporary home. Cracked, cold, concrete floors greeted him at his feet, and white, iron bars surrounded him. They were faded and stained in more of a yellow color. The paint was chipped in many places.

Trevor looked into the other cell and saw a man sitting with his back to him. He looked older but he couldn't tell. The sound of the outer jail door opened and he could see them bringing Josh down the hall. He braced himself for another fight. The officers opened the other cell and Josh entered it and stared at Trevor anger.

"You boys play nice." the officer said, as he walked away.

Only the bars between the cells separated the two men. That gave Trevor comfort, but he wasn't afraid. Josh continued starring at him and Trevor just smiled.

"Want me to kick your ass again?" Josh asked him with a smug smile on his face. Trevor sat down on the bench. "That's what I thought."

The man in the cell with Josh spoke from his sitting position. "I see you two know each other." He turned around and faced Josh. As soon as he turned Trevor thought he recognized him. It was the same man from the theater. But it can't be, he thought, there's no way that could be him. The man looked over at Trevor with exactly the same look that the man at the theater had given him. Despair came over Trevor.

"Look, he's scared of me. Even in jail he's scared, what a wimp." Josh mistook Trevor's puzzled look, thinking it was because of him. Trevor hardly noticed Josh's comments as his eyes couldn't leave the old man's stare.

Finally the man turned to Josh. "What's your name young man?"

"You talking to me old man?"

"Well yes I am. My name's Levi, and yours?" Levi extended his hand for a handshake. Josh walked away, leaving him hanging. "No need to be rude. It's not very polite."

"What's it to you? I'm only here for a short time. No reason to make friends with strangers."

"I understand, but you seem to know that gentleman over there," he said, pointing to Trevor.

"Oh yeah, he's the asshole who got me locked up. That's how I know him," Josh said, as he took a seat on the bench along the wall.

"So, we're not all strangers after all, how nice." Levi said.

"Like I said, what's it to you?" Josh said, keeping his angry vibe and trying to command the room.

"Name's Trevor," he said, interrupting Josh's power-play, and trying to get a bead on the man who called himself Levi. Trevor made sure to hide his uneasiness about the old man.

"Nice to meet you Trevor, as I said, my name's Levi. The young man in the cell with you is Bobby. He doesn't like to talk much, but he's a smart kid. Say hello Bobby."

Trevor looked at the Bobby, but he never responded to Levi's request. He only rocked back and forth as if he was meditating. "Like I said, he doesn't speak much." Trevor looked back at Levi and noticed that he looked more and more like the man at the theater.

He kept his thoughts to himself, but his curiosity took over. "How long have you been in here Levi?" If it had been longer than a few hours Trevor knew that he couldn't be the man from the theater.

"Well, I've been in here for three days now. I was gonna get out yesterday, but the courts were tied up and they say my paperwork wasn't filed properly. Now that it's Saturday, I'm stuck here until Monday morning, at least. No judges or courts on the weekend."

"You mean we're stuck in this hell-hole until Monday?" Trevor asked.

"This isn't a hell-hole, as you call it; there are far more hellish places than this. Getting out of here depends on what your charges are. Sounds like you two had a fight. If that's the case, you'll be here until Monday, too much paperwork to file for something like that on the weekend." Levi spoke clearly and confidently.

"That's a lie," Josh said, "my wife is gonna post bail soon. I'll be out in no time."

"I hope it works out for you that way, but it's been my experience, that over the weekend, this place is just a holding tank until Monday.

"Not for me it's not. I'm getting out of here." Josh said as he stood up and paced around the cell.

With Josh talking about his wife, Trevor's thoughts turned to Stacy. He got his customary one-call earlier, but Stacy didn't answer. He left a message explaining what happened. There was no way to know if she got the message or not. He hoped they would let him make another call soon. A lot was going through his mind and to add to it, the unsettled feeling of who Levi was, was working on his mind too.

"Since we're all getting to know each other, Bobby over there is a regular. He is in here again for public intoxication. They'll let him sleep it off over the weekend."

"What are you in here for Mr. Levi?" Josh asked in a condescending tone.

"Well let's just say, I have some demons that just won't let go."

"Demons? You mean drugs," Josh said with a laugh, "you're hooked on drugs I bet."

"Many things can act like a drug in this world; it's all about how you handle them. But rest assured, we all have demons that hide within us. Some people face them, some choose to brush them aside and avoid them," Levi said, as he turned around and looked at Josh directly. "But, they will never go away unless you face them."

"So what are you saying? I have demons? Listen, I got my life under control buddy, make no mistake." Josh was offended by the comment Levi sent in his direction.

"I have no doubt you have things under control Josh. You are a lucky man to have that power."

"Wait a minute! How do you know my name? I never told anyone in here my name." Josh said and moved towards Levi.

"No worries, I overheard the policeman say your names before they brought you in. If that is Trevor then you must be Josh." Levi was unafraid of Josh's bravado and smiled at him. Josh didn't know how to respond. For the first time he felt an uneasiness about Levi.

Trevor watched intently. It was good to see Josh back down from someone, plus it gave him time to figure out why he felt the connection between Levi and the man at the theater. He looked over at Bobby who was still sitting there with his head down slowly rocking back and forth.

"I am one who truly believes, and knows, all things happen for a reason," Levi said. He began to take command of the jail cells in a subtle, but confident way. He slowly walked in a circle, his right hand in front of him with his index finger pointing upward, eyebrows raised. He looked like a preacher, but more like a prophet.

"Sometimes people are brought together for certain reasons, some of them out of our control. The reasons why, we don't know."

"What are you, some kind of preacher?" Josh had to chime in. He wasn't going to let someone outshine him.

"No Mr. Evans, I'm just an old wise-man who has seen and learned a lot of things over the years. I'm just here, passing some things on that I have learned."

"Well maybe we don't want to hear them."

"Ah, do you speak for the entire group now?" Levi stopped walking in his little circle and turned towards Josh.

"I think I'd like to hear more," Trevor said. He wanted to rile up Josh, but he also wanted to unmask whoever Levi was, to get him to speak more. Maybe something would help ease his unsettled feeling about him.

"So, I guess you don't speak for the group Mr. Evans. As I was saying, there could be a reason we are all in here together, and then there may not be. Only the future will tell."

"Like I said buddy, my future will be those cell doors opening, and me walking out of here, while you losers sit here all weekend."

"That very well may be true. I believe you have a bit of prophet in you," Levi said as he smiled, his perfect white teeth gleamed in the light and his eyes sparkled with a confidence carried by very few men. The way he looked at him gave Josh the creeps, but he wouldn't let it show.

Bobby began laughing out loud. All three men turned to look at him.

"He does that from time to time. Usually in response to something he is thinking about, or has heard, maybe, from within his own mind."

He's probably just as crazy as you," Josh said as he turned and walked back to the cot. He was putting on a tough-guy attitude, but he was hoping Sharon would get him out of there soon.

Bobby never raised his head, and soon his laughter stopped, and was back to mumbling to himself in a very low tone. Trevor shook his head and then looked up at Levi. Levi was staring at him intensely, as if his eyes were burning through him. It scared him, he had to look away. Levi walked over to the bars that separated the cells and grabbed hold of them on either side of his face. He pushed his face as far as he could between two of them. He looked right at Trevor.

"No need to be afraid Trevor. I feel you understand what I speak of. If this is true, then you have nothing to fear," he told him with a smile. He looked completely different than the man Trevor had just seen. Almost, like he transformed from one to the other.

"I already told you. Trevor, or whatever his name is, is a punk, a sissy. Anybody that would blindside someone has to be a punk." Josh spoke up, not letting Trevor steal the show. He just couldn't help himself.

Trevor had enough. "Listen asshole, you want to talk about blindsiding? What about when you used your girl as a shield and then snuck that sucker-punch in on me? That smells of a pu . . ."

"Gentlemen!!" Trevor was interrupted by Levi. "Please! All of this vulgarity and anger? Life is too short to allow anger to consume you this way. You may not want to listen to me, but I can tell you, you are too young to go through life this way. It's all about making the right choices and getting your house in order."

"Now he's a preacher," Josh said with a laugh.

"You should listen to him," Trevor told Josh, "he probably knows a lot more about life than us combined."

Josh walked towards Trevor's cell, brushing Levi with his shoulder as he did. Trevor met him at the cell bars. "It doesn't matter what he knows. All that matters is that you are a punk and you got your ass kicked!" Josh said as he got as close as he could in Trevor's face.

Trevor smiled, although his anger was at its highest, he decided to try and kill him with kindness. "Yes, you kicked my ass, and I know you are very proud of it. You deserve a parade and a key to the city," he said in very condescending way.

Josh didn't take kind to the Trevor's little joke, so he spit in Trevor's face. The spit hit Trevor in his right eye and cheek. Trevor jumped back for a brief second and then jumped right back at Josh as the spit ran down his face.

"You stupid son of a bitch!" Trevor yelled, trying to get a hold of Josh's throat. Josh didn't back away and he tried to grab at Trevor through the bars.

Levi jumped into Josh to try and break it up before the guard could hear what was going on. "You have to stop this nonsense!" Levi said. Josh turned and grabbed Levi by the collar, shook him, and then threw him to the ground. Levi was angry for the first time, and jumped back up and right back at Josh. Josh wasn't as nice this time and shoved Levi hard, in the chest. He flew back and hit his head against the cell bars and fell to the ground.

"What the hell is wrong with you?" Trevor told Josh and stepped towards Levi. He couldn't reach him from where he was. "Hey, hey Levi, are you alright?"

"He shouldn't have messed with me. That's what he gets," Josh said as he walked away.

"Are you that heartless? Check on him, make sure he is okay." Trevor had more anger in him than before. Levi rubbed the back of his head and mumbled something. The blow had momentarily dazed him. Trevor looked down and saw that Levi had dropped something out of his pocket, a shiny, green envelope. "Levi, you okay?" Trevor asked again.

"I'm fine. Got the ole boy riled up I guess," he said, referring to Josh.

"Yeah, he's stupid," Trevor said, as Levi raised himself up. "Levi you dropped something." He pointed down to the envelope.

"Yes, I have a couple of these in my pocket." He bent down and picked it up. "Yes, this is one of two that I have." Levi's face turned more serious, as if he had never banged his head against the cell bars.

Josh was sitting and looking at Levi, making sure he didn't try to rush him.

"Don't worry Josh, I will not retaliate, that's not my style."

A tall, well-built policeman walked down the short hallway and shouted in their direction. "What's going on down here?"

"Nothing, nothing wrong at all officer. Everything's fine." Levi told him with that sly smile. Trevor, Josh and Bobby all watched as Levi talked to the officer.

"What was all that racket down here?" the policeman said, looking skeptically at all four of them.

"Just a little disagreement, nothing that can't be fixed. It will be worked out, I can assure you." Levi was smooth with his delivery. Just a couple of minutes ago he had his head banged against the iron bars, and now he was going on like nothing happened. As he spoke to the officer, Trevor watched him, his smile, his eyes, the way he handled himself. He didn't know how, but he was sure that this was the same man at the movie theater. It didn't make sense and seemed impossible, but he knew it was him. "Please, don't let us keep you from your duties officer," Levi said smiling.

The policeman had his hands on his belt and eyed Levi, searching his eyes for more than he was telling. He took one last look around. "Keep it down." Satisfied, he walked back down the hall.

Bobby returned to his rocking and Josh stood up. He wanted to let Levi know that he better not try anything. The one thing he didn't do was apologize. "You're pretty slick, old man," Josh said.

Trevor watched Levi, and how he carried himself with the upmost confidence, he was the proverbial: calm, cool and collected.

"No need to get others involved in our issues. Sometimes, the more people that are involved, the more the complications."

"We don't have any issues. I've already taken care of them." Josh was still as arrogant as ever.

"No we don't have an issue as I can see. What we have is unfinished business. I walk with purpose and direction. I have things to do and I get those things done," said Levi.

"Don't look like you can get much done in here," Josh said with a laugh.

Levi stood in the middle of the cell and smiled at Josh, then turned his head towards Trevor, his smile never leaving his face. "Maybe I am here for a reason. This may be the place I need to be, to get things done." That sent a chill through Trevor's veins.

Bobby began laughing out loud again at those words. His laugh was short, but Trevor started to think that Bobby knew something about Levi that they didn't.

Levi spoke again. "I know that we all have troubles in our lives. Some of those troubles have led you here. Anger can consume people, if they let it. It can drive us to do things that we normally may not even consider. But there is a much more evil thing than anger . . . greed. Greed can lead a person to trouble. The power of being greedy can make a person take risks, the kind of risks that can propel them into a very dark place. A place where they find themselves so far down that no matter what they try to do to get out, it's like standing in quicksand, the deeper they go." Levi stood silent, looking down at the floor.

Then, in a loud outburst, Levi pounded his fist into his open hand.

"IT WILL BE THE DEATH OF YOU! IT WILL SEND YOU ALL TO HELL!"

Levi's body shook as he looked up at the ceiling, his fists clinched tight. It almost looked as if he was foaming at the mouth like a rabid dog. Trevor stood up. Josh stepped back, for the first time he was afraid of this man.

As quickly as the outburst began, it was over. Levi, his eyes closed, his face dripping with sweat, lowered his head and spoke again. "Luckily for you I have a way out, it's simple really. From this point on, your future comes down to a choice you will make. Will greed make that decision for you?" More and more, Levi sounded like a preacher or prophet. Trevor was glad he was on the other side of the cage. Josh knew something was strange too, but he chose to keep his tough exterior. Levi stepped to the corner, where the two cells met.

"As you saw just a minute ago, I have a green envelope, but I also have a red one." He reached into his jacket pocket and pulled out both envelopes. He held them up like a pair of cards and smiled. "One for each of you. Please, come closer." Josh and Trevor both looked at each other with apprehension. For the first time they seemed to be thinking the same thing. But, Trevor knew more; the way Levi held up the envelopes and smiled was the exact same way the man at the theater did it. Trevor would play along, but with caution. "Don't worry gentleman, I don't bite."

"Yeah? Who says I want to play your stupid game anyway?" Josh said as he walked towards Levi, trying to hide his curiosity.

Trevor knew that Levi was up to something and wanted to find out, so he planned to use psychology on Josh. "Okay, let's say we go along with your little game, there are three of us here, counting Bobby, who gets left out?"

"Very good question, but Bobby is not involved in this. This is between the two of you," Levi said. The green and red colors of the shiny envelopes reflected off of the light and caught their eyes as he dropped his arm to his side.

Trevor stepped close to Levi, only the cell bars separated them. Josh, not one to be left out, moved in closer as well. Trevor didn't care about the envelopes, he was baiting Josh in, hoping to play on his greed, and find out what Levi was up to.

"This is how it will go," said Levi, "each of you will pick an envelope, inside each are two very different things. They may not seem extravagant or powerful, but believe me, they are. Green or red? Red or green? Which will it be?" With that, Levi raised his hand up quickly. The plastic envelopes shined in his hand, forming a perfect V at his fingertips. "Pick one!" Levi said, raising the envelopes just a little higher. Trevor hesitated, and Josh pounced on his opportunity, snatching the green one from Levi's fingers. Trevor was counting on him to pick the green one, knowing that he would think the green one to be better than red. Trevor took the red one from Levi's hand and stepped back, still curious.

Josh walked away and opened his envelope. He pulled out a small piece of paper and dropped the green envelope on the floor. He unfolded the paper and read it.

"What's this?" Josh said as he turned, holding the paper out in front of him, a look of disbelief and contempt covered his face. "This is stupid. What's with all the theatrics? A piece of paper with words I can't even pronounce, and movie tickets? Hell, that's what got me in here in the first place!" He dropped the paper, tickets, and envelope to the floor and kicked the envelope. "All of you are losers, stupid losers." He walked over to where Trevor was standing. "So you gonna open yours or not?" he asked Trevor, who was holding his envelope in one hand, and tapping it against the palm of his other.

Levi stepped back to watch the exchange between the two . . . strangers.

"Well yours must not have been anything you liked, or you would have kept it. I have no idea what's in here, but I can bet you'll like it more than yours," he said as he shook it. "Yep, it feels a little heavier than a little piece of paper." Trevor smiled. He could see the anger, but, curiosity building on Josh's face.

Levi could sense the tension building again and smiled.

A guard walked down the hall. "Evans! Get ready, you're getting bailed out. The guard turned and walked away.

"You see what I told you? I'm getting out of here. I won't have to put up with any of you lowlifes anymore." Josh looked at both of them with a wild and crazy look in his eyes.

"Well, it seems that time is short for our little group. Trevor, will you do us the honor of opening your envelope and showing us its contents?"

Trevor waited, and thought about it for a second. He didn't want to give Josh the satisfaction of showing him what was in it, but he knew that whatever its contents, it would make Josh look like a fool for snatching the other one so fast. "Sure, I'll be glad to."

Trevor stepped closer to the bars that separated the two cells. He reached through, extended his arms, and brought them together at either end of the red envelope. "Well, here goes nothing."

Levi watched with great anticipation, but he moved aside to let Josh and his curiosity, step in closer. Trevor, ever so slowly, slid his finger under the flap of the envelope until it opened. He looked at Josh the entire time. He reached in slowly, taking his time, and he could see that Josh was getting antsy. His hand touched, what felt like money, and something else. When his hand emerged it held some dollar bills and two tickets of some sort.

"Let's see," Trevor said, "we have two tickets to the PSR Nascar race for tomorrow, front row, and," Trevor counted the five, crisp and clean, twenty dollar bills. "$100! Very nice!" He stuffed them back into the envelope, smiling at Josh.

Josh reached out and took it from his hands. Trevor was startled, and pulled his hands back into his side of the cell.

Bobby laughed out loud from his corner of the cell. His laughter was louder and more hysterical this time.

Josh gave him a quick glance and then turned to Levi. "This is supposed to be for me. I was gonna pick this one, but I grabbed the wrong one."

"You're full of shit! That belongs to me!" Trevor was surprised at how angry he was.

"He is right," Levi said, pointing at Trevor as he walked to the middle of the cell, "that one belongs to him. You should return it now."

"Screw you old man. I'm getting out today. You three might be stuck in here all weekend, so it would go to waste anyway. I might as well keep it," Josh said, as he walked away folding the envelope, putting it in his pocket, and sitting on the edge of the cot.

"Are you sure that this is what you want to do? Levi asked Josh.

Trevor had calmed and knew that Levi was up to something. There was something about the connection to the movie theater, something about the way he carried himself, and something about those eyes.

"I'll tell you what." Josh got up and walked over to the green envelope on the floor. He picked up the envelope, tickets, and the note, and stuffed them back inside. "You can have this one. Fair enough trade because these won't expire by the time you get out and I'll be able to make the race. Besides, I love NASCAR!" Josh almost sounded civilized.

Trevor didn't know why, but he took the envelope from his hand, feeling it was the right thing to do.

"See there old man, problem solved!" Josh said.

"If Trevor has no objections?" Trevor looked at him and shook his head. (as if to say: I don't need no more drama.) "Are you sure Mr. Evans" Levi asked.

"What are you deaf? This is mine," Josh said, as he pulled the folded, red envelope out of his pocket, and raised it to the air.

"Very well, we are done here," said Levi.

"Josh Evans, step to the front of the cell. You are a free man, for the moment." The guard said. The cell door slid open and the guard stepped aside to walk Josh down the hall.

"Well I guess it's the end of the road, for our little party. It's been great, but I got to go." Josh was back to being arrogant and as he walked out the cell door, he stopped and turned to Trevor. "Enjoy the show." Josh smiled, turned and walked down the hall with the guard. The cell door slammed shut behind him. Bobby laughed out loud, once again.

Trevor was tired and lay down on the cot. He was glad Josh was gone and was hoping Stacy would be there soon, to make him a free man. It was finally quiet and he drifted off to sleep.

He didn't know if he was dreaming or not, but a gray, misty fog floated in the cells. He glanced over to where Bobby was sitting. He was gone.

"Looks like you'll be on your own."

Levi's voice startled Trevor. He looked over at Levi, who was brushing off the sleeves of his suit. "My work's never done," Levi said.

Trevor wanted to say something, but the words wouldn't come out. He felt trapped laying there.

"I guess you'll be headed to the movies Mr. Hammond. I've got some business, or work, if you will, to take care of at the racetrack. Enjoy your time." Levi never looked towards Trevor, but he didn't have to. Trevor knew the face of the man he saw at the movies, the same face of the mysterious man about to walk through the fog and into whatever world he came from. A chill ran through Trevor's body. The chill wasn't from the fog . . . it came from Levi.

"Hammond!" the guard yelled.

Trevor woke up and found himself alone in the cells. The fog was gone and the place was well lit, compared to earlier.

"Get ready to get out of here. Your wife or girlfriend is here," the guard told him.

Sweet words to Trevor's ears. "How long have I been sleeping?"

"You've been sleeping off and on through the night. It's Sunday afternoon," the guard said, with a little laugh.

"Sunday afternoon? I've been asleep that long?" Trevor couldn't believe it.

"We thought you killed over once, but we checked on you," he said, laughing again. "I'll be right back."

The green envelope that was sitting on Trevor's lap fell to the floor. He picked it up and opened it for the first time. There were two movie tickets and a small, folded piece of paper inside. Levi's words came back to him. I guess you'll be going to the movies. Trevor made the connection about Levi. He didn't fully understand it, but knew there was so much more at work than just some old man rambling in a jail cell.

"Let's go Hammond!" the guard hollered as he opened the cell door.

Trevor was shaken from his deep thought. He held the piece of paper from the envelope in his hand, and was about to read it.

"Remember your sparring partner that got thrown in here with you?" the guard said as he stepped further back into the hall.

"Yeah, why?" Trevor said, looking down at the paper as he stepped out of the cell, not paying much attention to the guard's words.

"Thought you might like to know, he was killed in a car accident about three hours ago."

Trevor stopped walking and looked up. "What??" Disbelief hit him.

"Yeah, he was headed out to the NASCAR race on 107th Avenue and Southern and got t-boned at the intersection. He was hit on his side, died on impact. His wife is in ICU, she should make it they say.

Trevor stared at him in stunned silence.

"It was a hit-and-run, they haven't found the driver of the semi that nailed him, and that's strange because I can't figure where the driver could have gone in all that dessert. They were on the scene quick. It was like he disappeared."

Trevor heard, and understood the words, but he knew Levi was responsible. The whole thing was creepy and shocking. He looked down at the note.

"You all right?" the guard asked.

"Yes, can you give me a second?"

"I'll be right down the hall. Hammond . . . I guess you really are a free man."

The guard walked away as Trevor, still stunned at the news of Josh, and at knowing that it could have been him. Josh would probably be alive if he hadn't stolen the red envelope.

Trevor read the words on the piece of paper from the envelope.

"So are the ways of every one that is greedy of gain; which taketh away the **life** of the owners thereof."

Trevor's hand shook, and sweat poured from his forehead, as he read the words. The piece of paper slipped from his fingers and floated slowly, to the ground.

It all finally came together in his mind as he stared blankly at the paper; knowing he had escaped death, knowing he had escaped . . . Levi.

As he found himself leaning against the cell bars relief set in, realizing, he was truly a free man after all.

Don't Bug Me

"I'm just starting to scratch the surface of what's going on here."

Travis sat on his sofa on a Wednesday night watching TV. There wasn't much on so he was flipping channels one after another, hoping to settle on something before the microwave binged signaling to him that his dinner was ready. He came across one of the upper channels that had a special on insects and bugs.

Travis has a phobia about bugs and has always had a genuine fear of being eaten alive by them. The thought of bugs eating through his living flesh scared the hell out of him, but he was very intrigued when he ran across a program that was about the very thing that he feared most.

"For every human on earth, there are well over one million insects or bugs. That's for every one human," the program host said. "With over nine million species roaming the earth, it's no wonder why there are so many incidents and reports of human infestation and diseases related to them." Travis put the remote down on the coffee table and crossed his arms to listen more closely. "Hook worms expel enzymes into the human skin to allow them to burrow through the skin and into the bloodstream. They usually reside in the small intestine and from there can travel to the stomach and eventually, in some cases, to vital organs, where they can cause extreme illness and even death."

As the host of the show spoke, the screen was filled with computer generated images and video of the Hook Worm's travels through the human body. Travis got the chills and began rubbing his arms as if scratching, but he was glued to the screen, fascinated by his own fear.

"Another, that you might say as common, infestation of the human body comes from the human botfly, also known as Dermatobia Hominis. Botflies deposit eggs on a host. Larvae from these eggs, stimulated by the warmth of the human host, drop onto the skin and burrow underneath," the host of the show said.

The visuals and the words were enough for Travis. He grabbed the remote and quickly changed the channel. His biggest fear was his biggest fascination, but he could only look so long. He rubbed his arms again and focused on the baseball game. He was expecting his girlfriend to come over and have dinner. Patricia liked hanging out with Travis on the weekdays because the time was more relaxed and laid back. She knew of his phobia about bugs, but she did not have the same fear. Other than his hang up with the insect world, she found no other faults with him.

Travis got up in between innings to go to the bathroom. He washed his hands as always, and as he looked into the mirror at his face, he did a double-take. He leaned in closer to the mirror. He focused on the area just above his eyebrow. The skin seemed to raise just a bit, then move to the right. It happened very quickly and he immediately ran his fingers over the area, but it didn't feel any different, it felt smooth and normal. He shook his head and wiped his face. I must be tired, he thought. Mirrors can play tricks on a tired mind for sure, but what he thought he saw gave him enough of a scare that he looked in the mirror one more time, just before he turned off the light.

Patricia knocked at the door of Travis' apartment holding a pizza. She was hungry and was looking forward to spending time with him. Travis looked through the peephole and opened the door.

"There you are," Travis said, "just in time for the game." He gave her a kiss on the cheek.

"I'm starving, forget the game. Let's eat," she said smiling. She walked to the couch and sat down, putting the pizza on the coffee table. Travis went to the kitchen to grab a couple of plates and some soda. As he reached into the cabinet a small spider drifted down from above.

"Shit!" Travis jumped back.

"What's wrong? You okay?"

"Just a spider," he said. Travis knocked the spider to the ground and smashed it with his shoe. "Got it!" he hollered. He tired to sound manly to Patricia, but the spider scared the hell out him.

"You're so scared of bugs; you should get this place exterminated more often." She was joking, but didn't feel as much sympathy as she probably should.

Travis was a little on edge after watching the documentary, and after his little scare in the mirror. He really tried to be "more of a man" about it, but it was something he had always scared him for as far back as he could remember. He came back into the living room and sat next to Patricia, hoping she wouldn't bring anything up anything else about his fear. Normally she liked to have a little fun with him about it, but she let it go for the night.

"Your Yankees are already losing," she said. "I thought you said they were going to be better this year."

"The game just started, give it a bit," he told her with a laugh.

"Alright, we'll see."

As Patricia said that, Travis felt a small bite near his elbow on his right arm. He didn't react in front of her like he would have if her were alone. Casually, he reached over with his left hand and scratched the area without looking. What is going on? He watched the game and smiled, but his mind was in a very different place. The game played on and the night passed by with only a couple of other small incidents that Travis was able to keep to himself. Patricia went home after the game and she glad they got to spend a lazy evening together.

Travis felt good the next morning. He slept well, having no incidents, no itching or feeling bites anywhere on him. He woke in a good mood. He started some coffee and walked outside to grab the newspaper. He was a tech and internet guy, so he only took the paper on the weekends when he was home for most of the day. He saw Ms. McChessney sweeping her porch next door.

"Good morning. How are you today?" Travis asked her as he waved to the seventy-year-old woman.

"Good morning." She waved back. "Nice out today don't you think?"

"Yes, very nice out. Have a good day!" Travis hollered knowing she was a little hard of hearing.

He turned and walked back inside as he read the headlines in the paper. Travis was feeling good and was looking forward to going to the movies later with Patricia. After his coffee was done, he mixed it with just the right amount of sugar and creamer and sat down at the table to read the paper. While reading the sports page, he felt a very slight twinge on his neck. He immediately slapped at his neck. He felt around, but there was nothing there. Suddenly, the great feeling he had for the day disappeared with the itching. He had no idea why he would over react, but it was how he felt. The feeling of a bug crawling on him, or even under his skin, was something that he had the most absolute fear of. He took a quick sip of coffee, trying to ignore what he felt.

No one knew just how bad Travis' phobia was. Most that knew of his fear, especially Patricia, thought he was just afraid of bugs, but his fear went much further, much deeper, deeper than even he knew. His real fear was that a bug or insect would get into his skin, crawling and burrowing under. The thought drove him crazy at times. No one knew this side of Travis.

Two weeks had now passed since his last episode. Travis was able to keep that one from everyone. That weekend Patricia was out of town visiting her parents. Now he was getting the signs of another episode starting again.

There it was again! This time on his calf. He felt it, something sliding along the back of his calf. He reached down fast and scratched the area, nothing. He stood up and walked to the living room. It was getting to him again. His mind was running way ahead what of was actually happening. He paced around the room. He put his hands to his head and tried to think.

I have to get myself together. I can't let it do this to me again. I have to beat this. Travis was only talking within his head for now, but he knew that would progress to talking to himself out loud, if he didn't get it under control.

His phone buzzed. He picked it up and read the text message from Patricia. Good morning... Love you... He replied back with his standard I love you too! He meant what he sent to her, but his mind was wandering in a way he hoped would not show itself. He knew he better try and keep busy.

After reading the paper and finishing his second cup of coffee, Travis decided to work out on the treadmill. He set it for three miles. The sweating and running, plus listening to some heavy metal, really took his mind off of his hallucinations, as he called it. The sweating really made him feel better. He figured that if there really were bugs crawling on him, or under his skin, the sweat would keep them away.

The three miles took a little more out of him than he thought it would, but he felt good and headed for the shower. Travis always made sure to keep lotion on his skin after a shower. He didn't want anything, like dry skin, to cause him to itch and scratch. He decided to run to the store and pick up a few things he needed before he went to the movies with Patricia.

Travis grabbed his keys and headed outside to his car. Ms. McChessney was still out in her yard working on her flower bed. He decided to avoid the awkwardness of yelling out loud to speak to her.

The day was clear and a lot cooler than the last few, maybe summer was breaking. Target was his destination this morning. He preferred Target over the other stores because it was closer. Usually on a Saturday morning there were a lot of people, but that day there was not very many at all. He grabbed a small basket to carry; he didn't need the push carts. After getting some toothpaste and deodorant, the feel of something biting his arm hit him again. He immediately smacked down on his arm and as he did, the basket fell and crashed to the floor. A woman standing ten feet away gave Travis a worried look. He was still looking at his forearm and scratching when he realized that the woman went from a worried look, to scared, as if he were some kind of crazy person. He was scratching so frantically that she moved a few steps away instead of closer, after she noticed how hard he was scratching. He had no idea how he looked to others when his mind left him like that.

He gave her an apologetic look and picked up his basket. His face felt like it was on fire because of his embarrassment, so he walked down the aisle in the other direction. After turning the corner he stopped and looked down at his arm again. The only things there were the scratches that he had just put there. He hadn't realized how hard he had scratched.

What the fuck? I need to get out of here, he thought. He made his way to the checkout and even the twenty-items-or-less line was long. He contemplated just leaving and coming back another time, but he really needed what he got and he was already there. By the time he made it to the cashier he was sweating enough for her to notice. She scanned his items, one by one, as he looked on impatiently. That's when it hit him again. Travis felt a sharp pain on the backside of his thigh. This one was much more painful, and for whatever reason he was able to keep himself composed and not go into a scratching frenzy.

With the sun shining bright in Travis's face, he walked at a hurried pace, got to his car and after throwing his bag in the backseat of his car, he sat down and quickly began to scratch at the back of his leg. He could still feel the sharp pain and literally dug his nails into the skin. He knew that it was starting up again. The crazy feeling, the one that almost drove him crazy two weeks ago, was coming on again. Nervous tension and anxiety set in on Travis as he looked out the windows of his car to see if anyone saw his abnormal scratching at his leg. Paranoia was getting to him as well.

I need to get home. I have to lock myself in and fight these bugs. I can't let anyone see me like this. Travis' thoughts were running wild, just like they had before.

The traffic wasn't bad really, but to Travis the ride home was as bad as rush hour traffic in L.A. When he finally got to his neighborhood he breathed a little easier. Have to get inside, have to hurry. Taking a hard left into his driveway, a nervous Travis felt a sharp bite on his neck. The sharp sting felt like a mosquito was biting him. He hit the brakes in his driveway and slapped at the spot, curling his fingers, trying to grab the culprit of the sting. He looked into his hand, it was empty. Travis knew it would be empty, but he also knew that sooner or later, the disgusting little creatures would show themselves. A quick look up into the rearview mirror revealed the red, panicked eyes of a man, who just two hours ago was in perfect control of his day.

"Okay, okay, okay. I made it inside," he said to himself. Feeling safer and secure in his house, he was now talking out loud. No one would be able to hear, or see him scratching, and most important, ridicule and criticize him. "I have to shower; I have to get them off of me."

Travis ran to his bathroom, stripped and ran the water very hot for a shower. The hot water caused steam to build in the bathroom and thick condensation formed on the mirror. Although very hot, the water, Travis felt, would kill the bugs that plagued him. "Yes, yes, yes, this will do it!" He rubbed and rubbed using soap and whatever else he could find in the shower to cleanse himself. The feeling of invisible bugs crawling all over him made him rub and scratch faster. The overwhelming feeling became too much to handle and he began to cry, falling and sliding down into a sitting position in the tub. Hot water continued to shower down on him from above. He knew he was in for a long night.

The sound of the cell phone vibrating on the nightstand woke Travis, who lay exhausted in his bed. Half-asleep, he reached over to the stand and lifted his phone. The aqua-blue display showed Patricia's name. He set the phone back down. Talking to her right now was not an option. This had to be taken care of before he could talk to anyone, especially Patricia.

Patricia didn't know of Travis's last episode, but she knew of his phobia, and twice in the past she had seen first-hand, what his fear could do to him. The first time it really frightened her and her compassion for what he was going through drove her to get him help. He knew that the help would do no good, but he had to give it, and Patricia a chance. Nothing was found to be wrong with him physically, so his mental health was next to be tested. This, Travis refused to do. He knew no one would ever understand that the bugs or insects were real. Patricia became irritated at his lack of belief in the possibility that it could all just be in his head. She became angrier with him after his second little episode. Again she was afraid, but this time, her compassion was shorter and again he refused to see a shrink. They split-up for a while, but eventually saw past their anger and refocused on their relationship. Travis knew though, that from that point forward, he could never tell her when another attack hit him. As far as she knew, he hadn't had one in a long while. The latest one was the worst of the three. He was scarred on his arms, legs, and chest from scratching and luckily for him, she was out of town during that time. If only she knew, he thought.

"She's probably calling to make sure we are still going to the movies," he said. "I'll have to call her back soon, make up some excuse." He paced around the room trying to figure out what to say. "If this keeps up there is no way I can go out in public."

Two weeks ago, the last attack began just like this one, a bite here or there, one by one until his entire body was under assault form the burrowing insects and bugs. Travis knew his body well, but most important, he knew them better.

"I have to keep moving. It seems like they don't get to me if I keep moving." He looked out the front window. A sharp, pinching sensation hit his right side. Again, he slapped at it, his hand landing flat on the bare skin with a loud pop. Travis scratched and scratched but continued to look out the window. If he didn't answer his phone, Patricia would be driving up at anytime. He looked down, assured he would see the bug crawling around his fingers.

"Fuck, it feels like the bug is under my skin, like it's trying to crawl out, but every time I look, nothing's there. No fly, no spider, no bug, and no blood! Damn! Am I losing my mind!?"

He walked to the door and examined it. "They have to be getting in here from somewhere. Yes, they're getting in the house, maybe through a hole in the screens. I have to look." Checking each window and any place he felt that the insects were getting in, Travis moved fast through his one-level home in a frantic effort to find the source of his terror. Each time he stooped to look at a possible entry; he scratched and rubbed different parts of his body. The bugs were getting to him by the minute.

"There's no way they are getting in. I can't find it. What the hell!?"

A knock sounded at the door. He looked at the time on the stove. "Shit! It's Patricia" They weren't due to go out for another two hours, but she always worried about him and lived close enough to stop by if he wasn't answering her calls or texts.

After finding a wrinkled shirt on the arm of the couch, he went to the door doing his best to not scratch or let slip what was wrong. He opened the door.

"Travis, are you alright? I called and sent you text messages."

"I know, I'm okay I was in the shower and forgot to look at my phone. I was going to call you back." Travis's face felt like it was on fire, sweat was building on his forehead. He wanted to scratch his neck. Oh, how he wanted to scratch it.

"Are you lying to me Travis? Is everything okay?" She had a genuine look of concern on her face.

"Yes I'm fine," he offered. She glanced down at his right arm and grabbed it. The skin on his forearm was raw and red and looked like it had been scraped by a cheese grater.

"What the hell in this?" She looked closer at his arm. "Travis, don't tell me . . ." She let go of his arm and looked into Travis's scared eyes. "How long has this been going on? Have you been hiding this from me?"

"No, of course not. I just, sometimes have to scratch. I promise it's not like it was before."

His answer was weak and he knew it. Patricia grabbed his arm again, lifting it up so he could get a better look. "You call this not as bad as before? Look at it! Look at your arm Travis!" She was scared for him, but also very angry at him for not talking to her like he had promised so many times over the last month.

"I don't know what to say to you. I didn't want to worry you about this. I figured I could handle it," he responded.

"Look, if you don't want my help that's fine, but don't keep things from me. This is about trust here and me wanting to help you. But, when you hide it from me like this . . . damn Travis." She threw her hands up in disgust.

Travis reached up behind his neck and scratched. He couldn't wait any longer, that bug was burrowing deeper under his skin. Patricia walked to him and grabbed his hand.

There was nothing in it. She turned him around and looked at his neck. The only thing there, were red lines from his scratching. "So where is the bug that just bit you huh? If you scratched, it should be there right?" She was angry and patronizing him, but she felt she had done everything to help him, committed so much time to get him past this, and now, he was still hiding his little secret, and much worse, hurting himself. "Like I told you before, you need help. You just don't want it."

Travis wanted to argue the point, but it wasn't worth the time and words. What he wanted at the moment was for her to go so he could get back to ridding himself of these bugs, and find out where they were getting in from.

"Are you even listening to me?"

"Listen Patricia, I want to get better, but I need some time to work it out, time to make it better," he said and grabbed her hand.

Patricia's anger wavered some in the moment, but she knew the only way to get him to take notice was to show her anger and disdain for the way he was handling it, especially the way he shut her out. She let go of his hand. "Look Travis, you have to get the right help. Until you decide that's what you need, you'll never get better."

"Babe, I am going to get better, please trust me."

"Bullshit Travis! You need help. It's all in your head. Can't you see that!? You better wake up." The spirit of her anger surprised even her. But, in her mind, it was well warranted. "Until you decide you need the right help, don't bug me!" She turned and walked out, slamming the door.

Even in his present state of mind, Travis couldn't help but see the irony in her words, "Don't bug me."

He was sad that she left so angry and disappointed in him, but he was glad that he was alone again. Now he could get back to finding how these bugs were getting in, and back to his scratching.

He stopped in the kitchen and reflected. "Patricia is right. I do need help. I just have to figure this out alone for now." He walked to the back storage room and began poking at the baseboards with a broom. "Come on you bastards, I know you're here somewhere."

Another hour had passed, it was getting dark outside. Travis had scarred his body badly from his face to his feet. Most of the scratches were on the surface, but a couple of them were bleeding a little. He had almost torn his house apart looking for the hole that he bugs had come in from. He sat on his sofa naked; the only way for him to get relief from the scratching was by taking a shower and then letting the cool air hit his skin.

The next wave hit him a few minutes later. Travis had drifted off to sleep when he was awakened by something moving just below his ear. He sat up quickly and reached up to his neck. This was different, it wasn't a bite. It was moving under his skin. It was big enough to raise his skin as it crawled. Travis pressed his hand to it and could feel the hard scales of the bug through his skin. It scared him, he let go. The bug burrowed down his neck, Travis was stunned, sitting as still as he could, then he slapped at the insect that was paving its way under his skin. It startled him even more when he heard the bug make a hissing sound. Travis stood as the large bug made its way from his neck and across his shoulder. He cupped his hand and put it over the insect and kept it in place just under his skin. He ran to the kitchen frightened, but at the same time excited. He was now about to have proof.

Travis, frantic for evidence, and desperate to prove to Patricia that he was not crazy, opened a drawer and pulled out a fillet knife. Placing fingers on either end of the bug, he sliced his skin. The pain was almost unbearable, but his adrenaline was so high that he didn't hesitate one bit. Blood let out from the sliced skin first. Then, as if by magic, the skin stretched and the dark, slithery insect poked through. First came the antennas, then the head. Then, all at once, the insect jumped from Travis's shoulder and landed on its back at his feet. He reached down quickly to pick it up. Blood ran down his shoulder and on to his chest. Grabbing the bug between his index finger and his thumb, Travis brought it close to his face to see exactly what has been causing him so much anguish. The bug, hissing and squirming between his fingers, looked similar to a cockroach, but had more of a slender shape and also had two pinchers, much like a beetle.

"There you go you little sucker. I got you now." Travis spoke to it like a human. His eyes looked crazed and deranged. "I got you, you son of a bitch. Now I can show Patricia. Now she won't think I'm nuts!" He walked with the bug to the counter and grabbed a glass. He dropped the weird-looking in it and covered it with a small plate. The dark brown bug ran in circles at the bottom of the glass.

Very satisfied with his catch, and not giving a damn about his bleeding shoulder, Travis called Patricia.

"Hello"

"Hey it's me," he said. "I want you to know you have been wrong all this time. I have proof now, if you would just come over, I can show you."

"Travis, I told you that I wasn't going to be part of your obsession."

"Yeah I know, but now I have proof. I caught a bug that was inside me."

"Did you say, from inside you? You mean you have one there now that you caught, which was crawling under your skin?" she asked sarcastically.

"Yes I do, pulled it from my shoulder."

"You know what Travis? You are really going too far with all this. You need to get help. When you are ready for that, call me." Patricia hung up on a stunned Travis.

"Hello? Did you hang up on me??" There was no answer. "What the hell else to I have to do!!?" Shocked that she still didn't believe him, he was pacing the kitchen floor when he felt a sharp and deep pain in his leg.

Patricia felt bad for not listening to him longer, but she had made her mind up when she left the house earlier that she wasn't going to enable him by pretending to believe him. She planned to call him later despite her feelings, just to make sure he was okay.

This time the pain came from Travis's thigh. He looked down and saw the skin pulsing up and down. He reached down and scratched at it, it moved. He grabbed at it this time and trapped it in place under his hand. He reached for the knife and just as he did, he felt something moving in his ear. That movement caused Travis to stay still, this was new. Never had he felt something moving in his ear. With his left hand he kept the bug in his thigh in place. With his right hand he slowly reached up to his ear. The little pricks he felt there were moving closer to the outer part of his ear. If there was pain involved with this creature crawling through his ear canal, he didn't feel it. Travis tilted his head to the right to try and help release the bug. He put his fingers to his ear and felt a sting on his index finger. The bug bit or stung him. He pulled his finger away and looked down at it. The bug was yellow, at least three inches long, and attached to his finger with two pinchers. The slimy insect's body wiggled back and forth from where it was attached to the tip of Travis' finger. He looked on in horror as the bug bit down harder.

Travis came to his senses and shook his hand frantically to shake the bug loose. It wouldn't let go. He walked to the kitchen counter and grabbed a small pan, held his finger out, and smashed the bug with the bottom of the pan. Yellow liquid, the inner guts of the insect, squirted out in all directions as the bug exploded. Travis jumped back to avoid the liquid and realized he had let go of the bug in his leg in order to kill this one. He looked down and saw his lower stomach pulsing up and down.

"Shit! It's moving up to my heart. I have to stop it." He quickly placed his hand over it to stop it. He noticed that when they came to the surface, he could hold them there. They didn't burrow back down deeper into his body.

Travis grabbed the knife. "This is gonna hurt." He sliced around the shape of the bug. "Oh my God this hurts." Holding the bug in place, he cut around it in an oval shape. Once done he let the bloody knife drop from his hand and grabbed the creepy-crawler between his fingers along with the sliced piece of skin. He couldn't see this creature very well because of the blood and skin, so he dropped it in another glass and covered it. Once shedding the skin, this bug looked similar to the first one that ran circles in the jar next to it. Only this one had one huge eye, looking like a bug's version of Cyclops.

Travis grabbed the knife and backed away from the counter, still bleeding from his shoulder and stomach. His arms shaking, he moved to the living room and looked at his face in the mirror. A shadow of his former self is what he saw. He saw a scared and confused man with no one to turn to.

"No one will believe me. Everyone will think I've lost my mind, especially Patricia."

Travis was a beaten man and slumped down to the floor with his back to the wall, the knife still in his hand. The familiar feeling of insects crawling on and under his skin grew worse. It felt like there were hundreds attacking him at once. He knew he had no way to fight them, no remedy. All that he could do was scratch, and his in his most chaotic moments, cut them out of him. He looked next to him and saw his phone on the floor. He thought of Patricia and grabbed it. As he pulled it back he saw two different spots on his arm, where the skin was rising and moving towards his hands. Nothing surprised him at that point, but he couldn't give up, he had to try.

The knife sliced easily into the skin on the back of his hand. The bug slithered out and dropped as it made hissing and clicking noises, before it ran across the floor. Blood poured from his hand as he placed the knife to his forearm to get the other. In a weird thought, Travis was pleased at how easily the knife cut through his flesh. It almost gave him a smile.

The insect fell to the floor and crawled towards him where Travis promptly smashed it with his hand.

Travis cried out loud. "Why is this happening? Why won't anyone believe me?" His cries were heard only by the creatures that lived inside his body. His body scratched raw, wounds open and bleeding, Travis looked and felt like a dead man. Bugs were now crawling at will under his skin, from his head to his feet. He would get to them in a minute, all of them, but first he needed to talk to Patricia.

"Baby?"

"Yes Travis?"

"I need you. I need your help." Travis said with tears streaming down his face, trying his best to not let her hear him cry. She had told him before; he had to be strong, after all.

"Yes I know Travis, but like I said, until you really realize you need help, it won't do me any good to try and help." Patricia felt bad for holding her ground like that, but she felt she had to. She had no way of knowing his true condition.

"Please," Travis begged her. His voice cracked, she could hear his emotional plea. "Help me . . . please."

The call ended before Patricia had a chance to say more.

Something is not right, she thought. No matter what her feelings were, she had to go check on him. She wasn't at home; if she was, she would only be fifteen minutes away, but from her location it would take her at least forty-five minutes to get there. She grabbed her keys and headed to Travis'.

After a quick cry and feel-sorry-for-myself moment, Travis refocused on the bugs taking over his body. "I'll get you all, you sons of bitches!" Travis was already lost mentally and after the call with Patricia, his only friend was his trusty filet knife. One by one he cut the bugs and filthy insects from his body. One by one they fell to the bloody floor and squirmed away. Travis kept up the good fight, taking out at least twenty or more of the hideous insects, until he couldn't hold the knife any longer. The knife made a small splash in the pool of Travis' blood that surrounded him. As he faded in and out of consciousness, the hissing sounds from the creatures that infested his body grew louder. Travis had no more fight left in him.

Patricia made it to Travis' house in less than an hour. She drove faster than usual and ran a couple of red lights. On the drive, her fear grew worse by the minute. She had tried his phone several times.

She ran to the front door and knocked. "Travis, I'm here. Are you okay?" she called out. She knocked again, but there was no answer. "Travis, it's me Patricia, please open the door, you're scaring me." Patricia had an extra key and fumbled for it in her purse. Her hands were shaking badly as she tried to line up the key to the latch.

Finally she got the key in the lock and turned. The sound of the deadbolt unlatching was deafening. She hesitated before slowly opening the door, she could hear the TV. "Travis? It's me," she said as the wooden door creaked open inch by inch. As soon as she got the door a few inches open, a handful of roaches ran out the doorway. She stepped aside and let out a quick scream. Her heart started beating faster. Now she was hearing the hissing. She stepped from behind the half-open door. The first thing that hit her eyes was the hundreds of bugs, roaches, and insects that were climbing the walls, furniture, and scattering across the floor.

"Travis!" she called out. Roaches, or what looked like roaches, crawled all around her. She took small steps, walking on her toes, tears welling in her eyes. "Travis!" She kicked at the creatures to keep them off of her. As she made her way around the couch she saw Travis, or what was left of him.

Patricia screamed. The bloody mess that was Travis, sat in a heap in the same spot that he had called her from.

"Travis nooooo! It can't be . . . noooooo!" Patricia cried out. Bugs and insects of all kinds swarmed Travis' bloody corpse. In total shock and horror, and oblivious to everything around her, Patricia moved closer to Travis. "No, no, no, no baby, no." She wept; her hands shook as she put them to her mouth shaking her head no. Roaches, spiders, and centipedes covered the walls and floor. The knife and phone lay next to Travis. His body was gashed and cut all over, his head slumped down, chin to chest, as insects of all kinds feasted on him.

Patricia felt dizzy and light-headed. "Travis? Please, are you okay baby?" She was now delirious; talking to a dead man. The blackness began to cloud her vision. The hissing and crackling made by the insects was getting louder. Just as she blacked out and fell to the insect-infested floor, the narrator from the TV documentary spoke.

"We hope that when the insects take over the world, they will remember that humans are partly responsible for providing their food supply."

Author's Note

The idea of writing in the horror genre, and telling scary stories is something that has always stirred in the back of my mind. Finally, I have taken the time and presented some of those ideas to you. The stories in this book have been inspired by many different people, places, and things. Inspiration for a story can come from a casual conversation, a dream, or sometimes it's visual - seeing something that sparks my imagination, and soon it takes off on its own story. All of the above have helped make this book possible. I have burned the midnight oil many nights putting this together. Sometimes the words flow effortlessly, and other times I hit the proverbial wall. But no matter which, for me, writing is an absolute joy and pleasure and carries a passion that is necessary to write a poem, song, or a book. Thank you for taking the time and reading "Purgatory". I hope you enjoyed the stories within the stories, and only you know what movies played in your mind as you read each page. There will be more to come, so keep your eBook readers charged, your reading glasses clean, and your mind open, to allow me in your world again.

Upcoming works by A. Lopez, Jr.

"NIGHT DREAMS"
Horror/Thriller Series

A novella series that follows a Dream Psychologist, Dr. Peter Branigan, who has no choice but to live out the nightmares of his patients in an effort to cure them from their own demons. Dr Branigan is bound by their demons while he struggles to make sense of the nightmares that plague his own life.

"31 DAYS"
Horror Novel

"Tomorrow starts the countdown to Halloween folks," the radio DJ pronounced to the listening public. "Yes, tomorrow is October 1st, bringing in the cooler temperatures, shorter days, and that one creepy night of the year that we love so much…beware of the goblins!" the DJ playfully warned his audience.

Little did he know that the countdown had already begun, long before he spoke his prophetic words.

The terror that was coming was far more hellish than he, or any of his listeners could imagine. The terror that *is* coming…begins in 31 Days.

For more info please visit us at: ace-hil-ink.com

Made in the USA
Charleston, SC
26 January 2012